THE ROAD DOG

A Novel By

Mike Johnson

Copyright © 2023 *Mike Johnson*.
michaeljohn@scratchline.com

All rights reserved. No part of this book may be reproduced, stored, or transmitted by any means—whether auditory, graphic, mechanical, or electronic—without written permission of both publisher and author, except in the case of brief excerpts used in critical articles and reviews. Unauthorized reproduction of any part of this work is illegal and is punishable by law.

ISBN: 979-8-89031-360-7 (sc)
ISBN: 979-8-89031-361-4 (hc)
ISBN: 979-8-89031-362-1 (e)

Because of the dynamic nature of the Internet, any web addresses or links contained in this book may have changed since publication and may no longer be valid. The views expressed in this work are solely those of the author and do not necessarily reflect the views of the publisher, and the publisher hereby disclaims any responsibility for them.

One Galleria Blvd., Suite 1900, Metairie, LA 70001
1-888-421-2397

*I wish to thank the following for
their meaningful contribution to this book:*

My bizarre childhood and all who contributed to that condition.

Johnnie Walker *black label* whiskey.

A small black and white cat.

The fine city of London.

My aunt Jeanine.

*"I'm going back to California, going down behind the sun.
Going to speak with Jesus Christ about the bad things I have done?"*

CHAPTER ONE

"Only a fool would go into that bitter place again; I was there for a small time before houses and fences were on the land; I will not go there again." Many months passed before she understood the meaning behind John's words.

Mary smiled as she took his hand before sitting beside him on the rough wooden bench. They waited quietly for a few minutes while an evening breeze scurried around, still warm from the late September sun. Old Cherokee John gazed into some distant horizon as the silence built between them. She remembered the first time they spoke, about a year ago, probably soon after she moved into this quiet agricultural community. She saw him on the bench, a slight figure bent with age reminding her of an old crow. Later, with familiarity, her delightfully ruffled old crow of a man spoke of many things. He told her of the ancient machinery working endlessly beyond the ridge, and never to go there, never to go where the land does not want you, and how her neighbor would invite misery and great harm if he insisted on exploring there. Cherokee John told other stories of the old years and tribal suffering, disease, and a more recent history of death and his wife and daughter. His past was carved into his face, and every deep line became a chapter in his life.

When he spoke, his black eyes glittered and sometimes brimmed with tears. He laughed loudly when she called him *"Mister Cherokee John."*

"No mister, no Cherokee, no John, I was Kipo'Mo, not Cherokee but Chumash. Antap. My family is Mohave, although we are one people." The old shaman reached into his poncho, withdrawing two large black feathers from the garment's folds. "Crow feather," he announced, handing both to Mary. "Now, write your words; tell your tales as I have done."

Mary would write her stories, and whenever she did, she pushed a large crow feather into the hair bunched behind her ear. As she wrote, the old man's words returned, and Cherokee John was not forgotten.

"Only a fool would go into that bitter place again,"

Em-Jay was not a fool, but he was a cement-head at times. So, of course, he knew better, wouldn't listen to the warnings, and, like my husband and many other men I know, stubborn as a railroad mule. After he rode through the gate, and later, when I brought him home from the hospital, he told me what he remembered about his ordeal. These were not paragraphs ripped from a psychiatric confessional or fluttering echoes in an alley; this was his story, said to me clearly, and I promised to take the time and write it all down for him. When we lay together in the quiet time just before sleep, he told me about his visions, voices, and the nurse at the hospital, how that haunted desert place frightened him, changed him, and then gave him hope. He described how Annetta and my Alan stood at the gate, watching as he vanished. I'm afraid he will return there; if he does, I may go with him, for I doubt he will ever return.

He was younger when he traveled beyond a needle's sting and the first breathtaking rush. He told me he used opium and sometimes shot heroin to raise his consciousness, and he said it would lift him up, take him to another time and a better place. He always found enough pretty words to obscure the truth or deflect questions. He would wander along dark, littered trails, out behind the whiskey and cocaine, and In the empty hours, after the warmth of morphine had cooled, leaving silence and desolation, he found other roads to travel. Through it all, what did he learn? As if learning was ever the goal. He was sure his way of using junk was safe. His trips would begin with new needles, always sterilized if reused, with close to pure pharmaceutical products as possible, and mixed only with distilled water. He climbed these paths to madness without guile or direction, believing some great truth would be revealed. At first, it was the experience, the thrill and excitement of another reality to explore, and always the incredible pleasure of floating on a vast lake of warm color and emotion. Friends warned him, pleaded, and yelled at him about the real and obvious dangers of addiction.

He knew better; he always did, explaining that he had no problems with heroin or morphine. Perhaps *others* did and became addicted, but not Em-Jay; he delighted in his immunity, believing he was unique, and maybe he was. Perhaps *others* were not concerned with clean needles or measured quantities. He was. Perhaps *others*, cowering in doorways or skid row shelters, were too far gone to care.

Others needed the rush; he wanted only the opportunity to explore and experience the enlightenment he knew was waiting for him. His friends were not convinced, but the passion and conviction of his denials carried him forward.

The final truth and great enlightenment for Em-Jay were that wanting, having quietly become needing, threw him against the rocks and washed him ashore. Another loser, another junkie, swept out of sight to join *others* in the same gutter. If any truths were revealed, they vanished quickly, without substance, and what was left for him were memories and a few travelers' tales.

So, in the end, all his years of worldly experience, the geometry, physics, and sciences he championed were for nothing. I believe he convinced himself his aberrant behavior could be excused, and changes to his physical appearance would go unnoticed. Perhaps I'm unfairly critical, but I do know for sure; that fear makes cowards of us all.

Through it all, he has endured, and his experiences are material for this story. He remains forever changed but is willing to recount his adventures for you and will do so humbly, with humor, and without regret. Talk to him for a while, and you will find an honest man who has experienced more in five years of his life than most do in a lifetime. That is undoubtedly one of the reasons that I fell in love with him. Although this is his story, you will hear other voices reaching out from the pages, each with a legitimate or compelling reason to claim your interest.

Okay, okay then, enough from me. I'm sure you'll enjoy the book, and well, you should, because as I said in the beginning, I will take the time to write it. So, the writing was my promise to Em-Jay, but the book is for you to enjoy.

Remember though, not everyone had a brightly lit, secure childhood, and not every fool is unworthy of salvation.

"A journey of a thousand miles begins with a single step." A quotation that is usually attributed to Chinese philosopher Lao Zhu. The actual origins are suspect; writings from such a learned source date from about 500 years b/c. Historical truths may dissipate over the years, but the intent of this simple message never falters. Any journey must begin with a single step, but the desire and commitment to take that first step are all important. During any lifetime, any journey starts beneath one's feet. I've found many other journeys are possible, borne on currents of one's imagination. Some imaginative journeys should never be started, and some never finished.

My repetitive go-to-work journey of seventy-five miles would end at my job as it did most weekdays and some weekends. Get up, get dressed, and go to work. Sometimes I would leave in anger, soon evaporating as my journey unfolded. Other times happily, with a repressed sense of excitement for the coming ride. In retrospect, searching back over the many years riding and driving these roads and freeways, one defining quality was that miles driven or ridden were never dull. I could tell of so many experiences that moved me very deeply on a personal level. Sections of any road driven at any time may seem straight without bend or purpose, boring to some, and predictable to others. Those travelers had chosen to ignore or perhaps couldn't hear the endless song of the highways that sing of life and death.

These Roads I ride are never quiet, never at peace, and never will be.

THE ROAD DOG

Roads absorb the sweat and smell of humanity and quickly become stained by the continual struggle with moving traffic. Highways and freeways, country lanes, and city streets are conduits of life. We have fought and died, loved, laughed, and given birth on the roads. Hopes and desires achievements and terrible losses. All these realities, thoughts, and emotions are continually played out on our highways, and it has always been so. Each path has a personal signature. Each road sings a different song. Roads are important to me, perhaps because I spend a long time on them.

Anyway, about thirty-five miles riding through California's high desert hills and canyons, navigating the narrow lanes and back roads that eventually reveal a neglected, overgrown on-ramp connecting to a minor two-lane freeway. Another thirty miles south, before joining the main intersections that spasmodically vomit traffic onto perpetually congested city streets.

Three more slow miles now on two wide neglected boulevards. I pass molesters, vagrants, and refugees from the previous night that are made unhappy beneath the morning daylight. There is nowhere to hide their litter or cover any nocturnal transgressions and nothing for them to do now but wait for the evening, then take shelter in shadows from flickering streetlights and barred doorways. They remain as they always do for nightclubs, motels, and late-night markets to entice a multitude of sinners with false neon promises.

There is some slight distraction on the streets outside the cheap motels. Wave to the women gathered there, I see a few familiar faces in the little groups, and I have probably become a familiar figure to some of them as I pass by on the motorcycle. I like these working girls, these colorfully decorated ladies gossiping and laughing so early in the morning.

Some wave back, and others stare past me through tired, vacant eyes. With regret, there is no time for me to stop and chat with them or listen to their stories. I must move on again with the hustle and flow of traffic, past dingy gas stations, fast food restaurants, liquor stores, and grim broken housing projects.

I see fragmented outlines of people walking or leaning, talking, and gesturing with meaningless puppet hand movements at every intersection and stop sign. There are darker mornings when the world around me splinters and breaks apart; at those times, I know we are all joined by a common thread of failed humanity. None of this matters because babies will be born here, and they will bring hope. Ignorance, hardship, and poverty shall not triumph; empty threatening words will echo in the streets without consequence. Children will emerge strengthened, resilient, and angry. This dismal ghetto land is a window in time, nonjudgemental but intolerant of weakness or fools. Many will fail, Some will succeed, and a few will shine like diamonds. Like a boiling pot, discontent and rage at the conditions they helped create will spill over and purge all that is here; and again, the cycle will continue.

There are many other mornings when brilliant summer sunshine will paint the city brightly, the streets will shine with golden, nothing should be taken seriously, and everything can be forgiven.

So I move on from my reverie, turn under a small railroad bridge and follow the tracks from a narrow, littered gangland street for about a mile—these few blocks reek of inner-city neglect and capitulation to local government apathy.

In this depressingly dirty industrial area, any flat wall becomes a canvas for graffiti artists to showcase their abilities and proclaim their dubious gospels. In most instances, imagination and bright artistic colors bring sudden relief from the surrounding drab monotony. The murals also support sinister undercurrents of tension, which is entirely appropriate in this neighborhood.

These decorative displays identify tribal boundaries, as do occasional gunshots. Depressing and dirty, these few square miles are and, to me, seem linked to prevailing weather conditions. Perhaps because I pass through every day at about the same time, I notice changes. The streets reflect a vibrant, bustling aspect in the summer or spring.

The onset of autumn and winter reveals their depressed, dangerous personalities again. Moving slowly past a few walls of discontent and colorful decoration before turning into a fenced yard and car park. Walk through another small fenced section, across the concrete slab, and into the restricted area where I spend my day and waste my time. Reverse and repeat the process every evening to complete my daily grind.

CHAPTER TWO

My boss thinks highly of me, as I do of him. *Old school* he is, but seldom questions my judgment, and even when my behavior should give cause for alarm, I am tolerated.

"Em-Jay? Yeah, he's a good engineer, eccentric, and opinionated most of the time, but nothing that's a problem for us. Pain in the ass at times, but then aren't we all? Although he usually rides a big motorcycle and comes in looking like a Hell's Angel gangster, he's a nice guy, intelligent and respectful. Good with people, too, and even gets along well with Pat. Now there's a real character for you. Another biker. Hell of a craftsman, though."

Pat is also tolerated and thinks well of the boss.

"Yeah, he's a good ole cracker, I guess."

And so, I chose to continue along this path of comfortable mediocrity, gazing into a boring, predictable future. My judicious use of opiates usually dissipates the ever-present boredom. I was concerned but not unhappy with my choices and saw more good days than bad.

Choices, Always choices; most days, there was a choice of car or motorcycle; I was lucky I had both, an old Toyota with too many miles, crappy but predictable, perhaps predictably crappy, and a sweet Harley shovelhead with a loud voice, a baby that I love and cherish. I would usually take the bike if rain were not forecasted.

There were a few memorable occasions when I misjudged the weather and rode in heavy rain and snow. Sometimes howling winter winds would claw at my face with Satan's icy fingers reaching through thick gloves and heavy boots into my numb fingers and toes. My Harley-Davidson motorbike is a friend of long-standing. Many miles drifting through mountain passes and across deserts, winding along coastal roads and cruising freeways, have brought us close to a happy non-committal relationship.

Time on a motorcycle brings a different perspective and a very personal relationship between the highway and rider: an intangible quality, an appreciation of one's surroundings that must be experienced to understand correctly. Nice people with no tattoos or body piercings secure within better-paid professions do not ride motorbikes or wear scruffy leather jackets. They drive nice clean cars, returning to their nice clean wives and husbands after they have finished work.

One memorable Friday afternoon, having finished with the seemingly endless futility of my working day, I headed towards home, navigating heavy city traffic to reach the freeway on-ramp. After making the turn at a major intersection, I moved slowly past a large Ford dealership forecourt. A woman on the narrow sidewalk walked towards me, perhaps mid-twenties, medium height with short blond hair. No eye contact or any form of recognition occurred before she suddenly pulled her tank top to her chin, unleashing a prominent pair of chunky breasts.

Her Jutting brown nipples contrasted nicely against an expanse of rounded white skin. The happy moment passed.

Tempted though I was to investigate further, had I jumped the curb or jammed on the brakes, the pain from a probable accident far outweighed the possibility of a pleasurable encounter. I waved my hand in appreciation, watching her blurred image fade forever in my rear-view mirror. There is a little bit of Elvis in us all.

A Jehovah Witness looking to share a sanitized version of the gospels with a stranger?

A nun from a progressive Catholic order selling tickets for a guaranteed absolution?

Either possibility is doubtful, although I will never know for sure. I do know for sure that a delightful woman who chose to share a sudden and memorable example of her femininity brought unexpected joy to a hardened, cynical traveler and, at the very least, deserved my gratitude and thanks.

And the sweet jingle-jangle of her magic triangle could be heard all the way to the end of the street.

There is a common misconception that a woman's breasts are functional; their only purpose is to nourish offspring. This dreary biological concept supported by the medical professions and held as truth by members of most religious and feminist groups is wrong. There is a mystery beneath the veil, and as many women admit, their breasts are primarily recreational appendages. Most men and some women have a genetic requirement and great fondness for caressing, squeezing, and fondling those delightful adornments. More than that, though, they evoke feelings of security and comfort with their softness and warmth. Old subconscious memories of a helpless baby and a nurturing mother return us to the beginning of my observations.

Tits are wonderful things; they will bring a soft scented breeze to blowing or cause a gentle rain to fall, also confirming that the proud owner is indeed a woman or possibly a determined transgender. The lady who deployed her stuff for me was aware of that obvious truth. And yes, I know a woman is a woman with or without breasts; just that I have a natural inclination toward them.

So, lifted by tawdry visions of what could have been, I decided to stop at Pat's place. About ten miles riding in the direction I was now heading would bring me to the house. Pat's place is a welcoming oasis to a large, loosely bound group of acquaintances. A common thread retaining the group in friendship is an appreciation for fine sporting guns, art, music, motorcycles, liquor, and narcotics.

Pat Winslow is a biker and a long-time Harley rider who is large, tough, hairy, and never to be messed with. A jovial alternative persona lurks beneath a surly glowering first impression that occasionally sees daylight. His big arms are profusely decorated with dark-inked tattoos. The mandatory biker beard is missing, replaced by a rugged, unshaven face. His house appears suddenly at the end of a secluded trail. The property is bordered on one side by an abandoned industrial complex and the other by an exotic animal rescue. It is a small three-bedroom, single-story refuge sitting on half an acre of grassland.

Pat told me he owned the property outright and paid for most of it with cash from the accumulated proceeds of cocaine sales.

In the mid-seventies, life was good in Southern California if you were young and had managed to avoid residency in another political graveyard for American heroes, *The South East Asia draft*.

My bike pulled hard with boisterous enthusiasm, the rhythmic thud of the exhaust fading like an echo behind me before changing to a happy gurgle as we coasted downhill on a trailing throttle. Soon be with friends; soon be at Pat's place. If I sit at a restaurant table, I expect to eat. If I go to Pat's home, I expect that, in some way, I will be fulfilled. I don't have the Beatles, Elvis, Allah, Muhammad, or the pope. There is no Smith with golden tablets, Jesus, Buddha, or any recently manufactured television deity to lean on or guide me in my weakness. I know my empty glass will always be filled at Pat's place, and my words will be welcomed. These evenings sometimes stretch into days, for some, perhaps lifetimes. Friday evening is a good choice for me, leaving the weekend to recover if necessary.

CHAPTER THREE

Pat had two reliable income streams. The conventional prototype machining position he held and his retail pharmaceutical enterprise. He delighted in displaying his skill and ability to produce complex metal parts using a variety of machines. He also sold drugs, specializing in heroin, cocaine, morphine, opium, and marijuana. Pat was as proud of his machining ability as he was of the quality of the narcotics he sold. The drug dealing was, I believe, confined to friends and trusted visitors to the house.

"I ain't greedy, so no reason to expand, no point in flying into the radar." He always said. He was right, I suppose; it seemed all his needs were met.

His lifestyle was muted, and he eschewed extravagance. No expensive car. No gaudy clothes or flashy jewelry. His dress code was rudimentary, Boots, Jeans, and tee shirts. A thick brown leather jacket, worn in the winter or when riding his bike, gave protection from rain and cold. The only jewelry he wore was an old military wristwatch his father had given him. He kept a low profile, living beneath the conventional social radar as much as possible, everything he paid for by cash, but he was not a humble man for all his lifestyle understatement. At times he was given to unpredictable, almost psychotic bursts of temper and, as a sudden storm, would explode with violent displays of rage.

He would never argue.

Just a long icy stare, then his piercing gray eyes would shine with a dark, malevolent fire. At that point, there was no room for debate; any discussion was over. I soon learned that time spent with Pat in a public place carried with it the possibility of sudden mayhem. He was not a bully, drunkard, or troublemaker and was not unreasonably confrontational. He was a trouble magnet, though. I was with him when he threw a man across a crowded hotel foyer after a brief disagreement.

On another memorable occasion, he and I were sitting in a burger house, finishing a small unhealthy lunch. Just before we left, a tall, casually dressed customer mid-thirties with spiky red hair started to argue with one of the girls serving behind the counter. Their disagreement escalated, voices raised, and the aggressive spiked fellow yelled at the girl, saying she was... "*just another dumb black bitch with no business taking orders for customers.*"

Pat suddenly left our table and, before I had pushed my chair away, was standing next to spiky red.

"Mind your mouth, sit down, and shut the fuck up."

There was no anger in his voice, no warning, no hint of displeasure, just an ominous monotone. Red turned to Pat,

"Who the hell are you? Mind yer own goddamn business."

By the time I reached the counter, Pat had seized the fellow by an arm and wrist, propelled him through the front door, and hit him hard on the side of the jaw, knocking him down. Red lay unmoving on the sidewalk for many seconds.

All in all, this could have been a page from a movie script, except this wasn't any Hollywood action-hero exploit; this was a long-haired biker with a bad temper. The blood was real, and the scene was undoubtedly as real as it gets. We had both disappeared before the cops arrived. Although he would protest otherwise, Pat was at once a good friend and a terrible liability.

I've known Pat for about seven years. I first met him when I was hired as a development engineer at the same small company where he was employed as a machinist. My initial impressions were that Pat was an agreeable fellow, although his manner and appearance were intimidating. I once asked him if he had any diplomas or grad school certificates. He thought for a moment,

"No, but if the paper makes me a better machinist, I'll bring some with me tomorrow morning; I'll bring a roll of soft, too, if you think that will help."

A shared interest in vintage firearms and a love of Harley motorcycles soon had us on the familiar ground; we both walked with confidence. I was invited to his house during the second week at my new job.

"Come on over to my place for an hour or two, just off the freeway in the same direction you're goin."

Quite an honor, as I was later to discover. Over the years, there were only two people from work Pat invited to his house. I was one; the other was a young Mexican boy Philippe; he started as a janitor about the same time I was hired.

I found the house quickly enough, although I was surprised by the sudden quiet after leaving the freeway. Shutting the engine down, I stood for a few seconds listening intently—no sounds of music, no laughter, or any other indication the house was occupied. The stillness was all around me; no traffic noise, birds, or insect sounds. A wide concrete pad at the side of the house was used to good effect as a parking lot. A dark-blue Mercedes rested elegantly next to two custom Harley motorcycles. A bracket and chain held a well-worn heavy punch bag from an adjacent wall.

CHAPTER FOUR

Before I could ring the bell, the door was thrown open, framing a grinning Pat Winslow. "Glad you could make it, limey. That ole pile o shit yer ridin makes enough noise to stop a clock."

He laughed loudly, beckoning to me. "Come on in."

I followed him into a large untidy living room; one wall was lined with a sectional black leather sofa. Two neatly dressed folks about thirty years or so lounged comfortably. Both nodded in my direction as I entered. There were no other occupants in the room.

"This limey is Em-Jay, the engineering dude I work with." Then turning to me,

"On the seat are two Jews, back in a few, gotta piss."

Having finished the formal introductions, he spun around and disappeared through a side door.

The fellow sitting nearest to me got to his feet, shaking his head, a big man with a pleasant manner. He stretched his arm and shook my hand.

"Glad to meet you, Em-Jay; I think this makes me Jew number one. Names Dave Zimmerman, this is my brother Mark." Mark shook my hand and laughed.

"That makes me Jew number two or the younger Jew, I suppose."

We all laughed, and I was happy with the easy familiarity between us

Despite Pat's brusque introductions, we quickly fell into a pleasant conversation. I learned they owned a small sheet metal fabrication business. Their shop was located about five miles from my workplace; I had unknowingly passed it every morning on my way to work. We chatted for several minutes. During our conversations, we speculated that Pat would be better employed in another occupation rather than a machinist. Perhaps a customer service rep at the department of motor vehicles or behind the front desk in a busy doctor's office.

We were still chuckling when Pat returned to join the conversation. He pulled a chair from the other side of the room, placing it in front of a glass-topped coffee table. Reaching into his back pocket, he produced a small glass vial.

"A little bump for you assholes?"

Mark laughed, "see how things change around here? First, we were Jews; now we're assholes."

"Can I be an asshole too?" I asked Pat.

"You already are." he replied, "Now there's three of you."

He tapped the vial on the glass surface until a small mound of glittering white powder spilled out. "Coke?" I asked.

Pat nodded, grinning. I reached across the table and took the vial from him.

I'm not an expert, but this was unlike any blow I had seen before. Holding the glass tube to the light, I saw large flakes that shone and sparkled with a bluish-white light. My experience was that coke was a dull white fluffy powder.

Pat laughed, "what you see, limey"?

I shook my head. "Never seen coke like this."

"Probably won't again. Like the rest of my stuff, this shit is from a good source; a lot of it goes to Hollywood movie jack-offs before I get mine." Laughing again, he opened a heavy paper fold and produced a single-edge razor blade. It took him several minutes to chop and part a long line on the table.

"Em-Jay, ask the Mexican gyp in the kitchen for straws."

He pointed to the door through which he had recently disappeared.

I wanted to ask what a gyp was, a gypsy, perhaps? Anyway, through the door I went. To my right, a short passage with a closed door. Bedroom or bathroom, probably. Ahead was a large area, obviously the kitchen. *Obviously*? Well, there was an old-fashioned cooking range and other cooking-like appliances surrounding it. Standing at the range with a straight, almost military-like posture was a slim woman, her glossy black hair woven into a long thick braid. Probably she was the Mexican gypsy.

Her back was facing me, so I coughed to announce my presence, hoping not to startle her. She remained facing the range, unmoving as if she had never heard me.

"Hello, sorry to interrupt, but..."

"You are mister pat's boss, then?" She asked without turning from the stove.

"No," I continued, a little taken aback by this strange encounter.

"Not his boss; we work together but in different departments."

She turned to face me, smiling gently—dark skin, thin, rather angular features about thirty or so with large gentle brown eyes.

"You are Em-Jay, then?"

"Yes, pleased to meet you." It was then I noticed her accent. Spanish, probably; if so, Pat's Mexican gyp comment was understandable. I offered my hand as she reached for a towel. Both her hands were covered with fresh blood. I stared in astonishment as she wiped her hands on a cloth.

"So sorry darling Em-Jay, you are having me at a bad time, I think. Look, I have for dinner tomorrow."

Still holding the cloth, she reached into the sink to her left and produced a brown cat, obviously dead, swinging from the back legs she held in her hand.

"Just started to cut and skin when you came. Sorry if I am rude."

"You eat cats at your house"? It was her turn to stare.

Suddenly she laughed with a delightfully warm melodic timbre.

"Darling Em-Jay, there are many things for you to learn. Pat say you are good engineer; I think you may be, but you must learn the important difference between a kitty and a rabbit, yes?" She walked to me and kissed each cheek, leaving a streak of blood on my forehead. Quickly running a little water and wetting a paper towel, she wiped my face like a baby, laughing as she did so.

"Perfect, and now all happy and clean, eh? My name is Annetta."

"Dear Miss Annetta, very pleased to meet you. I am Em-Jay. For some reason, I'm happy you don't eat cats. Pat sent me to ask you for straws. By the way, what is a gyp? Is that a Mexican gypsy?"

She turned suddenly without answering and walked quickly back to the range. Pulling open a cupboard door above the hot plate, she reached for a torn cardboard box and roughly drew a few straws. Some fell to the floor. Something had suddenly changed. She was no longer smiling; her demeanor was tense and angry, her movements stiff and deliberate.

"Here, tell that pig that sends you I will one day find a place between his ugly ribs for this blade. Ask *him* what is a gyp if you did not know."

Her brown eyes now shone with fury as she thrust the straws at me; she held a short kitchen knife in her left hand. I stepped back hurriedly, now thoroughly confused.

"Annetta, I'm very sorry if I offended you. Believe me. I did not intend to. You are a beautiful lady, but remember, you are talking to a fool who doesn't know what a gyp is or the difference between a cat and a rabbit. Please forgive."

She stared at me for a few seconds, then ran to me, throwing her arms around my waist, kissing my lips quickly, and laughing.

"Let us both go in peace and with love, darling fool Em-Jay; we meeting again soon, I know."

Pat laughed loudly when I returned. "Shit, she must like you; she gave you the straws."

"She likes me because she gave me straws? You asked me to get them for you."

"Did she tell you to fuck off?"

"No."

"Then she likes you. Lighten up, Em-Jay, not so serious; ain't we all friends here?"

And, of course, we were. The memory of the knife and the flash of anger behind her brown eyes were not diminished by our friendship, though.

And when the coke was gone, we were all still friends. Pat cut another line. He did not use a straw. He just rubbed a small amount on the inside of his mouth. Brother Mark, the Jew number two, and I were the only ones to inhale the lines. I looked at Pat, "nothing for you or Dave?"

Pat shook his head. "Don't do any of that shit, never did, a beer or two sometimes, nothing else."

Dave laughed. "Yeah, same for me; I'm dumb enough without dope."

"More power to you, gentlemen. I use it because I like it, a character flaw, I suppose."

Dave nodded. "A good reason, Em-Jay, long as you don't use it because you think you need to. Opium ain't too bad occasionally; *smack is*. Stay away from that crap. Stay away from the skid row caviar *speed*; almost as bad as smack, in my opinion. Coke is okay sometimes, like fine wine, but don't get caught up in it, and don't smoke it.

The problem is, most street stuff is cut with junk—anything from cornflower and talcum powder to speed. The bastards use anything to take yer money. That's the thing; good blow will cost the same as the shit. About the only reasonable source around here is the Pat man." He laughed, nodding to Pat. Then Turning to me again, he continued,

"Look, man, don't think I'm sticking my nose or lecturing you. Just my opinion is all. Just saying."

"No, no problem at all, Dave. I appreciate your opinion."

And so the evening continued. Neither Mark nor I did more coke. This stuff was long-lasting and about perfect. The sweet, strong taste and numbing sensation of anesthetic at the back of my throat, a great sense of euphoria, and a pleasing camaraderie told me everything was very well with the world.

When Pat left the room, Mark lowered his voice speaking quickly to me.

"The woman Annetta, the girl you saw in the kitchen, she's Italian, not Mexican, studying fine arts at the University UCLA. Pat can't stop; he has to goad her. Don't get me wrong, I love him like a brother, but he can be a real asshole at times.

He's lucky she puts up with his crap." Dave grinned, nodding in agreement.

"Yeah, like a big kid. If he don't get a reaction, there's no fun in it for him. Nothing personal, just the way he is. Example… know what a gyp is, Em-Jay?" I shook my head.

"See over on top of that little white wood cabinet? Have a look at the photo there." I did as he suggested and examined an ornate folding frame that held a close-up color photograph of a brindle dog. "Pit Bull, Em-Jay. Pat had a couple of em here a while ago. The one in the picture is a female. Old-time dogfighters called em gyps, never bitches." Understanding was coming slowly to me, and I thought of my recent introduction to Annetta. "She's Pat's woman, then?"

Mark shook his head vigorously. "Nah-no way, she just…Before Mark could finish his sentence, Pat returned, interrupting our conversation with beer, Led Zeppelin, and a local bluegrass band.

At least two thirty when we all went our separate ways. Next week, I decided to ask Pat about his Pit Bulls and his relationship with Annetta. I also decided to take Annetta in my arms and kiss her with great feeling and affection when another opportunity presented itself. With any luck, I would avoid the pain of a knife between my ribs.

I swung onto the freeway and headed north. There was nothing between me and the road as I sat on a whispering cloud of motion. We sailed the gentle freeway tide singing a short, sweet song. The wind at our back took us forward; the breeze in my face brought clarity, filled my lungs, and gave me hope. The sounds of a far distant engine exhaust hung on a cool evening many miles behind.

Eventually, the wind brought us to familiar twisty back lanes beneath a clear night sky. A dull orange moon and countless incandescent stars lit our path. Everything was in its proper place that evening; everything was good.

I sat on the back porch swing, staring up at the sky. It was a blazing field of light above me, so close I thought I would reach up and touch it. If I did, I might feel the tiny pinpoints of bright burning starlight.

As I watched, I realized everything was in a gentle rolling motion. In fact, the great blanket of light above me was a vast luminous ocean, part of the freeway sea that recently brought us home. I wondered about that, wondered at what point and where the sky ocean flowed down into the freeway. I needed to talk to someone and discuss the unique abstract thoughts that had just occurred to me. I was alive at four in the morning, dancing with light and filled with nervous, sparkling energy. This was my, being the living motion that gave me reason. Here at this time, at this moment, I knew the purpose, if not the direction of my life.

I thought about the evening at pats. The conversations and music returned clearly. Jokes bought laughter again. I knew I would return to that house many times. I knew I would see Annetta again; shadows were all around her, and she was obscured by a mystery I did not understand. Questions waited for answers, and there were many feelings between us that could only be resolved in the bedroom.

Sleep came to me later, but it wasn't easy to find. Peace came to me later in my life, but it was a long time coming.

CHAPTER FIVE

It was early next week, Tuesday, I think, when I found an opportunity to ask Pat about the mysterious gyp and the Pit Bulls.

"Better than tell you I'll show you," he said in response to my question. "What brought that up?"

"Remember at your place when I went for the straws? I asked Annetta if a gyp was a Mexican gypsy. Big mistake; I thought she would stick a knife in me."

It seemed like a long time before Pat stopped laughing.

"Yeah? Well, that explains why she wouldn't talk to me for a couple o days. Fuckin gyps are all the same." Another long laughing session.

"Look, Em-Jay, Saturday, me an the cop is going to Tehachapi, about two hours from here. We all meet here at seven sharp. Stop at the pie house, grab a bite to eat, then move on to Ruben's place. He always has Pit Bulls and usually has a good gyp or two."

Friday evening, I turned down an invitation to meet at Pat's place for beer.

"Not this time, gotta be up in the morning, going to the house of gyp."

A little before seven, I rolled into the parking lot.

Pat's bike was parked next to an old Ford F-150 truck. I stood my bike next to the truck. Pat, accompanied by a stocky, tough-looking man I assumed was the cop, walked into the parking lot from the street.

"Heard that ole scooter halfway down the freeway, man. This is Reggie. He should give you a ticket for disturbin the fuckin peace."

"Reg Brown." The cop shook my hand and grinned. "The wrong department for traffic tickets. Pleased to know you." He was probably in his early forties, about five-ten, with iron-gray hair that may once have been blond. A large disfiguring scar parted his upper lip, giving him the appearance of a battered street fighter. Well-worn jeans and a white Tee shirt enhanced the image. A sudden smile transformed his face; I liked him at once.

"Em-Jay," I said. "Glad to know you, Reg. Thanks for the disturbing peace pass."

During our conversations in the truck and at the pie shop over breakfast, no mention of gyps was made. Reg told me he was leaving the LAPD

"Been with em for nine years. Now they put me undercover. Tell the truth, Em-Jay, and I hate it. I'm thinking of leaving Los Angeles, perhaps back to New York. Even working the streets, I don't know anymore who the fuck the good guys are or who are the bad. I'm beginning to think there ain't no difference."

He told me he was studying for his real estate broker's license. For some reason, I felt inexplicably sad and very sorry for Reg.

He drove slowly through the pleasant green country until we came to a house at the end of a steep, impossibly narrow lane. The castle of gyp was a large single-floor house—a modern open-plan design, sitting on a large lot of uneven grassy ground. I was surprised to see about fifteen vehicles parked in front of the house. Three motorcycles stood alone at the side. Besides the bikes, an old John Deer tractor waited, a humble, patient icon dressed in faded green paint. Ruben greeted us enthusiastically. He hugged Pat and Reg and extended his hand when Reg introduced me. He was slim, medium height, and Hispanic-looking with oiled black hair swept back and tied into a ponytail. A heavy accent also helped identify him.

"Pat, tell me you come to see my gyps? Good, I show you, Sue, the one we use later, eh?"

I followed him to the back of the house, accompanied by Pat. In a large area of leveled ground, there were about ten dogs secured by chains and attached to old auto axles driven into the ground. Wide nylon collars were around the dog's necks and fastened to the chains. Large chain swivels allowed the dog free range without knotting up the chains, and there was enough area when fully extended to separate each animal from his neighbor. Each dog's space had a plastic barrel with a large hole cut into one end. These were filled with straw providing comfortable-looking shelter.

The animals were various colors; none were particularly big like Rottweiler's or Doberman's; some jumped about excitedly when they saw us; those that remained in attitudes of indifference followed us closely with bright glittering eyes. "You like what you see, man? You like my boys?" Ruben grinned and indicated the chained animals with a wave of his hand.

Not knowing what the hell to say to him, not knowing what breed of dog he had, I paused, shaking my head.

"About the best I've seen in a long time, Ruben. You know what you're doing, obviously a man who knows his dogs."

Ruben was delighted. He grinned hugely and slapped me hard on my back.

"Thanks for that, brother, means a lot. Yeah," he continued, "I've been with the Bulldogs for about ten years and been in the sport about seven. Most of my stuff is Crenshaw; some crossed out with Floyd's stuff."

I nodded slowly as if weighing this new information with expert understanding, unfortunately, not knowing at all what he was talking about. For sure, I saw no Bulldogs as we walked. A slight incline brought us to a leveled area upon which stood a large wooden shed. Ruben unlatched the door and spoke softly to someone inside, and then flipped on the light. A chain-link cage about six feet square housed a small red dog.

"There you go, Em-Jay. This is Sue. As good a gyp as you are goin to see at forty." I squatted in front of the cage as the dog greeted us happily. I shook my head, saying nothing, avoiding Pat's eyes as I held a meaningful conversation with Sue. She was a compact animal showing obvious muscle in her legs and chest. Thin, though, with ribs clearly visible.

"About half-hour Em-Jay, I'll bring her down for the weigh-in and wash."

I nodded to Ruben, not knowing the difference between a weighing and wash. *Probably better not to ask questions yet,* I thought, wishing fervently I had said nothing to Annetta about a gyp. Pat and I returned to the house.

"Nice looking gyp," I said.

Pat chuckled loudly." Which one? The red one or the Mexican."

He was still laughing as we entered the house.

At the side of the house, an electric roll-up door opened into a three-car garage. Wooden boards about knee height were arranged to form a large rectangle. Each panel was fastened to the next, creating a sturdy structure. Within the rectangular frame, a floor was laid with thick interlocking rubber sheets. A long strip of silver duct tape in each diagonally opposing corner was the line the dogs had to pass. *Scratch lines I was later to learn.*

A sturdy shelf ran the length of the rear wall behind me, forming a strong bench littered with various dog stuff, medical supplies, and collars. About fifteen people were milling around, some locked in animated conversation. There was a scattering of well-dressed women in the crowd and a few children, although the kids quickly disappeared. As I looked about, I saw some of the male attendees were also well-dressed. There were a few s uits and ties, but most wore jeans and tee shirts. Many of them acknowledge Pat with a nod or handshake. Reg appeared suddenly and stood next to me.

"Watta think Em-Jay ready for the show? Your first time, Pat tells me."

"Hey Reg, yeah, I suppose so; what the hell sort of show, though?"

"Bulldogs, man, you goin to see em in combat."

"Ruben has Bulldogs as well as the others, then?" I asked. Reg stared at me. "You ain't putting me on, pal; you don't know? Pat never said anything to you?"

I shook my head, becoming a little annoyed now by the whole situation.

"Okay, let's go outside for a moment. Let me explain what's going on here. First things first, then, Ruben is a dog man, a dogfighter. You knew that, right?"

"No, Pat said nothing to me, only that Ruben had gyps." Reg continued shaking his head.

"Okay, this is what Ruben does for a living, how he makes his money. Sells a few sometimes but mostly sets em down for cash. Puts his money up and bets on em. The more he wins more valuable his dog line becomes. All this is very much against the law, of course. Believe me, for you to be invited here without him knowing you just don't happen. Because of his friendship with Pat, I guess."

"He knows you are police Reg?"

Reg laughed, "Yeah, I've known Pat and Ruben for a long time. When I go to these functions or parties, I go as the man, not the badge." He continued, "These people fight bulldogs; most outsiders call em pit bulls. All the dogs you see around here are pit bulls bred by Ruben with me so far?"

I nodded, "Yeah, but I thought pit bulls were big with short ears."

"No, you're thinking of other breeds. Any short ears here are from surgery. Dogfighters have their own language, like engineers and cops."

He laughed as I nodded in understanding.

"The pit bull is the original old-time bulldog, not that fat greasy lump from England. You know what a gyp is now." It was my turn to grin as I nodded.

"The male is either a dog or a male. Look, when we have time, we can talk more. The show is about to start."

Back inside again with me only a little wiser.

CHAPTER SIX

An older man, tall with long gray hair, stepped into the arena, *the pit* Reg called it. He produced a small microphone and addressed the spectators in a deep southern drawl.

"Thank yall for coming. My name's Phil Massy; good to see a few familiar faces here. All interested parties have agreed that I referee both matches, so yall will see me again in a spell. Before we start, I ask all spectators to give a little room behind the walls. No holding or leaning, please." He paused, looking around, smiling.

"We have two contract matches for you today. First, two gyps." pointing to a corner behind him

"Behind me, Rubens Sue. In the other corner, Rowdy Kennels Black Belle. Gyps at 40 pounds, no forfeit called. Both gyps are washed; no taste is called. Handling for Ruben Castillo is Willie, Handling for Rowdy Kennels, Little John." The timekeeper for both contests will be Bobby Monday.

The gyps were in their respective corners, behind the silver-taped lines. Both were restrained by the handlers and faced away from each other.

"Corners make ready." After a few seconds, "corners face your dogs." and then "Corners, let go."

With the gyps now facing each other, both handlers released the animals, and no collars or leads were restraining them. Sue and Belle flew from their corners, meeting in the center of the pit. Sue dropped her head and grabbed a front leg, biting and twisting hard. Belle turned and bit down on Sue's nose. There were no cries or other indications of pain and suffering. Both gyps bit and shook, at times rolling on the floor, biting and wrestling for position. Ruben and Pat called encouragement to Sue at the far end of the pit. Both handlers stood close to their animals; the referee watched attentively, moving position and squatting at times.

For over half-hour, they fought hard without a break. Both dogs bleeding heavily, locked in a mad, violent dance, a bloody ritual tango without music: no barking or growling, just heavy panting and the sound of their claws on the mat. Sue was the small golden-eyed red girl, the same friendly tail-wagging creature that only a few minutes ago I was talking to and scratching her head. I wondered about the black gyp. Was she friendly like Sue?

It seemed to me Belle was tiring and breathing hard. I thought Sue was much fresher, always eager to engage with Belle. After another fifteen minutes or so, Belle turned her head and moved back several paces with Sue hanging on her rear leg. Willie called to the ref: for a turn. The handlers returned their animals to their respective corners.

"Black Belle to scratch," Little John released Belle; she stood panting for breath staring with empty, vacant eyes refusing or unable to move.

"Five seconds," the referee counted slowly to five, at which time he raised his hand.

"Rowdy Kennels Black Belle did not cross the scratch line. At forty-eight minutes, hard-fought and hard-won. The winner is Rubens Sue.

Willie grabbed Sue again, returning her to her corner. The spectators responded with applause and cheering.

The fight was over. It was then I realized my fists were clenched so tightly I could not open my fingers to clap. Reg and I walked to Sue's corner to congratulate Ruben. Sue was being moved to her holding kennel, the one we had visited earlier. She was covered with blood and limping heavily. Reg told me Willie would wash her with antiseptic and stitch any wounds as needed. It was then I first became aware of the smell. A peculiar and not unpleasant "wet dog" odor that I have smelled many times since, and each time I do, I am returned instantly to this place.

This whole dogfighting thing was not as I expected. It seemed to me the affair was conducted like a traditional, almost civilized sporting event with a referee and timekeeper of all things. I was amazed, *almost civilized except for the blood,* I thought. I would say the same for a boxing match, blood and all, a sport I dearly love. Had anyone previously asked my opinion of dogfighting, I would have immediately condemned the practice, ascribing it to a bunch of street gang thugs delighting in cruelty with no regard for the animals.

The next fight was between dogs at fifty-six pounds. An all-white against a brown brindle. This fight did not interest me as much as the first match because Ruben had no connection with either dog. It was one hour and fourteen minutes when the brindle corner pulled their dog to save it from further punishment—a vicious bone-breaking affair with the pit walls splattered with blood. Within twenty minutes or so, the crowd of spectators had quietly evaporated.

Remaining at the house, a few friends, and Ruben's wife. His young daughter was also present, talking in familiar terms with both handlers and referee Massey. The air was littered with bulldog talk, and the room was filled with *gyp, turns, scratch, holds, rolls, and weights.* I found this all quite interesting and absorbed as much information about these canine fighters as possible. Ruben's daughter Alice, a pretty dark-haired child about twelve years, started talking to me.

"What do you think of Sue?" She asked.

"An excellent little gyp," I replied, exercising my newfound vocabulary.

Alice nodded. "She's good, but Red Rosie was better for my money. Did you ever see her go?" I shook my head.

"Rosie had a harder bite, a true stifle dog. My dad sold her to a friend in Mexico. Sue is her daughter."

"Sorry, I never saw her; your father certainly knows his Bulldogs."

She nodded, "I'm going to be a vet when I leave school, but I think doctors make more money; what do you do?" It was then our conversation was interrupted by Pat.

"Time Em-Jay, what's new with you, Alice?"

"Hi Pat, Oh, nothing really. Do you have the bike outside?"

"Not this time, peaches. I haven't forgotten about our ride, though. Next time I bring the bike, you, me, down the road. Em-Jay rides a Harley. Talk to him about a ride."

Alice grinned, chattering innocently. "Em-Jay, would you give me a ride?" My dad used to ride a Harley, but he had to sell it when we got this house. Reg Brown has a bike, but it broke. Pat's fixing it for him. Would you *please*?"

What could I do?

"Here's an idea, Alice. I don't have the bike here. I'll come over, perhaps next week, if that's okay with dad and mom, pick you up, and we'll go to breakfast, just you and me."

Alice squealed with delight and ran to tell her parents.

Pat grinned. "Looks like you got another gyp, then; at least this one won't have a kitchen knife."

"No, but I'm sure she could borrow one from her mama."

After much discussion, the arrangement was cleared with Ruben and his wife, Dot. We exchanged phone numbers, with me agreeing to call and confirm.

"Tell you what; we can all go to breakfast then, my treat." Dot shook her head.

"Thanks, Em-Jay, soon, but not this time. This will be a big deal for Alice, a grown-up thing, and something to boast to her school friends about. We keep to ourselves mostly, and this place is isolated, as you can see. Not much chance for Alice to make friends other than at school, human ones anyway. Oh, I know she isn't thirteen yet, just a baby, but this will be such a treat for her."

I chatted with Ruben for a half-hour before Pat called time again. After the handshakes, thanks, and good wishes, Reg, Pat, and I boarded the Reg truck, and we made for home.

Not much sleep for me that night. I found a small joint in the kitchen drawer and smoked it. Mary Jane of any color is not my favorite high; I've tried a bong, pipe, hookah, and papers. They all make me cough. After the coughing stops and feeling like an idiot, I stare fixedly at distant objects, unwilling to converse or interact with anyone.

Waves of self-consciousness engulf me. I know everyone is staring at me, and I must remain very small and quiet. These feelings are always the same, no matter the occasion. There is no pleasure for me at the end of the bud or leaf. If I smoke, my pleasure is a small rolled cigarette with good tobacco and about half a milligram of white Mexican smack.

Why I smoked that night, I do not know. So many new experiences, perhaps, so many feelings to recall and examine. This had been one hell of an interesting day. At the time, a joint seemed an appropriate punctuation mark—only a little coughing and not too much staring. As there was no audience, the self-conscious feelings never bothered me. I sat on the back porch swing, gazing into a moonlit sandy landscape surrounding me.

I thought about my new friends. Three good people, each as far from the social mainstream as one could get. Each with fine qualities, each very different from the other. And me, I was as different from them as they were from me, or perhaps there were no differences at all. A cord of common trust ran between us all, it seemed. If not for the trust Pat and Reg felt in me, I would never have met Ruben, certainly not at his house with the dogs.

I remember Reg grinning, "You did good Em-Jay. Didn't run your mouth or ask questions about anybody. I think Ruben and Dot really like you."

"Yeah, Alice sure does," laughed Pat.

"Why don't you guys come next Saturday? A great run and a good breakfast on me."

"Can't-do?" said Pat. "Got people coming over."

"Me either," said Reg. "Unless we go in the truck. Still waiting for Pat to finish the valve seat inserts."

So I gazed past the sand and moon into the infinity of dark sky, thinking about Bulldogs and the dog pit. I became lost in a peaceful floating sensation that carried me to Annetta. I never remembered going to bed, but I knew she had come with me. The following morning I could smell her perfume on the pillow and lingering faintly in the bedroom.

CHAPTER SEVEN

Another week had passed. Saturday morning, a little after nine, when I rolled into Rubens's yard, a great fanfare of barking dogs greeted me. Dot and Alice came to the door laughing. Alice ran to meet me before I shut the engine down. We walked hand in hand to the shed where Sue was recuperating. She was chained outside, jumping and barking with few signs of her recent ordeal. Talking with Ruben for a few minutes and petting Sue was more than Alice could stand. She was jumping up and down, begging me to start the bike.

So with Alice secured behind me, we rode away, stopping for breakfast at Aunties burger and sandwich shop. She seemed overwhelmed by this great adult adventure and obviously uneasy with the sophisticated ambiance of the burger house. Sitting opposite Alice at the clean plastic table, waiting for our clean plastic food, I stared at a hollow-eyed face, a haunted child with eyes ringed by dark circles. There was a sickness over her, a bad feeling of impending tragedy close to me. We chatted about her school and the teachers she liked.

She told me she now had a cat. "A little black and white male. Found it wandering around the house. It won't go away," she laughed, "so now I keep him and call him Bobby. He isn't afraid of the dogs either."

After food, we rode slowly through the surrounding countryside for about half an hour. Eventually, we returned to the house, Alice babbling continually to her parents about our ride and the recent breakfast. Everyone was happy. It seemed everyone except me. I could not shake the ominous feeling or the specter of distant misery unfolding. I said nothing about my feelings or observations to the family, Just that we had a good time, and thanked them for letting me take their beautiful daughter to breakfast. I was still questioning my vision of an innocent little girl in the middle of all this illegal dogfighting activity. Her parents seemed to be loving, honorable folk, obviously concerned for their daughter's well-being, but there was a most disturbing aspect of the situation I found difficult to accept. A pretty little schoolgirl is wandering nonchalantly through a pack of wolves—goodbyes time and now, hugs from Ruben and dot.

"Mi Casa Es Su Casa," Ruben said earnestly. And Alice plaintively "Please be careful Em-Jay, and please don't crash and fall off."

"I will be very careful and take you for another ride soon, sweetheart."

With happy faces and waving's, I trickled down the steep lane to find the highway once again. I was beginning to love this ride, green, for the most part until the city boundaries on then through familiar high desert highways to home. Two weeks had elapsed before I heard from Ruben again. Wednesday, I think, just after lunch when he called.

"Em-Jay, come on out Sunday. I'm goin to roll a few, nothing special, but probably worth watching. If you tell Pat, I'll call Reg. After we finish with work, we throw some chicken on the fire an drink a few cold ones."

"Sounds like a perfect Sunday, friend; anything you want us to bring?"

"Not a damn thing, amigo. There's food, beer, and good people."

Reg called. His bike was not quite ready for the road.

"If you bad boys like, we'll take the ole truck again. Not much point all going in separate vehicles."

Everything was arranged. It just needed a Sunday. As luck would have it, just beyond Saturday, a Sunday suddenly appeared. Reg and Pat were at my house a little after eight. A few miles later, we stopped at a supermarket for beer, and We bought four six-packs despite Ruben. I suggested a bottle of red wine.

"You are one fucked-up hombre," Pat said, laughing. "This ain't a fagot ballet were goin' to," Reg grinned at me.

"Yeah? We're both fucked up, then, I guess? I drink more red wine than beer."

"Perhaps we should invite Pat to a cheese and wine party then?" Reg nodded, "suits and ties only."

"Yeah, maybe shave and a haircut" Pat shook his head, muttering about "having to ride in a truck again with two wino assholes."

Another slow drive on a beautiful morning. Another day of illegal activity was waiting for my participation. I wondered about the implications of the coming dog thing. Neither Pat nor Reg had explained the meaning of a roll, and I was too embarrassed to ask Ruben. Whatever it might be, I was sure it would have two distinct qualities. One, it would be illegal; two, it would be enjoyable.

I realized then how far removed I was from my previous life in England. So far away from my repressed upbringing in London's city and suburbs. A million miles distance between the dogfighting pit at Rubens and my mother's church benefit tea-and-cake mornings on the back lawn of her house. Everything seemed much simpler then. My wants were few; the air was cleaner, and life was miserable. The happy gossiping church folk, the old worshipers, secure beneath the words of their imaginary gods, inane parrot chattering bringing happiness to some, distress to others. I despised their hypocritical yapping, yet there was comfort in the ritualistic performances. There was comfort in the misty rain, the smell of cool early morning, and the bright green grass freshly cut. When I remember these things now and think of my parents, I am sad but sometimes find a small measure of comfort there.

These two groups, dogfighters and worshipers, were not so different, perhaps. Just people meeting for a common purpose, neither group interested in the other. I wondered how I had come to this place in my life, where I had gone wrong or just gone. Here I was, a young, almost respectable mechanical engineering graduate with a job, house, and mortgage. On the surface, the chains of capitalism were already beginning to tighten with respectability, waiting around the corner. Later a wife and children would secure balls to the chains. However, my love for motorcycles and a fondness for narcotics held respectability temporarily at bay.

In retrospect, I suppose I was never really respectable. The value or condition of respectability was a quality held dear by my mother and impressed into me every day, like table manners and cleanliness. I think my stepfather's influence and my mother's need to rise above her dirt-poor days in Dublin were her reasons for giving such importance to respectability. I listened to stories she told of my father, Jim O'Connell making gin in the bathtub, drinking in the bars, and their life in the slums. Respectability must have been an unknown and unnecessary concept in those days.

I followed many overgrown twisting trails that eventually brought me to California. In England, my love for motorbikes steered me toward a career in mechanical engineering. There is an eloquence in design and functionality not found in any other utilitarian transport, except perhaps a horse. I never rode horses in England, only motorcycles, and now I ride motorcycles in Southern California. I have used drugs in England and used them in the USA. I found opium and hash in the Navy, heroin, morphine, and cocaine at my job in California.

The over-prescribed painkillers and sleeping pills hold no interest anymore. At one time, they did. A while ago, the Percocet and morphine tabs were my friends. Stupidly lifting a heavy rotary table from a mill bed, I twisted as I set it down on a bench a few yards away. Never again.

The following day I was all but paralyzed. X Rays and Cat scans told their story, and spinal injections and a body cast helped me heal. Morphine and Oxycodone shut most of the pain down. The problem I found was that my body adapted to the meds, and every week, I would increase the prescribed dose. At one time, I was taking six Oxycodone tablets washed down with a large glass of whiskey. The only way I was able to sleep.

The doctor told me I would stop breathing if I continued, but *he* continued to prescribe them, no doubt trusting me to listen to him and pay my bill before I expired. An attendant problem with these prescription opiates was awful constipation. I never experienced that problem with heroin or coke. I was told many users crush the tabs mixing the powder with a little water and injecting the mix—apparently an amazing, if dangerous, experience. I never did try that. I thought about it, though.

So, no more of that modern medical stuff for me. I stopped *cold turkey*, full of anger and depression but free. Now, no more of the beloved antidepressants, tranquilizers, or any other addictive painkilling doctor drugs recommended ostensibly for medicinal purposes.

I prefer quality cocaine to inhale, perhaps heroin to smoke, although I have tried tapering off. Like the heroin, I continue to smoke opium in limited quantities. Ask me why I would do this; well aware of the dangers these practices involve. Later, I may tell how I first saw the devil cat, the God that changed my smack habit. It was after shooting a little number four heroin. I don't use the needle anymore; that cat experience was enough, but I smoke a little. My failings are indelibly written on the pages of my life. The pages are not clean; none are pristine, and there are a few I wish I were able to rip out. But we were on our way to Rubens, and this was not the time for introspection or self-pity. And as I was drifting and reminiscing, I fancied Annetta's voice whispering quite clearly, "dream on, my darling fool Em-Jay. The best and worst are yet to come."

CHAPTER EIGHT

Little Alice squeaked, gurgling and laughing uncontrollably when Pat threw her into the air catching her and throwing her again. Ruben heard the clamor of our arrival and came from the house accompanied by Philippe. Ruben hugged us; Philippe shook our hands. Pat told me later

"Ruben hires him for weekends. He works hard, don't say much, and for sure don't drink red wine. The little bastard lives in some shithole garage and sleeps on an old mattress like a bum. I'm goin to give him a room at my place soon, plenty of work for him outside to earn his keep."

"A big step up for him then should work well for both of you." Pat nodded in agreement.

"Yeah, there's something about that kid that tells me he'll do good, even though he is a fuckin beaner."

A roll had no connection with cigarettes, food, sex, or tobacco. It was a test, a sparring session, a tryout to see if any dog had outstanding abilities. Also, to see if any lacked the inclination to fight. Fifteen minutes for each pair of animals. The pit was set up like the last match, except there was no referee this time. Reg kept time. So the morning continued with Philippe handling one animal, Ruben the other. Three experienced match dogs were used to test two rookies each. Six new dogs were tried, no gyps this time. At the end of the proceedings, we all helped dismantle the pit—only a matter of unhooking each section and storing it on an overhead shelf. The floor was simply a many-sectioned interlocking rubber affair, like sixteen large jigsaw pieces about half an inch thick. These were stored atop the wooden pit sections after we hosed them off—all in all, a neat, practical arrangement.

Ruben was pleased with the results of the roll. Two dogs he considered above average, four mediocre.

"I'll keep em; all of em are just over a year old. The others may show well in another four months."

I asked Reg about the roll. "What if a dog won't fight?"

"Most of em do." He replied. "It's their nature, what they're bred for and have been for hundreds of years. The few that don't work out are buried. A bullet in the head solves all the problems quick an painless. Cull hard, same as scent hounds or bird dogs. The only way to breed and keep a good strain alive. Ruben don't breed junk, never has, can't afford to."

"These dogs are expensive, then?

"Not too bad. Ruben would probably let you have a pup for fifteen hundred or so if he thought you would put it to good use. See, it's not so much the cost of the animal. It's raising and conditioning, vets fees, food, an all the rest of the expenses, not to mention the time. This is a professional operation Em-Jay. Between the two matches you saw, over a hundred thousand dollars changed hands."

At the rear of the house, beyond sight of the chained dogs, was a grassy area of level ground. It was here the barbecue was set up. A heavy-gauge steel barrel, about fifty-five-gallon size, was attached to a smaller one, each separated from the other but joined by a common chamber. Both had long, hinged doors. The larger drum sported a chimney about two feet high, and this device was mounted on an articulated four-wheeled cart. I stood to examine the thing for some time.

"Never seen one like this, Ruben. This is about the most elaborate barbie I ever saw."

"Yes, it is amigo, smoker, and grill, cooks very well. You ever meet Dave from DMZ Aero Fab?"

"Yeah, I met Dave and his brother a few weeks ago at Pat's."

"They make this for me, Mark wanted to make it from stainless, but the materials alone would cost over eight hundred bucks. This is all from scrap at their shop. Cost me nothing. Never charge for their time, Nada. They should be here in an hour or so."

We all sat around on folding chairs. Two children, Alice's friends from school, the Jew brothers, Pat, Ruben, Reg, Philippe, and Dot. Mark and Dave came on their bikes, the same custom Harleys I saw at Pat's house on my first visit. Music was from an old CD player, and beer was from a large ice chest. All the kids were playing baseball, shouting, and squeaking as kids do. Overall the smell of barbecued burgers and chicken descended unseen, adding to the warm quality of a dreamlike peaceful afternoon. As the sounds and smells faded, I saw the ghosts of a hundred pit dogs rising from the blood-soaked ground beneath them. Each stared back at me from the ridge on the hill.

The vision slowly faded, and the dogs returned to the ground without malice. I wondered if this place on the ridge was a doggy graveyard. Perhaps I would ask Ruben later…perhaps not.

Out came the paper plates, out came the plastic cutlery and glasses, and out came Philippe carrying two large trays of food. Ruben cooked the food that Dot had prepared. I believe that, to a great extent, taste and appreciation for food are determined by the occasion and the company. One could say the same for music, dope, and booze. A simple fish fry on the beach is as good as fish served in any Manhattan restaurant if the company is suitable for the occasion. So it was today—fine simple food shared by a few good people. Her school friends occupied Alice, so we didn't talk much. Dave and Mark chatted incessantly about everything. I was delighted to see them again and found their company as enjoyable as the first time we met. They insisted I visit their place of business as soon as possible.

I imagined my stomach as a small, transparent container filled with sandwiches, chicken legs, and other half-chewed food. The addition of beer floating on the food allowed any grease to solidify slowly on the surface of the liquid. An interesting, if unsettling mental picture. More interesting to me were the digestion processes and the rich history of social dining—the acceptable delivery system using cutlery, sticks, or fingers to pass food to the mouth. Then, from the mouth, having been processed violently between teeth, it's mixed with saliva before entering the stomach and colon for re-purposing into manure. A simple cycle that I'm sure you know well. The engine is fueled, fuel consumed, and any waste exhausted. The exhausted waste is promptly flushed into the great subterranean city colon. Oh, what fun our little brown logs will have, bumping and jostling with all the other logs of used food in the vast, echoing sewer. Many are happy travelers on the turbulent surface of their watery journey, rushing, giggling, and dancing. Others, weighed down by serious philosophical considerations, true seekers hoping for enlightenment, drift below the surface to be caught by a dark undertow before finally greeting light and finding the sea.

Oh, but can you imagine early Sunday morning before church? Move aside the heavy maintenance hole cover, and climb down the slippery iron rungs into the blackness beneath. The sound of distant machinery and running water is all around now, and as your eyes become accustomed to the poor light, you see choppy waters moving darkly a few inches below your feet. In you go, take the plunge because it's not as deep as you thought, just above waist high, feel the cold refreshing waters engulf you. Here is the ultimate baptismal experience, as you dive beneath the surface and become one with the little floaters around you. Reach out to feel their sensual, silky touch.

Time to rise from the waters and climb to street level again. As you stand triumphantly warming in the sun, raise your face to the sky and spread your arms. Give thanks to your God. You have cast off the chains of enforced cleanliness. Celebrate this new-found dirty with a great shout of gratitude.

Questions must be asked, for within the turbulent swirling symphony of crap below, perhaps there are lessons there for us? Life's impermanence, or the fecalaty of our existence? Yes, here is the first and most important lesson, keep well away from shit and sewers. There is nothing there for you,

no good will come from such a relationship, and your Mother will smack you.

On to the church now, share with the congregation your blessed experience, and revel in the freedom. Jesus loves you and would approve, although he may not approve of the smell.

As a child, I was blessed or perhaps cursed with the ability to see or imagine vivid, colorful images in my mind. Music usually triggers pictures as the sounds reach my ears. Smells and other sounds do the same. Over the years, I learned that not everyone has this heightened awareness. I remember listening to a jazz band on the radio. Alistair, my stepfather, was entering a ledger at the dining table. After the music had finished, I asked him what he saw. He had no idea what I meant.

"I see the table before me; I see my favorite little bairn. What else is there to see?"

"The music from the radio. You didn't see the little golden lady with the long ribbons jumping on the water?"

"Away with your nonsense, laddie. The only golden lady in this house is yer mother, an she's in the kitchen. No man alive can *see* sound. If ye see faeries coming from the radio, tis time to get a new radio or call the doctor," He laughed at his humor and hugged me quickly to end any further discussion about a subject he could never understand. *Ah, thank you, dear pedestrian Alistair. My mother has accepted you, so I must continue with the charade.*

I didn't discuss my condition with anyone. I simply accepted my sensitivity as quite natural. My condition exists without drugs, and so with the influence of narcotics and booze, these visionary pictures are magnified, enhanced, or distorted many times.

Maybe a topic for discussion on the swing with a pretty woman and plenty of red wine. Philippe came with another large plate of food for Ruben to cook.

"For you, mister Em-Jay?" Smiling as he passed.

"No, wait, let me see that plate" I stared at the plate uncovering a plump thigh and holding it by the bone.

"You okay, then, mister Em-Jay?"

"Yeah, just for a moment, I thought that was Bess, a chicken I met at a party."

He stared at me for a long time and nodded slowly before returning to Ruben and the barbeque. I returned to my chair next to Dot, a little disappointed that my brilliant gringo humor had failed so miserably.

A hawk dropped from the sky, appearing a few feet from where Dot and I sat. A sleek, silent, golden-brown missile, leaving a small plume of gray feathers to mark the place where it landed. I watched, fascinated, as the silent airborne assassin rose again, clutching a large pigeon. A bright butterfly continued its ungainly flight visiting various wildflowers, a colorful idiot spectator, seemingly uncaring and unmoved by the sudden violent murder. A chorus of oohing and wowing filled the air, and there ensued a much-excited discussion about local predators and their prey. Eventually, the flood of conversation subsided to a trickle. It was time to go, a universal unspoken signal that the time for departure had come.

Chairs, tables, and plates were removed. There were huggings and goodbyes, hands shaken, and arrangements made. Philippe would ride with us and stay with Pat, who would bring him to work in the morning—refusing offers of drink when we eventually arrived at my house. Reg and his two passengers elected to continue home. Pat pulled a small joint from his shirt pocket.

"A little Thai for you, brother, much better than your goddamn red wine shit."

Reg shrugged his shoulders, rolling his eyes meaningfully.

I did not discover good Thai that evening. Work in the morning; leave the house at six-thirty, so get to bed early. Time for the mysterious Thai experiment Friday evening, perhaps. Work came and went, and the monotonous project given to me almost filled the void between Friday evenings. Annetta was always waiting quietly for me, just out of reach, hidden by the mystery surrounding her. I asked Philippe if she was sleeping with Pat. I was sure they were not married. He found great amusement in my question; I stared at him, this skinny framed kid with liquid brown eyes, innocents, held captive in a heavily pockmarked face. Suddenly his face was illuminated by a huge grin.

"No married or his girlfriend, Mister Em-Jay, sometimes they fight, she calls Pat a pig and don't like him in the kitchen. Sometimes they are like the dogs at Rubens House. They are both my friends, though. You know I stay now at Pat's house? I have a fine room and a bed. I work for Pat, and this is very good for me."

I liked the boy Philippe; there was an innocent simplicity in his manner. If he was a thief, he was not a malicious one.

Part of the Annetta mystery was solved then, not married, at least not to Pat. Next move, ask Pat about her. On reflection, no, I could imagine the conversation.

"Hey Mexicali, remember Em-Jay, the wino engineer I work with? The guy who called you a gyp, he wants a woman and thinks you might be okay to practice on."

A long silence, then a furious glare as she reached behind her for a sharp object.

No, much better if I talk to her myself. There would probably be an opportunity for that next time at Pat's house.

"You want her, mister Em-Jay? I tell her you talk about her. She is Italian lady, she tells me. Pat says Mexicana, but she should know, yes? Her voice is not from Mexico anyway; her speaking is very different from Spanish."

"No, Philippe amigo, say nothing to her, just wondering is all. I'm sure Pat would call her a Norwegian if it annoyed her."

CHAPTER NINE

Here was Friday evening; the Thai could wait. I had a date with Kerry. We would go to a nice place for dinner, then continue with the evening as the fancy took us. This was my first date with Kerry; I was not sure I liked her. She was an established local attorney with a small practice and carried the unmistakable confidence of a good-looking woman enjoying an elevated social position. We met in a small mall on a rainy Saturday morning. I, on my way to a coffee shop, she, having left an all-natural food store with a small bag of groceries in one hand and a laptop computer in the other. We were within ten feet of each other when she slipped. In a futile effort to save something, she dropped the grocery bag as the computer flew from her grasp. I caught it. A heroic save nearly fumbled as I managed to hold on. The damp air was filled briefly with exclamations of gratitude and some embarrassed laughter.

"Since you threw your computer at me, the least you could do is buy me a coffee."

She stared at me for several seconds, then shook her head.

"Oh no, I didn't throw it at you, I slipped and"... *Could she possibly be that simple?* I thought.

"I understand, just a joke, a touch of sarcasm, but since you *didn't* throw it at me, this must be fate. Please let me buy you a coffee instead. There's a little place just over the road."

"Thank you, yes, actually, I don't drink coffee. Do you think they would serve tea?"

Tea, coffee, croissants, and cupcakes later, we seemed well on the way to recovery from the initial awkwardness. An attractive woman for sure, a few years older than me, with long chestnut hair that she toyed with continually. She was below average height with a trim body, bulging comfortably back and front where women traditionally bulge. During our meal, she pulled a slim, deeply engraved silver case from her coat pocket.

"This is my firm." A nicely embossed business card proclaimed, "*Kerry Rice and Associates* A law firm." Beneath which, "Kerry Rice, attorney at law."

I was impressed, "You are Kerry, then?"

"That's me, yes."

"Do you represent clients in court?"

"Not me; my associates do, though. I have ADT and can't concentrate for very long; not a good thing if you are representing someone in court."

"ADT, is that a military expression?" I asked jokingly. She frowned. "No, medical,"

followed by an in-depth explanation of her ADD condition. I'm sure she thought I was stupid. Obviously, light satire was lost on her. A lesson quickly learned. I asked her to dinner and was quite surprised when she accepted. Perhaps she didn't think me totally stupid after all, or; maybe she was stupid for accepting. We agreed to meet on Friday at seven, outside her office.

A couple of miles from the little mall where we first met were a small block of offices. *The professional center.* A two-story block occupied primarily by lawyers and medical specialists. And there it was on the ground floor, the lair of Kerry Rice, attorney at law. Dark smoked glass window with ornate silver lettering. A conservative, professional façade that would undoubtedly inspire confidence in the clientele. Confirmation that all their legal needs would be addressed most properly. Suddenly there she was, clip-clopping along the tiled passageway in her high heels and pastel peach designer suit. We smiled and hugged briefly. I couldn't resist,

"You certainly are a beautiful little gyp, Kerry."

"Well, thank you Em-Jay; I think this will be a wonderful evening."

I was immediately sorry and a little ashamed of the smart-ass gyp comment, even though she didn't understand. Off to dinner we went having arranged to use her car with me driving. About twenty miles following a country road before the restaurant appeared out of nowhere. I had eaten there before, a delightfully secluded stone building in an ornamental garden setting. Inside we were presented with an extensive menu offering a variety of French cuisine and wines.

Kerry spoke French fluently, over two and a half years studying business management at the University of Sorbonne. The owner came to our table, insisting he would personally serve us, happy to converse with an elegant lady in his native tongue. Kerry was a delightful companion despite my initial misgivings. After I had adjusted to her personality quirks and probably her to mine, the evening was a great success. I raised a glass of expensive red wine and whispered a short toast to Pat and Reg. An appropriate gesture, it seemed to me.

Kerry laughed, "And I don't get to participate?"

So I repeated the toast loud enough for her to hear. Kerry and I touched glasses." Promise to tell about Pat and Reg?"

I nodded, "happy to, but not tonight."

After the food and wine were finished, after an espresso and green tea downed and the dark chocolate mints savored, we walked in the overgrown back garden for a while holding hands. The evening was evaporating before us, and soon time to return to her office and switch vehicles. Her Audi for my Toyota. We chatted for a while, dissected the evening, and concluded we had a wonderful time.

"Thank you, Em-Jay, for a fine meal and delightful company. I wish the evening didn't have to end."

"It doesn't come back to my place; we can sit on the swing, drink wine, and listen to music." Or if you prefer, back to your place.

She laughed, shaking her head. "Since we've only known each other for a few hours, I think a little more time would be appropriate. I'm not ready to jump into bed with you yet."

" Yes, of course, you're right, Kerry, and I respect your decision. But when did I ever ask you to go to bed with me? She stood looking at me for some time before she hugged me.

"Can we do this again?

"Tell you what. I'll call early next week. If you're not too busy lawyering, we could go out at the weekend; I'll take you on the bike somewhere." We kissed quickly, and off she went. From the darkness, a warning voice whispered the words "*high maintenance*" softly in my ear as her Audi sounded a long sweet goodbye in the quiet of the night.

Somewhere out in the distance, I thought I heard Annetta call my name, but I couldn't really be sure...

CHAPTER TEN

Against my better judgment, I did call Kerry as promised. Not early in the week, though, Thursday afternoon. And, probably against her better judgment, she agreed to a Saturday bike ride. She was waiting for me that morning at her office again. Her Jeans were partially hiding beautiful short crocodile boots, and a thin brown lizard skin jacket covered a white tailored shirt. All the subtle hallmarks of understated good taste. I stared at her, inhaling her beauty, savoring her perfume. We held each other for a long time. This was the same woman in the French restaurant but now so different. Different in the way she hugged me and reached for my hand. Different in the way we kissed. I saw in her an almost child-like animated facet of her personality, something new that I had not noticed before. The specter of a hidden attorney lurking just beneath the surface was nowhere to be seen. In our favor was a warm Saturday morning holding the promise of a beautiful day. First, stop at the little coffee shop where we recently sat together. Croissants and coffee for me, green tea, and cupcakes for her. We lost ourselves in animated conversation, with Kerry telling of her privileged upbringing."My parents are quite rich and still alive. Unfortunately, dad's in poor health now. When he dies, I will inherit just under six million. There are other assets and property as well; you might say I am a spoiled only child." She laughed happily, tossing her hair. "I don't feel bad about that. I have seen poor and want no part of it. There is nothing poverty can give me that wealth can't."

"Oh, I don't know, a sense of perspective? Perhaps a feeling for the greater part of humanity. Why would you expect poverty to *give* you? Is it your custom to always take or expect to be given?"

"Not to take no, but to be given? Certainly. Em-Jay, why are you so angry and contentious? Should I be ashamed of what I have or what I am? I'm just telling my little story; you did ask me."

"Ah, you're right, Kerry, yeah; sorry, I didn't mean to come off as critical or judgmental. Perhaps I'm a little sensitive, never having had much as a child. "We do have *something* in common, though; I also am an only child. Tell me why you became an attorney?"

"No, not over tea. Later, over dinner, if that's okay with you."

And it was. Now knees in the breeze, the highway was calling, anger and resentment would soon be washed away as it always was when riding the bike. That's the thing about motorcycles; they usually return the rider to a grounded reality. A squirt down the freeway heading south for about twenty miles, a turn past Santa Monica, then meandering through the city to the museum of fine arts. Kerry was delighted with the choice."

"Haven't been here for years. I love this place."

She also professed a great liking for motorbikes and seemed quite comfortable as a Harley passenger. For my part, the previous feelings of anger and resentment had almost evaporated in the face of Kerry's laughter. Later, having explored the museum, a lunch stop was required. Kerry chose a large Chinese restaurant in Santa Monica that she remembered served good food. She was right. I sat contentedly, gazing happily at a lovely painted doll in the opposite seat. Kerry was so much more than that, though, and I knew it. I was enjoying a good day so far, and not over yet, but still, a few strands of smoldering resentment remained.

Customers came and went. The ebb and flow of conversations mingling with the smell of food and noise from the kitchen seemed inseparable somehow. Our waitress, wrapped in a colorfully embroidered robe, clasped her hands and bowed repeatedly. She apologized for her lack of English fluency.

"No Chino, I am Mexicana from Jalisco."

Waves of babble flowed all around us. A thousand yapping accents and inflections from bleating talkers concerned only with themselves and the small worlds they inhabit. Sharp opinions and observations ricocheted past us, and nobody gave a shit. Your granddaughter is of no interest to anyone. The broken front door lock, your uncle's iniquitous medical insurance coverage, and even the rest of your life matter to very few. The battles fought and won are historical echo's now and of no concern to anyone but you, so important at the time perhaps, but now? Buried, between the pages of contrived revisionist history, an embarrassment to us who have to listen to you and feign interest. Apathy or disinterest is the price you have to pay in this culture. Your valor is considered unnecessary; your wars are discussed by children with no comprehension of anything except their immediate self-gratification. Perhaps in the next emerging generation, some will be required to spill their blood and repeat your mistakes. And, all the while, an orchestral flow of diverse languages competing for recognition.

So, until that time, stop your tongues and still your minds, darling diners. There are essential matters to consider quietly. And indeed, many questions to be asked. Does a one-legged duck swim in a circle? Is the chow-mien cooked sufficiently? Is the shrimp well seasoned and the steamed rice of good quality and separation, without clumping?

If so, be aware that in the ensuing silence, as streams of unnecessary discontent and anguish subside, the taste and perfume of savory pork dumplings, crab legs, and noodles will slowly rise and triumph, holding dominion over all.

And it was at that moment; I knew I should have been a philosopher, except philosophizing doesn't pay very well. About the same as a poet or a basket weaver, I think. So no, I'll stick with engineering for the time being.

"Well, did you?"

"Did I what?"

"Enjoy the food; you haven't listened to a word I said, have you?"

"Of course, I have my beauty, the food was excellent, and I love you now more than I did this morning."

Kerry laughed. "You lie, but because of your boyish charm, I forgive you. A wonderful day so far, don't you think?"

"Yeah, this has been great for me; I do enjoy your company Kerry Rice not to mention that you are one beautiful, educated lady. Ah, but you already knew that, though."

A short ride to Venice beach. We walked for some time along the shore, Kerry without boots, rolling her Jeans almost to her knees, looking for all the world like a happy kid. After the vendors and little stores had exhausted their charms, we ran laughing and holding hands. Suddenly it was time to go. A little after five, freeway traffic would soon become an exercise in misery.

Slow riding for about fifteen miles, threading our way through Saturday evening madness, brought us to a large hotel. We would eat dinner there, then go back to her office. The food was delicious—no cacophonous dining room to endure in this atmosphere of muted elegance. Tea and red wine reminded Kerry to further her inquiry about Pat and Reg.

"You promised in the restaurant last week, so, time to spill," I told of Pat and his penchant for occasional violence, his house, friends, and our drug use. No mention of his narcotic business or Annetta. I spoke of Reg and Ruben, my new friends with the dogs, and our recent barbecue. She listened in an attitude of disbelief, her head resting on her hands.

"So, I have just spent the day with an animal-abusing drug addict then."

I wanted to tell her she was wrong. Tell her she was talking with a sailor, a man who had seen and recently spoken to a great cat God. A man following a different path from the bleating sheep. An independent, not subscribing to the prevailing herd mentality she was obviously so comfortable with.

Instead, angry at her response, "Yes, however, your total and deliberate distortion of my words exemplifies your chosen profession perfectly."

I realized then how resentful and unreasonably angry I had become. The simple habit she had of playing with her hair infuriated me to the point that I wanted to reach over and slap her hand away.

Suddenly she smiled broadly, a totally disarming expression.

"Did you enjoy the dogfighting?"

"It was a unique experience, and I learned a lot, but I enjoyed the company of the people more. The little girl Alice worries me. I think she's very sick."

"Okay darling, I forgive you again. Would you take me sometime?"

"Would you go if you were invited?"

"Yes, as you say, a unique experience. Perhaps you could teach me the language."

Then, suddenly remembering the previous Friday and my gyp comment. *Careful Em-Jay, not so fast. Your mouth could quickly get you a bloody nose.*

"I'll see what I can do. These people are a secretive bunch. Not too keen on inviting strangers. I will try, though."

We chatted for a long time. She asked about Alice and why I thought she was sick. I tried to describe her appearance, the dark-ringed hollow eyes and a pale face. Mostly a gut feeling, though. Kerry shook her head, offering no opinion except the obvious one to suggest an immediate doctor's visit. During a brief silence, I tried to understand and analyze my anger and tried to reconcile feelings of resentment. And then I understood. I was jealous, jealous of her success and everything she and her family had that I never did. And in that moment of realization came acceptance and freedom from the *poor little me* mindset that threatened to ruin a fine evening.

She told of a failed marriage, no children, and an enviable education. Nearly three years in France, studying business management at the Sorbonne. Four years at Harvard law school. I was in the presence of beauty, money, education, and, once again, enjoying it immensely.

"I had a terrible problem learning anything." She continued, "It was a huge struggle for me. I had to work twice as hard as the rest of the students. This stupid ATD thing is a terrible curse."

She grinned at me, "What are you laughing about; Do you think this is funny?"

"I think *you* are funny; ADD must be a problem, although you seem to manage it well."

"Yes, tried therapy and drugs, both useless."

"You were probably using the wrong drugs, sweetie; I would have to recommend morphine and a little opium."

"Good heavens, would you, seriously? Well, thanks for that brilliance Em-Jay. Apparently, your treatment was a failure also."

Eventually, we left this pleasant place, promising each other that we would return soon. Time for the freeway again, head north, and find our way to her office.

"Glad to get off the bike and out of the wind, Kerry?"

"Actually, no, I'm not. Thanks for a great time, dear Em-Jay. So, Am I invited then?"

"Like I said, Kerry, I will ask if it's okay, then we go."

"No, not that silly, to your place. Drink wine and listen to music on your porch swing."

CHAPTER ELEVEN

A thousand swirling thoughts, *Was the house clean with paper in the bathrooms? Had the pile of dishes miraculously cleaned themselves?* It was what it was. We were going back to my place, even if I had to move the donkey from the living room and scrape shit and straw off the walls first.

"Is there a problem? You don't seem too happy at the thought."

"No, absolutely not. Just hoping that the house is clean and respectable is all."

"Ha, don't worry, Em-Jay, as long as *we* are clean and respectable, and I'm sure we are, eh?

So we drifted along country roads again to home. I had seen her lair; now, she would see my disorganized little nest. The house wasn't too bad. Untidy but forgivable, considering this was a bachelor pad. Kerry used the bathroom, giving me enough time to open two bottles of cheap red wine and pour a bottle and a half into a decanter. So now we had an exclusive red wine that I hoped would pass as such.

"This wine is pretty good, a little sweet for my taste, but good Merlot nonetheless. Did you get it locally?"

"Glad you like it, Kerry. Yes, I got it at the specialty wine store in the mall. Expensive but quite good, I think."

I poured two glasses, silently asking forgiveness but delighted the subterfuge was successful. The wine enthusiasts' placebo, *Two Buck*

Chuck, would never taste the same again. Out in the backyard, beyond grass, flowerbeds, and a small chain-link fence, half an acre of sand and scrub wait quietly, a magical, hypnotic view I dearly love. There are a few times when the scene changes, some evenings when the wine lays sour in my gut, and the wind moans all around me; melancholy fills the house. At those times, I look out on a harsh land of angry, twisting sand and splintered rock.

Not this evening, though. Gazing over the land from the patio, one can sense a dynamic quality, an ever-changing movement all around. Rabbits and squirrels explore trails through the brush, and sometimes a large lizard will flit across an old pile of wooden fence posts. Everything is tending to its own business and doing so without artificial time constraints, haste, or interruption. When the wind slides between the leaves on the big cottonwoods, I hear the hiss of the sea. Waves wash the shores, and sand returns briefly into an ancient ocean. Dry desert land becomes a sea again. For every change in cloud cover or moonlight, the scene before me changes. I think I spend more time on the patio than I do in the house. Let the house decay around me; the patio will endure. I will find solace in a sleeping bag by the swing.

Kerry and I sat on the swing drifting gently with the evening. In time to come, when speculators bring their construction equipment to level the land, and there are no more animals or plants to hinder their advance, lunch trucks, portable toilets, and litter will claim this fragile landscape. Sounds and smells of poisonous diesel progress will fill the air. And yet, when their lights are dimmed and work waits for the day's first post to sound again, ghosts will come to remind the living that theirs is not the only reality. Jazz, blues, and classical violin, the sounds of New Orleans and New York will drift sweetly across a dry unlovely California desert landscape. With regret, the ones building now will never know those living here before them, except by legend or faded photographs. We sat in silence, drinking our exclusive Merlot and squeezing hands, the silence of lovers before sleeping.

"Just perfect Em-Jay, a perfect day and a perfect evening. You do this often. Sit out here and swing?"

"Yeah, I do, often as possible. This little place and the bike give me ease; my work is nothing without this." My work is nothing anyway; just a means to pay for these things."

"Oh, I can understand that to an extent, but with your engineering expertise, you surely don't mean your work is nothing. How can that be? You have a nice house that is peaceful, comfortable, so relaxing, and supported by the job. I live in the town center with all the noise and activity. This is like a mini-vacation for me, Em-Jay." She was silent for a while before continuing, "Hmmm, thinking of that, perhaps I could spend a few days with you and commute into town. That would give me an extended vacation. Of course, if you think you could stand me for a few days."

"If you can stand me, I think I could stand you. In fact, that would be a perfect arrangement, Kerry. Just a matter of when your vacation starts and when it finishes then. For me, just a matter of when it starts. Perhaps there is work you could do here instead of at the office. I'm sure we could stand each other even with your STD."

"Oh, thanks a lot, Em-Jay, It's ATD, as you well know. I have to leave sometime Sunday afternoon. So, if we're still speaking to each other by then, perhaps give it some serious thought, eh?" We sat in peace, chatting and exchanging short histories and opinions. She asked me why I was cleanly shaven. "I thought all bikers had long hair and beards; you only have a trimmed mustache. Does this mean you aren't a proper biker, then?"

"Suppose so. I'm just a guy with a haircut who loves riding motorbikes. I never did subscribe to uniforms. Uniforms are for the military, police, or hotel doormen."

Kerry laughed, nodding her head. "You do have a certain roughness about you, though. Very appealing. I think rather than a biker, you are a dog, a dusty old road dog."

"Oh yeah, very clever, better than road hog or roadkill, I suppose. Much better than road rash, for sure."

I thought of Pat, the one percenter archetype, except he wore no identifying colors, nor did he belong to an outlaw club. Some would visit the house regularly, though. Pat was an original, the mold from which big bad bikers were cast. In any crowd, he would be unreasonably and unfairly seen as the troublemaking, grungy biker figure.

A vast yellow moon was climbing above the trees, and as we watched the magic together, I knew I was in love with Kerry, in love with the world and everything around me.

Like a promise remembered, I suddenly thought of the Thai joint Pat gave me a couple of weeks ago. I put it in the kitchen drawer and forgot about it until now.

"Feel like sparking a blunt?" I asked, grinning at Kerry.

"What on earth are you talking about?"

"Oh, sorry, that's junkie for lighting a marijuana cigarette. I just remembered Pat gave me a small joint a couple of weeks ago. Would you care to join me if I light it up?"

"Okay, I may try a little with you, although I haven't done any of that stuff since I was in college. You definitely are a bad influence, Em-Jay. Something I have to ask you now, very important, almost an emergency."

"Can't be that serious; we haven't known each other long enough for dramas."

She laughed before continuing. "Your name *Em-Jay*. What is that short for? Is it a stage name or something?"

My turn to laugh. "Just initials, sweetheart. My name is Michael John O'Connell. I was Em-Jay in school, and it stuck. My stepdad was John James O'Connell Jay-Jay."

"O'Connell, that's an Irish name, isn't it?"

"That it is. My grandfather was Irish; dad and mom were born in Ireland, but mom came to England after the war. I was born in Ireland but lived in England since I was about three years old." I smiled at her as I lit the joint.

I'm sure we both have good stories worth hearing. Family histories later, though, darling I want to hear yours first.

There was no coughing as I inhaled, but the smoke crashed into me with a sudden unexpected punch. I smiled at Kerry, "just a little, babe. This is strong stuff." I passed the joint to her and watched as she inhaled. This was no ordinary leaf, Thai, bud, or anything else. I felt sure the joint was heavy with smack. Opium was smooth and dreamy; heroin was always a rush in the smoke, much more so through the needle. Kerry coughed and gasped,

"What is this? It's like smoking an old shoe. Don't remember grass anything like this."

"See how it is, darling. It came highly recommended by Pat. If it's no good, I'll yell at him at work."

I watched, fascinated to see the world dissolve around me as I smoked. I saw Kerry as a translucent form shining and radiating light, swaying gently back and fro on the swing. She suddenly left the swing and walked, drifting across the grass into the roses by the gate, soundlessly disappearing as I tried to follow her. She may have become part of the rose bush or dissolved into the grass. I couldn't tell for sure. There was nothing after the few flowers and the roses, just the sandy desert ground as it had always been. Through the little gate into the moonlit sand and scrub, I went only a few yards before I became very tired and decided to return to the swing. My legs were so heavy the dull weight above my ankles dragged at my feet like an anchor.

From the swing, perhaps fifty yards of grass before the gate. Everything was clearly visible in the moonlight. There was no reason for my tiredness, and that thought spurred me further into the desert. All around me, small creatures stared curiously and whispered among themselves as I walked. Some pointed and laughed as I passed. In the distance, I heard Annetta calling to me.

"Don't go too far, darling fool Em-Jay. Easy to get lost out here. Come back to me now. I have dinner for us. Are you hungry?"

I stopped for a while, listening intently and turning quickly, thought I saw Annetta walking silently, a lithe black shadow in the distance. With a start, I realized there was no fence, gate, or house.

Not possible. I was walking within half an acre of fenced land. There were boundaries here that would be impossible to cross. However, here I was, desert all around, flat and shining with no fences anywhere. I stopped walking and sat on the warm sand. Staring around me, nothing was familiar. Far out in the distance, I could see an extensive mountain range in silhouette, on either side of me, flat desert ground. I must have sat for six months or more in the quiet of the evening. There was a sound now, light footsteps moving the sand behind me, and then a little laugh. Annetta sat next to me, smiling softly.

"Why are you here, Em-Jay? What do you need?"

"Not need, want. I want you, sweet lady."

"Then come to me. Not here, in the other place. I wait for you, Em-Jay, my foolish darling road dog. I waiting but for not a long time, yes?"

"What is this place, Annetta? What are those mountains in the distance?"

I pointed to the mountains in front of us. She never replied, turning again; there was no Annetta. I should have been terrified but felt only sadness because I never said goodbye. I realized that this strange state, these visions only existed because of the heroin I smoked. A familiar delusion I knew well without substance or reason in my world. But what about her "*ROAD DOG*" reference, then? How could she *possibly* know that? How could she have heard a muted conversation between Kerry and me? Nah, that was fanciful and distorted echoes from the smack we smoked, undoubtedly laced in Pat's joint. Of course, Annetta was never with me at all, a simple and reasonable explanation. The awful curse of impending sobriety.

To my left was a small clump of sage from which grew a few tiny yellow flowers. I moved and picked some dropping them into my shirt pocket. In just a few more minutes, I knew I would walk through the gate, back to the swing, and Kerry. There was thunder or perhaps a loud crack like a large wooden stick suddenly breaking. I think I shouted out as I grabbed the swing seat.

"You okay, lover? Were you sleeping? You nearly fell off the swing."

"Kerry babe," Breathlessly. Conscious now of my furiously racing heart and feeling as if I was in an aircraft suddenly plunging through turbulence.

"Yeah, I'm fine, honey, not sleeping, just thinking. How are you doing? It looks like you survived the smoke."

"I enjoyed it, still am. The only problem I have is the stuff tastes like crap, a bonfire of leaves almost. I didn't smoke much. Still half left."

She held up the remainder of the joint so that I could see.

Quietly reaching for the safety of the wine carafe, I poured another two glasses. We sat for some long-time drinking, both of us gazing across the land and thinking our special secret thoughts.

She called loudly from the bathroom. "You are a big slob Em-Jay."

"Slob? What did I do? Just took a quick shower, is all."

"Yeah, and left your clothes and a towel lying all over the floor."

"Oh, sorry, sweetie, I must have dropped them there by accident."

I felt sure my whit was not appreciated. I couldn't see her in the bathroom, but I could imagine the deep disappointment and sense of betrayal she must have felt by my flippant attitude when confronted by such uncouth slobbery. At the time, it must have seemed to her as if I just didn't care.

"Well, okay, then, babe, pick em up in the morning, please. Hey, do you want me to put the little flowers in water for you?"

"Flowers?"

"*Flowers,* five or six small yellow flowers on the countertop by the washbasin."

Kerry was awake before me, just before eight. She had made tea and coffee, stolen my old bathrobe, and contrived to look like an angel. We sat on the patio languishing in the soft embrace of a warm Sunday morning.

I thought of our time in bed and remembered the feel of her body.

"Five days a week, an hour and a half a day in the gym." She told me proudly. No wonder she was so firm and supple. That workout time had molded her to perfection. As she said,

"not bad for forty-seven years. You're not too bad either, for a baby biker Em-Jay. A little gray in that wavy black hair, but other than that, not too much fat. I like it very much."

Her sculpted body and total lack of inhibition made for a memorable experience.

I confess that several times, my first sexual experiences with women I have dated were much less than satisfactory. I know the problem lies with me. My childhood vision of Aunt Jen looms large to this day and probably always will. I will tell that story later when I find the courage to do so. And then there was Danny. A tale more easily told. Many years ago, my friend Danny told me of a miserable experience he had with a prospective girlfriend, a mutual acquaintance of ours.

"Waste of time. She lay there with her legs open. I did get it in, but she didn't respond. I think she was just a garage."

"Eh, a garage? How do you mean, Dan?"

"You know Em-Jay, a garage, a place where I could park my dick for a few minutes."

He shook his head when I asked him if she had died suddenly, and perhaps he never noticed.

"No, man, she sat up in the bed. If she was dead, I think I would have known."

I found his garage description so amusing; the visual stayed with me for many years. Often when I first enter a girl, *Danny's garage* bubbles to the surface. I want to laugh; the more I try to suppress the laughter, the more I need to laugh. I think my nervousness and fear of *failure to perform* also play a large part. Over the years, I've noticed that a woman is seldom pleased by her lover chortling and chuckling after he has just penetrated her vagina.

With practice, I have managed to disguise the mirth by pretending to cough. This ploy usually works but requires considerable effort. There was no garage or laughter with Kerry.

"You are a spectacular lady Kerry; Yesterday was so good for me. Last night was unforgettable. I want more, much more of you." She smiled broadly as I studied her across the small glass table. We sat at peace for many minutes drinking in the fine morning. Kerry and others before her have become part of my high desert home forever. Women I have loved and still do, sweet darling ladies I will never forget.

And the soft jingle jangle of their magic triangle calls to me loudly through the sweet desert air.

"She giggled, "Okay, darling, last night was free. If you want more, you gotta pay or at least buy a lady breakfast. Oh, by the way, I let the cat out for you."

"Thanks, darling. That was very thoughtful of you. The only thing is, I don't have a cat."

"Pretty little black and white thing seemed to know its way around. Came in through the front door, probably still in the garden then."

We walked to the sliding door looking by the swing and over the patio. No cat to be seen. Kerry shrugged,

"Okay, no cat, then, let's do breakfast."

And so we did, took the car, drove to Torrance, and sat watching the ocean from the balcony of a large crowded restaurant. First, a champagne brunch, though. The food was excellent. Perhaps it seemed so because we waited so long for it. Later a walk by the shore on a crowded beach before her wristwatch called her back. We drove to my house first so Kerry could collect the few clothes she had left there. Only about a half-hour ride from there to her office. We took the Harley putting easily through the lanes and twists, finally arriving at her office.

"Then I'll call you at the beginning of the week. If it's still okay with you for me to stay awhile, I'll make arrangements at the office."

We parted reluctantly, both of us tired but happy. Leaving her at the office, I rode home in the warm half-light of the evening. The house seemed empty without Kerry, without her delightful, quirky personality and delicious smile. I missed her and her ADT. Only one thing to do. Quick shower, then sit on the patio swing with a jug of red wine and stare into the night. There was sufficient exclusive Merlot left in the decanter for one full glass. I had another unopened bottle, but it just wouldn't be the same.

After some time feeling sorry for myself, I tried to recall the previous evening. Such an exhaustive effort required me to open the remaining bottle. Decanter or not, the wine was okay. The evening was improving with every glass. Shadowy Recall returned me to my conversation with Annetta; her evening ghost seemed real enough at the time, her voice soft and clear. She told me to come to her, and I knew I would.

My memory of the events had not diminished them; daylight had not reduced them. I thought of the desert in the clear moonlight and remembered picking the little yellow flowers and the awful breathtaking jolt as I returned to the swing. Kerry enjoyed the high, although I never told her I thought it was mostly heroin we were smoking. There was obviously some leaf or bud included because of the taste she complained about. It was then I remembered Kerry yelling at me from the bathroom.

"You're a slob. Do you want these yellow flowers in water?"

Not possible Em-Jay, *there could be no flowers. You can't bring flowers from a dream, no matter how real it seems at the time.* Feeling like a fool, I went to the bathroom and searched. No flowers, of course, not in a vase or the wastebasket. No flowers.

Within the hour, Kerry called. She told me she was "on the way to the hospital, so can't talk long." her father was sick.

"If you need anything, let me know. Would you like me to come with you?"

"No, darling, thanks. My nephew will drive, and we'll meet family there."

"Do you remember last night? You called me a slob and said I left my clothes on the floor."

"Yes, my darling, you are a slob, so no apologies."

"Do you remember yellow flowers?"

"You are a strange one, Em-Jay. Yes, I remember. I took them and put them in my handbag for a keepsake; there were four or five. I think I'll press them in a book. If they were important, you should have said something. You didn't seem too worried when I told you about them."

She left the remainder of the joint on the dining room table and tempted though I was, I did not smoke that evening.

Sweet honey goodnights, many years and a thousand miles before I would speak to Kerry Rice again.

"And the only woman I ever did love is on that road and gone."

She never did stay with me. By Tuesday, her father was dead. Prominent businessman and local historian Edward Alwen Rice succumbed to complications after contracting influenza. He was eighty-seven years old. I called several times, left messages of condolences at her office and house, and gave my home and work numbers. No response from Kerry. I waited for her to call me, not wishing to intrude on her grief.

CHAPTER TWELVE

Two weeks later, after surviving the crushing boredom of work and daily living, missing Kerry, and feeling a little sorry for myself, I arrived without an invite, as I was expected to do. It was Friday evening at Pat's place. To my surprise, Ruben was sitting with Dave and Mark. Much hugging, backslapping, and handshaking. It seemed everyone was well; Ruben said his family was thriving, as were all dogs, and his small world was good.

"Em-Jay, go to the kitchen an ask Annetta for a kitchen knife. "Scattered laughter in the room.

"No, why bother? I'll go to the door, call her a gyp, and bring back the one sticking in my chest." Great waves of laughter from all in the room. "Or, call her a Mexican instead."

Pat was delighted, "Em-Jay, seriously, if you are going to the kitchen, ask her for a couple of straws, mind you ask nicely, though."

I knew I would never hear the last of the gyp thing and prepared to endure the marginal humor. She was standing as I remembered her the first time we met. Medium height, slim and straight with jet black braided hair. As before, her back was to me. I stood for some time watching her.

"Hello, Annetta," my throat was dry, and I stumbled over the words. Two words, and already, I sounded like an idiot. She turned again with the flashing smile that lit her face.

"Em-Jay, you see, I did waiting for you as I told you, yes?"

She chattered excitedly, walking to me with arms outstretched. I understood nothing. It didn't matter because we were in each other's arms, holding tightly and swaying to slow music only we could hear. It must have been five or six hours, days perhaps before we parted.

"I sure you need straws, yes? Stupid Pat should keep them in the front room draw; then they will be for him easy, eh?"

"Please, yes. I'll take the box if you like. Will you come home with me tonight?"

"Forever?"

I nodded and laughed at a little girl in a woman's body.

"You will need clothes and other things, I can't carry big cases on the bike, but I can carry you."

"Okay, Em-Jay, go with your friends. I come soon, then with a small bag."

"Hey, we was worried about you, man. Did you get the straws, a knife, or just the straws?"

"Got the girl and the straws. She said it would be easier if you keep em in the draw on the side. She'll be here soon, told her I would take her for a run on the bike, sort of a peace offering." I listened to a round of muted applause and well-wishing from the company.

"How long you guys gone for then?" Pat asked.

"Not for long, just this evening, I think."

"Yeah, you probably wouldn't last much longer." More laughter and commentary for me to absorb. At that point, Philippe came to join us.

"Mister Em-Jay, come see my new room."

I followed him and Pat along the passage, passing the kitchen and Philippe opening one of three doors to my right. He proudly ushered us into a fair-sized room. A small single bed and cheap wooden furniture, a portable stereo player next to a vase of artificial flowers gave a simple, happy atmosphere to the room. Over the bed hung a large crucifix, probably made from bull rushes.

"This is perfect for you, Philippe, an excellent pad."

"And a window looking onto trees and grass. What I think is the best room ever, eh?"

"Yeah, it is. I'm glad for you, Philippe; you better get plenty of work done for Pat and bring a jug of tequila. Invite us to a room-warming party soon."

"Shit, don't tell him that; I'll have to pay for the fuckin booze."

Back in the living room, Pat cut a small pile of coke on the coffee table. Two long lines of glittering flake. "Here, same as before, same stuff." He cut a straw in half, passing one to Mark and handing me the other.

"You guys are the only bozos using here. Help yourselves, enjoy."

Can't afford the stuff anymore," said Ruben with a grin. "Not now; I'm a married man."

There followed a general discussion about the cost of living. I told the true story of a co-worker at my previous job.

"A young fabricator Brian used a lot of coke, but he was well-liked and very good at his job. One morning he approached the boss telling him he would have to quit. "I have a serious drug problem. I can't continue to work here."

"No big deal for us, Brian, we want you here. We'll get you into rehab or whatever it takes to help you."

"Thanks, boss, but you don't understand. My drug problem is that I can't afford to buy drugs with the wages you pay me."

After the laughter had subsided, Mark and I inhaled the lines.

Mark grinned at me, "That's a big step up the ladder for us, Em-Jay. Last time we were assholes, now were bozos."

"You're both still assholes, as well as bozos said, Pat." About that time, Annetta came in to join us. She sat for a few minutes, chatting with everyone.

From the tone of the conversions, she knew everyone and was well thought of despite the teasing. She had changed from a long print dress into jeans and short boots. A practical choice for a motorcycle passenger. Pat took her arm and pulled her to one side. He whispered something in her ear. She shook her head vigorously and then kissed him on the cheek. Everyone followed us to the door raising hands, grinning, and contributing suggestive banter.

"Remember Em-Jay; if you break it, you own it."

I laughed with the company and started the bike.

We drifted on warm air currents, buoyed by excitement and happiness, listening to the sound of a motorcycle far behind us. About twenty minutes or so and I pulled into a small roadside restaurant.

"Something for us to eat before we get home. Not much to eat in the house, plenty to drink, though."

We sat happily chatting in the quiet little café. This was the first time I was alone with Annetta, and I felt like a nervous child, much different with Kerry. I was concerned that Pat would be hurt or angry if I pursued a relationship with Annetta. I was, after all, a newcomer to the group and felt it somewhat presumptuous of me to invite her to my house. Perhaps I should have talked to him first. Maybe the threat of the knife still lingered, but more so, the effects of the cocaine.

I asked her many questions that would have been easier asked at the house.

"What did Pat say when you kissed him?" She laughed.

"Pat ask me if I needed money. Very nice of him, yes? I told him I had you and needed nothing else."

We both held hands, laughing together. I don't recall the few miles we rode to the house, only that the night air was warm, and I was unreasonably happy. Into the house, we went. Annetta stood for a while inside the doorway before closing the front door behind her.

"Please open any door and look around. This is your house as long as you're here."

She did so, but not before she performed the same odd little ritual when entering the front door.

"Beautiful house on quiet Indian ground," she said, smiling. "I am so happy to be here with you, Em-Jay."

"And I with you," I replied. "Why are we here together now or even at all? I'm still not sure. Two times we've seen each other is all" She laughed her melodic, soothing laugh.

"We have to be; there is no choice. I think you know that, yes?"

"Yes, I suppose so. I had the strangest feeling the first time we met, somehow knew we would be together."

"Oh, I remember *good;* you don't know what is a rabbit. Later I think of you much and laugh."

CHAPTER THIRTEEN

I poured wine into the carafe, now a standard procedure for me to convert poor wine into good. I seemed to remember that it was a biblical procedure, but I was probably wrong.

And in a loud voice, Jesus spoke to the disciples gathered at the table.

"I say unto you pour your bad wine from clay vessels into an urn of beaten gold. Do this in my name. Immediately, it will become good wine, far greater than any wine before it."

Now I don't know for sure that he did speak those exact words, but it sounds very Jesus-ish, and even if he didn't, I'm sure he would have done had he thought of it. He would have been correct, of course. I can attest to that, having recently converted several bottles. Now was the time to test a glass. Annetta would not sit on the patio until we had walked through the gate and into the desert beyond. She opened the gate and, as before, waited in the gateway before continuing.

"A strange little performance.

Annetta, you did that in every doorway in the house."

"A show of respect Em-Jay, a very old custom. Sometimes behind doors, there are those not wanting you to come in."

"Not in this house, darling. All the rooms are empty."

"No, dear darling, Em-Jay. Rooms with doors are never empty. Here in this desert." She indicated past the gate with a wave of her hand.

"Here is many things unseen, others before us we never see. Out there are diamonds and demons, yes?"

"No, out there is only what we see before us."

"And perhaps what was behind us, nothing more then? You know I call to you that night, we talk, so that is nothing to you?"

"That was the black tar. How do you know about that anyway?"

"I know I love you; I know you might love me in time. I know what is a kitty and what is a rabbit. I know only what I have been taught, and I have been told what is a *road dog*, eh? Walk now with me, darling."

I slipped my arm around her waist, and together we strolled along the perimeter fence, with me still thinking of a suitable response to her *road dog* comment. And for about twenty minutes or so, with my arm around her waist sometimes, holding hands. An easy loving feeling, a familiarity I felt that belied the short time we had known each other.

At the patio, we sat in moonlit silence across from each other at the small round table. There was a timeless quality about her, an elemental creature born of sand and dust holding sunlight and rain clouds in her hands. A very old soul at home in the mountains or valleys working in the fields of maize or dancing in a bordello. I knew then that I loved her. I gazed across the table, wondering. Long black hair pulled back to reveal dark skin and angular features. Slim and strong, a body not cultured in a gym but crafted from work and effort. From Tangier to Israel and all of South America in between. The perfect stereotype. Not a beautiful woman in any classical sense but an elegant, striking figure and one I most certainly wanted and wanted with a passion.

"I'll get wine for us, sweetheart. Will you tell me about yourself? You are surely the most mysterious lady and a lovely one." She smiled at me as I left the chair.

"I go with you, Em-Jay, so you not run away."

We walked together into the kitchen, returning quickly with the wine and her with glasses and napkins. We sat again at the table, feeling the evening and sharing a quiet, breathless intimacy as she began her story.

"My name is Annetta De-Fiore. I was born in a beautiful Italy, Parma. Even as a little girl, I love writing and drawing. Mother, like me, was tall and thin; here you call skinny, maybe? She was a strega. Father was a curator at a museum in the Palazzo Della Pilotta. He was very strict, but I love him. I wanted to study for a fine arts degree but said no. He say I study for a nurse or doctor, no arts."

"Okay, with you so far. What the hell is a strega, though? Is that some old Italian laundry maid" She grinned, then held both hands like claws and bared her teeth momentarily, a flashing whitened grin? I shook my head,

"Your mother was a bear?" She laughed heartily, clapping her hands.

"Oh, sorry darling Em-Jay. You would call here a witch or healing woman. No bear. I try to make a scare face for you. So, I am nineteen and marry a teacher from France. We live in France together. He was very handsome, and for four years, we are happy. With more time and he become tired with me. Look for other girls. I am leaving and going to Parma again for over a year."

She sipped her wine and smiled at me. I stared at her and, for the first time, realized that behind her smile was a kind, gentle lady far removed from the knife-brandishing devil girl I first encountered.

"I stop now, darling Em-Jay? So you see, I am not such a mysterious woman, eh?"

"No, don't stop, please. I want to hear the rest of the story."

After more wine, she continued her story. For me, a fascinating tale. But a family of witches???

"For write and painting, I learn some English and decide to study in California at UCLA program. My father helps me with government papers, although he is angry. I am accepted to learn, so all is okay but very much money. I am working two jobs, one cleaning houses and then in a big restaurant near Van Nuys as a waitress. Now I am tired to talking. You have to kiss me so I speak more."

"I kiss you anyway, honey, but I do want you to tell the rest of your story, especially about your witchy mother."

A long lingering lover's kiss, with the wine taste in our mouths. Her speaking was forgotten until after the third kiss. I poured more wine, and we sat again, smiling and at peace. She continued with her storytelling about how she met Pat and Reg. Apparently, she was trying to move a dining table into her newly rented apartment. Reg had parked his truck in an adjoining alley. Walking from the apartments, Pat saw Annetta wrestling the table on a flight of stairs. After some laughter and advice, they came to her rescue. During the table moving, they talked, and Pat suggesting she could have a room at his house in exchange for cleaning and cooking. Not only was his home closer to her work, but the savings were more than attractive to her.

Within two months, Annetta had moved in. She quickly discovered the downside to her new accommodations was Pat's uninvited commentary and his particular brand of doubtful humor.

"First, I thinking he is serious with what he says. I know now his heart is much bigger than his mouth, and I no more insulted." I nodded in agreement remembering how he was helping Philippe.

I kissed her again so she would tell me about her mother and also to celebrate the fact that I was not intruding into any personal relationships, and in truth, I wanted another passionate kiss before she continued.

"My parents moved from Verona to Parma when I was born. Ah, such a beautiful place in Italy. So, my mother was born into a line of women, as was I, the real stegra, for hundreds of years. Healers and makers of magic. She was very clever and educated, a beautiful woman. I have photographs. I think father was a little afraid of her. In the small village we lived, some people hated her and were afraid. Many loved her for the good healing she did, never for money as the doctors. She lives still with my father, although they both are old now."

Time for more wine and gentle swing therapy. We both sat in silence for a while, lulled by the movement of the evening. There was so much for me to think about. This month I had been with an attorney and her ADD. Now a writer and daughter of a witch of all things. It occurred to me that perhaps I was not destined for a relationship with an ordinary woman. I considered that carefully before admitting I would probably be bored to death. I asked Annetta to tell me about her night ghost and our recent conversation in the desert. She said she *felt me* and feared I might wander alone without direction. *Doing that very thing all my life,* I thought but did not interrupt.

CHAPTER FOURTEEN

She followed me for a while before sitting beside me and talking.
"You said you wanted me and would come. I was very happy and told you I would wait for you. Do you remember?"

"Yeah, I remember most of our talk, but I can't accept that we were together. Far as I'm concerned, those illusions resulted from smoking heroin. And that's all they were, just illusions."

"In a way, you are right. The heroin was the stage you decided to use to walk upon. I wanted to join you there and talk to you. Don't you wonder how I know what we said? Don't you think how I know about your avocado woman and her *road dog*?"

"My avocado woman? I have no idea what you are talking about, sweetie."

"No avocado darling, *avvocato* woman.
Your old legal Lady, avvocato, is Italian for lawyer, eh."

I was stumped again; she knew about Kerry saying nothing. She was correct; I just couldn't believe it, though, and told her so.

"Sorry, Annetta, I'm not quite ready to believe in magic yet."

"Magic is wherever you look. You will see in time. When we are together, we make our own magic, I think."

I stared at this Italian flower, this lady sitting next to me, and my heart overflowed. I knew she was right, knew she spoke the truth, and was afraid to admit or even open doors to those implied possibilities. Experiencing the smoke and the needle, the peyote, and tiny LSD tabs, I understood well there were many layers of reality removed from the only one I was forced to hold fast to. I did not want to look over the wall or experiment with Annetta's magic because, having done so, there may be no turning away. My fear was I might not want to turn away. I was comfortable here in my ignorance but did not know for how long.

"Do you have to go back on Sunday? I could take the car and drop you off at Pat's Monday morning if that would work for you."

"Let's make the most of tonight. I call Pat tomorrow after us deciding, you think is okay?"

"Sure, only wish you had more time to spend here" We walked out in the desert again through the small gate, which was taking on strange importance somehow. As we walked, it occurred to me that Kerry had studied long and hard, practiced, became fluent in another language, and worked for years to become an attorney. Annetta had studied and worked probably more so to learn customs and arcane knowledge from her mother and family. Aside from her artistic endeavors, learning English and working two jobs to support herself.

Two women so different, and each to be admired for achievements and expertise in their chosen fields of study. We walked in silence, holding hands, absorbing the unique ambiance of the warm desert evening. I would drink more wine with Annetta, probably stare into the evening, and talk with meaningless extravagance before going to bed. I seemed to have done a lot of that recently. As we walked, I became aware that the silence at first so noticeable had now given way to noise all around us. The wind suddenly blew across our path, insects chirping, and the rustle of unknown creatures in the scrub drew my attention. There was life and sounds of life everywhere.

"We go back now, darling Em-Jay first, a little magic for you."

She walked for a few yards, picked a fair-sized white rock from the ground, and placed it within a few feet of the gate. She took my hand again.

"More wine and swing, darling, then bed for us, yes?"

I laughed and nodded enthusiastically. The perfect scenario. Booze and sex. Under different circumstances, a resounding yes, but suddenly, I felt a strange reluctance to go to bed with Annetta. Almost as if I was afraid to change a delicate balance in our relationship. If balance were a consideration, more wine would probably change my outlook in that regard. We sat together on the swing in delightful harmony, with my arm across her shoulders, sipping red wine.

"So, where is this rock magic?" I asked.

Without speaking, she beckoned to me. We left the swing again and strolled to the gate. She pointed to the place where she had placed the rock. Nothing but the sand and scrub now so familiar to me—no white rock. I shook my head, staring at the place on the ground where I was sure she had placed it.

"Where's the rock, sweetheart? I saw you put it on the ground there just in front of the gate." She grinned, nodding her head.

"Yes, but you can't see or hear over the wall. Only on the other side and if you are there."

I pushed open the gate and walked a few yards. As I expected, nothing. Turning to the gate again, the white rock was clearly visible, reflecting indistinct moonlight. A small sentinel guardian about twice the size of a man's fist, set in unmoving defiance and contesting my recent view of the world.

"Annetta," I shouted and again, but no reply. I walked to the rock picking it up, feeling the weight and the uneven surface texture. Without question, This was a rock, a simple white rock with no properties other than the rockiness that it possessed for millennia as far as I knew. Replacing it on the ground again, I opened the gate and found Annetta, who was leaning over the fence nearby.

"What happened? I saw the rock, picked the damn thing up, so I know it's there."

"Yes, darling baby, like any rock, it will stay there unless it is moved. Look over from the gate again."

The rock had vanished from my sight as before. I am not a speculative metaphysical type, much preferring the solidarity of geometry and physics in a world most folks are familiar with. This had to be a quality of the prevailing light. Refraction or a reflected image, whatever it was, it was a condition of uncertain ambient light.

Fuck this trickery. I'm too tired for these circus games.

Taking her hand, we walked to the swing and sat silently for a while. There was silence all around us, now different again from the sounds in the desert beyond the gate.

"Please don't be angry darling Em-Jay. I not try to joking with you; just these things are real. I do not make them."

"Not angry, love, confused, yes, but not angry. One more glass, then bed. Not very late, look, only just after ten."

We sat at the table with more wine—the last for this evening. I was deliciously happy, tired, and excited now at the thought of taking this woman to bed. Just after eleven when we went to bed and just after ten when we got up. A night of loving and laughing, sleeping briefly, then loving and laughing again. This delightful process was repeated until the morning. We showered together quickly, dressed, then had breakfast at the local golf club. I don't play golf, but I do occasionally eat at the member's restaurant.

Annetta and I sat at a window table, not saying much but grinning at each other as we remembered the last night's loving and morning showering. Staring from the small window overlooking the green, I could see athletic creatures swinging clubs, often whacking balls. A fine morning soft and warm, perfect for ball whacking, I supposed, but I was happier with Annetta sitting next to me eating a fat country omelet. All around us were golfing diners eating and talking, discussing golfy matters—a pleasant, quiet atmosphere with most patrons appearing reasonably normal. I think we were the odd ones at the table dressed as we were in shabby biker chick—a slow ride in the sun back to the house and ready to call Pat.

As expected, all was good at the Pat house. He did have to cook his breakfast, complaining bitterly about such a tragedy. Apparently, Philippe had found a girlfriend.

"Yeah, now we got a fuckin Beaner and a Beaness."

Dave Zimmerman suggested that Pat keep em apart.

"If they have kids, you have Beanetts or Beans to contend with." Pat sounded amused by the whole idea.

"Yeah, an the little fucker found himself a cat now," he continued.

"Wants to keep it in the house. I told him the first time it shits inside, both of you are sleepin' in the garden."

"This could be a good thing, Pat. Why don't you get yourself a nice goldfish? No, much better a hampster. Get a little plastic cage and a treadmill; give some meaning to your life."

"Yeah, thanks; you already got a hampster, a fuckin Mexican one. See you at the shop."

Reg had finished his bike, which was now road-ready. Pat suggested Reg come to my house tomorrow afternoon and bring Annetta back. A good idea. Reg would be able to give the Hog a thorough road test after the engine overhaul and save me a lot of travel time.

With Annetta happy to stay with me until Sunday, I elected to drive into town and load up on red wine in honor of the Reg coming. Also, a few groceries I was told were necessary for my survival. Two hours later, I was back at the house with all the supplies.

Meanwhile, Annetta had cleaned the kitchen and bathrooms, unloading a mountain of advice and instruction on how not to live like a pig. At least I avoided the recent slob label. She managed to find time to concoct a colossal lasagna, which was slowly baking in the oven.

"Enough for us tonight, and tomorrow afternoon, Reg will be able to eat with us."

And so, good things continued throughout the day. I saw her briefly standing before the oven with her back to me, exactly as I remembered at Pat's. Slim and straight with a long black braid. I stared for some time, wondering whether to ask for straws. She spun around, suddenly facing me. She had a huge grin and arms outstretched as she danced toward me. Both hands were empty, and I was not afraid. I was not afraid on the patio when she unleashed the lasagna. It was so good I considered a fast-food take-out for Reg, but Annetta would not hear of it. We ate and complimented the food with exceptional and exclusive house red wine from our urn of beaten gold. I think Annetta liked my house and certainly liked the swing. She insisted we walk into the desert for a while before the exertions and comfort of the bed.

"If we are going to do that, I will either smoke dope, drink whiskey, or otherwise disrupt my normal mental functions.

"You have *normal* mental functions, darling?"

Oh, a great wave of biting sarcasm from Annetta. I was momentarily confounded, unable to reply.

"I think, so sweetie seemed to remember one functioning some time ago. Normality was suspended when you came to the house, though."

And so the banter continued without malice or sharp kitchen knives.

"Okay, a compromise then, another glass of wine, and off we go."

Through the gate and into the desert we went. The first thing I saw was the white rock where it had remained since yesterday.

My innocent four-foot chain-link fence and gate had now acquired a considerable significance becoming, as I saw earlier, a mystical barrier between our world and the unknown. I noticed how these magical properties increased; the more wine I drank, the more opiates I ingested. So, very simply, all things magical were, as I had long suspected, derived from narcotics. Annetta would surely disagree with me, but she only drank wine, as far as I knew. I was satisfied with this logic. There was nothing beyond the gate except drug-induced fantasy. And so we walked arm in arm as before, a shared feeling of happiness and peace between us.

"So, do you use horrible mind-altering drugs, my sweet?"

She shook her head, laughing.

"Only a little wine, nothing else, I have tried, but these things make me stupid."

"That's the reason I use, makes me stupid as well, but the challenge is to think through the stupidity and function normally." she thought for a moment frowning.

"If you are wanting the challenge, then to join the army, but if you look for normal, then stay without drugs. You are normal, then. Em-Jay darling, you know you cannot think through heroin, eh? And you know heroin will soon destroy your life?"

Once again, she was right. My reasoning was slightly faulted, but only because I had drunk too much wine. This evening there was no magic. No sudden winds or strange noises, nothing but the good old-fashioned desert sand as always. All very normal. That was another reason for my drug use. I was born with an overabundance of normality and inherited volumes from my parents. Luckily narcotics helped balance that tricky situation.

There must be something to blame for this social aberration, peer pressure at school, violence glorified in the popular media, and an unhappy childhood. A medical or psychological condition, possibly. For sure, this drug-crazed, lecherous self-indulgent wretch is the result of external influences, and qualified analysts will unearth a cause. Blame the nasty motorcycles so abhorred by my mother and the neighbors. Blame my rowdy friends who rode them. Blame the Navy and my three years at sea.

Of course, Em-Jay cannot be held personally accountable for what he is or has become. That just wouldn't be fair.

CHAPTER FIFTEEN

Back through the gate again, and to my great disappointment, the pig-shit white rock had disappeared from my sight again. Thankfully Annetta had not, and together we walked to the swing. I resolved to find the cause of this strange rock behavior, later though, when Annetta had left.

The swing is my long-standing friend: a special place and refuge. If there was magic, it was on the swing, not behind the gate. In the evenings after work, I would fill my glass, sip wine or whiskey and inhale the peace around me. There was a downside to doing that. A tranquil evening or warm afternoon, the results were the same. Booze, coupled with the gentle movement of the swing, would lull me to sleep. Only for a few seconds, though. As the glass slipped from my lifeless fingers, I would jerk awake to the familiar sound of breaking glass. The broken glass would contribute to a growing pile of shards and spilled drinks. This process would continue until the pile became a talking point for visitors and an embarrassment to me. I would then remove the glass, clean the mess, spray insecticide to remove the ants, and buy more glasses. Since this situation could not continue indefinitely, I made a change.

There were reasonable alternatives. Should I drink from a tin cup on the swing or drink at the table before sitting on the swing? I chose the table. With my darling companion beside me, there was no need to enforce the table rule. Annetta and I both engaged in conversation, and wide-awake, sipped our wine from glasses without mishap.

Another delightful evening for me in the company of a special lady. Another delightful night although offset somewhat by feelings of sadness, knowing she would be gone in the afternoon. Came the morning with quick showering and breakfasting. This time in town, at an I-Hop restaurant. For all her gourmet cooking and culinary expertise, Annetta seemed to prefer simple meals. She may have tried to accommodate me, though, as my preference is for simple, greasy, and quick. Food! Not girlfriends. A quick scoot to the supermarket for a few items, then back to the house. I hadn't been back for more than five minutes when Reg called.

"Be with you guys in a couple of hours; keep the beer cool."

Just after three when Reg arrived. "Shit, I heard that bucket o bolts halfway down the fuckin freeway, man."

Reg laughed, "Okay, Pat, thanks for the heads up."

He rode a sweet hardtail pan-head, a gem of a custom machine. We sat discussing Harley's and engine rebuilds for a while, interrupted by the arrival of the lasagna. Reg heaped praise on Annetta's fine Italian cooking.

"If I decided to marry again, I would find a girl who could cook like Annetta."

They exchanged glances. Annetta, suddenly ill at ease, lowered her eyes, finding something fascinating with a small corner of her napkin.

"Yeah, Reg, the problem is I eat so much with her. I need another wardrobe," Reg grinned and nodded. Whatever passed between Reg and Annetta was already forgotten. A glass of wine before Reg was ready to go. We clasped hands, and I wished him an easy ride. He stared at me for what seemed a very long time before he nodded. "No problem, Em-Jay. I'll take good care of your lady." I watched them to the end of the road until the Harley disappeared like a white rock around the corner. The big engine left its steady musical signature in the desert air until the heavy echo faded and disappeared. Again I was left with an empty house. Her perfume hung lightly in the bedroom to remind me of some other time, but I couldn't quite remember when. Her shadow remained in the kitchen and waited for me on the swing. I mooched around the house, finding many subtle traces to remind me of her being. I realized my sudden sadness and depression would remain until I saw her again.

As arranged, she called from Pats to let me know she had arrived after an uneventful but enjoyable ride with Reg. They stopped for coffee in the city.

"We no eating not possible for us. Lasagna fills us too much. I want to be back with you, Em-Jay. Next week is possible? I am making more Italian food. I love you so much."

"Anytime, love, see when you're working when your next semester begins, and I will come for you. Sooner, the better."

Monday morning in my little office at about ten-thirty or so. Pat stayed for an hour chatting about the weekend.

"Shit yeah, I miss the cooking, but little Philippe cooks. Not like your Mexican hampster woman but good enough. The kid ain't afraid of working either. So, what the fuck you goin to do, brother? I think your gyp would leave tomorrow if she could.

"Perhaps, but we can't do Pat. I live too far from UCLA and too far from her jobs. Something to think about, though. If we come up with a plan, you will be the first to know." Pat nodded; the rest of our conversation was devoted to the sweet Reg Harley and his engine rebuild.

There was mail lurking in my mailbox waiting, poised to infuriate me with overdue, pay now, buy this, and subscribe. The always discrete *enlarge your penis and rejuvenate your sex life, invest in penny stock.* An envelope embossed with the legend *Kerry Rice Attorney At Law* reduced all other letters to insignificance. Peel back the wrappings and reveal a letter from Kerry Rice herself. She had thoughtfully stapled a business card to the bottom of the single page, but there were no yellow flowers enclosed—my darling Em-Jay. I should have read *Dear John.* Maybe I was a little over-sensitive, overly optimistic with unrealistic expectations perhaps, but as always, ready to move on. She continued by announcing how devastated she was by the death of her father. She was sure I would understand why she could not stay with me as arranged. Was sure I understood the problems with the millions to manage, the family estate, and the awful attendant paperwork.

Oh yes, of course I did. Poor Kerry, my little waterproof lamb; I understood precisely how those nasty millions would weigh so heavily on such delicate shoulders. Life was most unfair at times.

After a quick prayer of gratitude that I was not similarly burdened by great wealth, I reverently placed her letter in the waste bin. At least she wrote to me, a fitting end to a new exciting, and short-lived affair. I think closure was the word I searched for, yet I remembered the fire and passion and knew sorrow at her leaving.

I used to imagine the dating process to be a hunt. Identifying and then stalking the prey, a delightful period of friendship and mutual discovery, then a clean capture, bedtime being the worthy objective. After the first sexual experience, a slow period of disappointment seemed inevitable. A culmination of time and effort to achieve the ultimate conquest, then with familiarity, the anticipated disillusionment, a self-fulfilling prophesy for me, perhaps but an enjoyable one. Usually, imagination is better than reality. Not so with Kerry. Not yet with Annetta. I think this scenario applies to either sex. I also think cynicism fits me comfortably, like an old pair of slippers. I have matured over the years, realizing a much deeper need and a selfless response rather than sexual gratification and the thrill of the chase. Growing up then, perhaps?... *Nahhh*

Thursday evening, I came for Annetta. This time in the car, she wanted to bring clothes in two cases near impossible to carry on the bike. There were two visitors in the front room when I arrived. They were strangers to me, both wearing club colors, both outgoing and friendly, and both Harley riders. Pat was his usual exuberant self, asking if

"that piece o shit I rode had finally given up."

"You better hope it hasn't, brother; you'll have to fix it."

General amusement in the room when Annetta came with her cases. Huggings, quick kissings, and introductions all round. She handed a yellow pad of lined paper to Pat. On two pages were detailed instructions on how to warm the food she had prepared and its exact location in the fridge. He grunted, shaking his head

"This is written in English or Mexican?"

"Oh, I sorry Pat, it is in English, but I forget you no read. Give to Philippe he can read English and Spanish. I draw a map where the refrigerator and kitchen are so you find."

Pat's reply drowned beneath sounds of laughter from the visitors. Our drive home was uneventful, the car filled with excited babbling about her stay and punctuated by a stop in town to eat. I do have a refrigerator. Unfortunately, it was not equipped to accommodate visitors and contained only beer and a few ancient leftovers. Perhaps I would persuade Annetta to stock it with a huge lasagna. I was more than happy she was at the house again. Before entering, she performed her small, respectful rituals to acknowledge any unseen inhabitants in the rooms. I realized now any time spent in her company was a pleasure and becoming more so as days passed. We had no exciting developments to discuss, and our conversation in the car and at the restaurant exhausted all current topics.

Unfortunately, plans for a permanent houseguest were not practical yet. Simply a matter of geography and her schedule. The best we could hope for at this time was two or three days and some weekends.

CHAPTER SIXTEEN

By unspoken agreement, we gravitated to the swing, wine in hand. The customary walk in the desert waited for our participation.

I wondered about the white rock. Distracted by the Kerry Rice manifesto and the pressure of doing nothing productive at work, I had given no thought to any magical stuff beyond the gate. Thanks to Pat's ongoing generosity, I had the necessary ingredient to make our special magic at any time beyond any gate. That and a box of matches would ensure fairyland was just a step away. The joint came with the Pat guarantee.

"Here, limey, you thought the last one was good; this motherfucker is better. Save the fuckin thing for a special time."

His words held the promise of an interesting and relaxing weekend.

With Annetta by my side, things could not be better for me, with or without the special magic-joint. Any speculation at this point was far away and meaningless. Now for a walk in the desert. A good time just before nine, with perfect stillness everywhere waiting to cover us with a precious silent evening. Through the gate and past the inevitable and infuriating white rock. She squeezed my hand.

"You are good man, mister Em-Jay thank you for my staying. I have something to tell you when we are with the swing again."

"I have the bargain, darling. The company of a fine, intelligent lady, a crazy loving girl in my bed, and the best Italian food this side of Italy." The words were wrong, somehow all jumbled and strange to my ears. No smoke and only one glass of wine? Time for something more powerful, perhaps, If this was sober clarity, it was not working for me.

"Annetta, what are those mountains in front of us? I saw em the other night when I was out here. They're not there during the daytime. I don't think they should be there at all."

"They are where they have always been, darling. You see with the different eye; you see instead of looking." She thought for a moment, "You say in America, the elephant in the room, yes? Before you, but you do not see it."

"This is a freaking mountain range, not a white rock. Are they visible to aircraft?"

"Must be darling Em-Jay, also to divers under the sea, not in the place we see it, though."

I understood nothing, but it didn't matter. I was with Annetta, and we had the weekend in front of us.

"You take the car tomorrow. I'll take the bike. Thinking about that, I'll take a half-day. There's nothing that can't wait at work. Be home about twelve-thirty."

We retraced our steps slowly, holding hands and enjoying our together beneath a quiet, mysterious evening. As before, on the other side of the gate, no distant mountains or white rock. I needed reliable witnesses to resolve this matter. The welcoming swing, the signature red wine, and a remarkable woman. All these things conspired to make a memorable evening. Everything was special that evening. Everything was set firmly in position, awaiting celebration and gratitude. It did not come easy that night.

"And what do you have to tell me, darling?"

"I must tell of my affair to you."

"Your affair? Speak on reggae; woman tell me anything; I am ready."

"I was with Reg for a time, about three months. I am no more with him now. He is a good person and, like you and me, splintered by this world. He is a friend still."

There was no happiness for me at that time, although there should have been. The feelings I had were on a cold, raining night on the city streets of West London. A little boy walking with head bowed against the wind.

"Keep your scarf on; wrap up well, or you'll catch a cold."

Walking home from school, numb fingers and dripping clothes would have him standing at the front door of an empty house. He would hurry past other houses with their curtains drawn against the night. Light would suffuse the windows with a welcoming orange glow that told of children inside. They were eating dinner, talking about their school, and of many tiny dramas that filled their days. They were warm and dry as children should be, well-fed and happy as children should be. Their houses were never cold or empty.

Hurry past the dim flickering streetlights in the alleys. Hurry through the rain and darkness

"Don't be scared, boy. The dead won't hurt you; it's the living you have to be afraid of."

In the early years, I had become accustomed to standing on the outside looking in. A small waif of a thing, a little insubstantial pale ghost, is flitting sadly through the wet cobblestone alleys and onto the streets. If a child is cut, the wounds heal and hold no importance. If a child is cold, hungry, and afraid, these wounds are difficult to close, and the child never forgets.

"Oh, dear me. Did I hear an echo of self-indulgent sniveling? Was this pathetic whining necessary? Well, apparently, it was. So, you were, to some small extent, deprived as a child? Too bad. Get over it."

Deprived by western standards is, by comparison with children of many other countries, to be indulged and pampered. My melancholy reached between us, touching Annetta.

"What is the *wrong*, darling? You pull away from me; you are angry with me, yes? Are you angry with Reg? This sadness you feel is...." She paused, searching for words. "Is destructive to you; it is a bad indulgence. If you need me to leave, I will but not happy."

"I need you but not to leave. Don't leave, darling. I need a little time to think about you and Reg and why the hell you didn't tell me before he came to the house last time. I like Reg; I think of him as a friend, but it's just the thought of him knowing you as well as I do. He would be thinking the same but with the advantage of me knowing nothing."

"Ah, advantage? You are jealous then, my darling, thinking of Reg loving with me. Ha, like every man I have ever known, jealous. But I, Annetta, thinking of you with another woman, perhaps a rich old lawyer?... *Oh, don't be silly, my dear, that was nothing.* Phaa. That *was* something, of course, eh?"

I tried to explain myself before continuing; I don't think she understood me, though.

"Annetta, What I'm telling you now, has nothing to do with you and Reg. The evening is warm, but suddenly I'm freezing inside. If I'm sick, I'll stay home tomorrow. I don't know what the problem is or why I feel like this, but I've felt this many times recently. Just remembering my early childhood makes me sad. In later years, I was happier. Much happier when I was older and self-reliant."

There was quiet now, and some time elapsed before either of us spoke again.

" I'm sorry for spoiling this evening, Annetta. I'm so happy you're here. I really am."

She reached for me and kissed me holding my hands. "No evening, spoiled darling, but I have to tell."

I nodded because no more needed to be said at this time. I was determined to ask searching questions about her relationship with Reg when the time was right.

Two more glasses of wine, and we were ready for bed. The wine caused several dogs to bark way out in the distance; their noise dispelled any ruinous childhood echoes and any *jealous of Reg* thinking. I was happy again.

"You have to tell to me Em-Jay, the time when you were small. Tell to me about your family."

"Okay, sweet. Not tonight, though. When I get home from work tomorrow, I'll tell you."

"Promised to me."

"I promise to you."

She never saw two fingers on each hand were crossed behind my back, thereby negating any verbal or written promises. A slick lawyer trick I learned from Kerry Rice.

CHAPTER SEVENTEEN

Morning came, and with great difficulty, I left the bed. Annetta was beside me with her hair cascading like shining black liquid over the pillow and her skin dark against the pale sheets. That vision was my inspiration for the day and is with me still. She smiled sleepily, reaching for me as I searched for my clothes. A sweet moment forever is frozen in my memory. This precious moment of mine was a picture, but beneath the image was feeling and emotion much more profound than any visual layer.

Work came and went. The simple pleasure of the bike ride each way through light traffic and the thought of seeing Annetta again when I returned made the miles easy. Riding north on the narrow freeway, my thoughts returned to our walk in the desert. The mountain range I saw was inexplicable. This country was rocky with hills and a few small mountains but nothing approaching the peaks I saw. Almost as if the Himalayas were relocated to my backyard. I continued my journey troubled by many unresolved questions.

There would be no empty house this afternoon when I stood at the door. Annetta was jumping with excitement, expressing in her particular way the simple joy of being here with me. The house was alive with light that shone from every room. She had cleaned and cooked, driven to the supermarket even chilled the wine, something I never did or even thought of doing. We sat at the patio table. Even that was improved by a small vase of bright, happy wildflowers waiting in greeting: chilled wine and a warm Annetta waiting for my pleasure.

"Are you hungry, darling?"

"Perhaps in an hour or so. Now I want to enjoy the afternoon and look at you." She nodded, laughing.

"Perfect afternoon Em-Jay. I think of you much when you work."

We sat in peace as we had done before, talking, laughing, and drinking wine.

"Now, my darling, tell about your family how you come to California."

I tried to invoke the secret finger cross. My attempt to explain proved too much for me, and I found it easier to unearth dusty old memories. So I reluctantly began to exhume the great O'Connell Irish saga for Annetta.

"The ancestral Irish curse often referred to and occasionally invoked by my Mother was, in reality, a crutch upon which our family would frequently lean. I believe it gave them a reason and a small measure of comfort to justify personal failures.

"The curse of bad brains from the taverns and peat bogs followed me here to London,"

She would mutter to herself in times of trouble. True, my birth father was born in Ireland, but far from any peat bogs, although there was indeed a preponderance of bad brains and taverns in the neighborhood. She told me that a miserable slum in Dublin near the old Sherif Street area was my birthplace and undoubtedly an area no decent man would choose to frequent.

July 1945 was the year of my birth. 1945 just as the war ended. A time when poverty, always biting deeply, led most men to despair. Despair was the name of the creature padding softly through the narrow, dirty streets, searching through the slums to feed upon ragged, desperate people.

I never knew my birth father, who remained a mysterious shadowy figure throughout my life. Mother never revealed the truth about him or discussed the details of their relationship.

As I grew, I could only assume my father was in jail, perhaps confined to a mental institution.

"Yer father's dead."

That was the extent of the available information. As time passed, I resolved to discover the true family history. My interest waned with the passing years, and I never pursued my childhood resolution. At some point in time, it no longer held any interest for me.

I'm sure I remembered Jimmy O'Connell clearly, although there was some doubt as I was no more than three years old when Jim was killed. It was the name O'Connell that I was given, not my real father's name, Riley. Mother would tell me stories about the legendary Jimmy smiling and laughing with me as she remembered him. He was described as a large, boisterous man, often participating in outrageous displays of public drunkenness.

Most evenings, he would take his clothes off and juggle hard-boiled eggs naked in the street."

"Eh? What are you talking, Em-Jay? What eggs?"

"Ah, just checking if you were paying attention, my darling."

"You are very disturbed, my dearest Em-Jay. This is a most interesting history for me. So! Do you continue or go hungry?"

"I will continue; I work for food, but please understand the effort to recount this murky history is exhausting, time-consuming, and painful."

"Oh, I do understand, my dearest. Cooking Italian food for an English man is also painful, time-consuming, and exhausting. I am sure you understand this, Eh?"

"You make your point succinctly, beautiful lady. Okay, if you want me to continue with this stuff, here goes. Do remember, though, all this info about Jimmy, Just my mom's opinion. As said to me by her." And so, I continued with the story.

"Jimmy could often be found drinking whiskey with friends in the local public bars, sometimes brawling in the streets. At home, he would distill copious amounts of gin from an old family recipe, sharing his abundance with friends and neighbors. His gin was available four times every year in large quantities. Mother said it was a great inconvenience for her as the bathtub would not be available for washing, and the house would smell for weeks of berries and flowers. She would have to wash me in an old galvanized tub in the garden, a reasonable sacrifice as the gin was well-liked and appreciated probably because it was free.

So, Jimmy was the man mother had taken up with and would eventually prove to be her salvation.

He was a meat cutter, and a good one, employed by a small processing plant. Because of his agreeable personality and inclination for hard work, Jimmy always remained when others were discharged or replaced.

"Yer with us fer life, Jimmy lad," the manager often told him.

And so it was, for on a cold April morning, an *F.W Woolworth* delivery van driven by a young, inexperienced driver rounded a corner at the intersection of Wicklow Street and Grafton where the old hotel used to stand. Unfortunately, Jim O'Connell was halfway across the wet cobblestone street when the speeding delivery van drove into him.

A broken rib or two would be the major injuries he would have suffered had he not fallen backward, cracking his head on the stone. He lay in the street, gazing into the cloudy gray sky, unable to move.

Jimmy was just too far. Too far from a priest and too far removed from the church to receive absolution. Too far from the hospital to receive immediate medical attention.

Too far from his friends to be carried to the tavern on the corner.

As he stared at the changing cloud patterns above him, he became lighter. The lighter he became, the less noise from the street concerned him, and smells from the brewery faded.

I'm dyin', he thought. *Dyin in the streets of Dublin with the daylight in me eyes. No word of comfort in me ears, without the taste of good whiskey in me mouth, and no prayer on me lips.*

This is not, by any means, the way I wanted to go. In uniform on the battlefield or savin the life of a beautiful lady, perhaps. Mebby in the excellent company of me friends in the saloon, but not struck down by a Yankee, penny-a-pound store delivery truck.

His other regret was Maggie and the boy Michael was not by his side to say farewell.

He was floating now, able to look down at the scene below. He gave thanks that he was drifting ever closer to the clouds, not being pulled into the ground by the weight of his sins.

This ain't so bad; I'm on me way to the angles gate without ever settin foot in the big Whitefriars church.

Now, of course, Mother could not swear the words and feelings of dying, Jim was *exactly* as she described them, but as she knew him so well, she thought they probably were.

She said that as Jimmy floated into the clouds, he smiled broadly. Four young men from the small crowd that had gathered loaded him into the back of the delivery truck that struck him. He was driven slowly to the hospital and then carried inside on a makeshift stretcher.

About twenty residents provided a noisy entourage that followed the truck slowly through the streets, for Jim was well thought of in Dublin. Jimmy never left the hospital and never felt the comfort of the bed provided by a concerned Woolworth company.

Most in attendance at the wake said he was a good man, and he was.

Most in attendance at the wake said how much they missed him, and they did.

Most in attendance at the wake told of a beautiful, heartwarming ceremony, but, in truth, most attending the wake was too drunk to remember.

"Remember, sweetie, you asked me. All this anecdotal information was told to me by my mother and stepdad. Mother mostly because Dad never knew my Mother until they met in London. I don't know how to shorten the story. Please stop or interrupt me if you're tired. We can always finish after dinner."

Annetta insisted I continue. I did so reluctantly after my empty glass was filled again. And that in itself was a small problem, for the more I drank, so my memory was diminished. To compensate for this inconvenience, I embellished and exaggerated, hoping the dear girl would tire of my nonsense. Unfortunately, she did not. Annetta was relentless, insisting I continue.

"*Okay, then, beautiful lady,* my mother Maggie, Jimmy's unofficial wife, felt the cold comfort of the money the company reluctantly offered her. It was just sufficient to buy a steerage class fare to the prosperous, sinful city of London. Mother, never shy or unwilling to express her opinion, negotiated for three weeks with company executives. She argued convincingly for more money and a general letter of introduction, extolling her excellent character. Also, there were Woolworth stores in London.

Anxious to divert the growing tide of bad publicity, the company also provided her with a letter of recommendation extolling her capabilities as an exemplary employee to any Woolworth store in London.

The year of forty-six found London seemingly depressed. It was, by most appearances, a ruined city. In the east end, several streets were cleared, although many houses had fallen. Blocks of rentals and public housing stood vacant. Some leaned precariously with broken walls as if a great slice of the building was taken, giving a miserable view of the deserted rooms inside. The larger bomb sites, having been quickly fenced, displayed the rubble that was once a store or large house. Tortured twisted pipes and heavy electrical cables poking through the debris were a continuing attraction to the schoolchildren playing in the ruins.

I was one of them and remembered this clearly. In the bombed-out ruins, there was magic waiting for a child with nothing except the friends he played with. In the Kilburn area where we lived for some time, the shattered buildings were my playgrounds for several years.

Alongside that depressing backdrop, a current of activity ran. There were the necessary construction and public works projects, and stores opened again, although food and luxury items were strictly rationed. The undercurrent of euphoria, so noticeable at the end of the war, was now tempered with reality as life slowly returned to a degree of normality. The poor struggled as they had always done; the rich were sometimes mildly inconvenienced.

May 1947. My mother, Maggie O'Connell, crossed from Dublin to Liverpool with her little son Em-Jay. The waters were rough, and the weather rainy and cold. Her new life started with cold, freezing winds and the loneliest feeling of desperation. She knew she was a woman alone in a harsh world but never as sharp as scratching for food on the miserable streets of Dublin. She said those days were the standard by which all bad things were measured.

Over the years, as I grew, she and my stepdad described their life vividly. The memories remain with me clearly to this day."

Mother told me that a steam train left us at Paddington station on a gray Monday morning. She and I had arrived in central London with wet clothes and heads high.

I don't remember anything about the ferry crossing, the station, or our arrival, but I have been back to the station many times. It never changed, as I recall—a huge echoing concrete and steel-framed structure with an enormous glass vaulted roof.

A venerable mainline terminal for noisy steam trains. Pigeons would roost in the high beams and walk the platforms without fear, forever searching for a generous bread or cake handout. One thing they shared was a uniform dirty gray color. I think this was smoke from the engine's coal fires and oily steam exhaust that permeated the station and covered the pigeons with sound and smell. All that has changed, I'm sure. Steam trains exist only in the imagination, having made way for diesel-electric. If there are any pigeons now, they are probably much cleaner.

"Beautiful Italian Annetta, Realize that this story or stories are from the time when I was a baby or small child. I have to go back so many years; there is so much detail that I have probably forgotten."

So, a room in Hammersmith was our home for two weeks before mom moved us to a small self-contained flat behind the Edgware-Road. A large bustling Woolworth store sat proudly, a neighborhood landmark about ten minutes walk from our new home. Eight-thirty the following Monday morning, she presented herself to the assistant manager.

No more than a boy, she thought, surprised by his youthful appearance. A boy perhaps but a handsome one, black hair slicked back, even white teeth when he smiled. He was also quietly spoken and with a sense of humor. Alistair McFadden gazed at the woman seated opposite. Here was a pretty Irish lass with her long auburn hair half-hidden by a little red beret. Pretty she maybe, he thought but with purpose and hidden strength—not exactly a beautiful woman, but a damned attractive one. The few lines etched into her face seemed to add character to her personality. He saw every line as a testament to her fortitude and courage.

The two introductory letters surprised him, an almost unheard-of recommendation from head office suggesting most strongly she be hired without delay. He handed a simple questionnaire for her to complete and asked that she return the following morning.

They shook hands briefly as they stood, and she thanked him for his help. *Something very special about that* one, he thought, gazing after her slim retreating form. She started stocking shelves and was soon promoted to the counter register; Mother was a happy girl. Happy for her little home and happy to earn enough money to feed young Michael without begging. She would walk in the streets through Hyde Park and explore the ponds and paths in Regents Park. Now, often to be seen in the company of Alistair McFadden.

May first on a Sunday afternoon in 1950. My Mother and Alistair were married. The company allowed a week to enjoy a quick honeymoon, and for the last time, either of them would ever visit Dublin. *I suppose they took me with them, I never asked, and they never told me*—a bittersweet sentimental journey for mom and a chance to proudly display her wonderful new husband. The dismal old streets she knew so well gave no welcome or reason for her to stay.

Alistair never adopted me or had my name changed. "The wee bairn is happy enough for now," he would say. And so I was, for I had grown to accept my new father. I think my new father was learning to love his new son. As our family fortunes improved, we moved from Alistair's small rented flat in Sussex Gardens. A quiet corner of West Hampstead, at the end of Aberdare Road, would be our new home. Mom and dad rented a basement flat, two large ground floor rooms in a red brick house with the use of a fenced back garden—plenty of room for me to enjoy and a little cheaper than Sussex Gardens.

"Now, my darling, I must stop to eat. I can't continue this nonsense without food and drink. Also, a long, lingering kiss would lighten the load."

Annetta provided all three quickly. She had made a large pot of seafood, prima-something in a white cream sauce—another delicious meal contributing significantly to my rapidly expanding waistline. And so, after great feasting, I continued the story of my family's early days in London. Telling how father would walk to the underground station, taking a train to Edgware Road.

After a few months, he decided to buy a good used car. No more rain-drenched walks to the tube for him. Also, he could take us in style to explore the countryside. Our family Rover 16, born in 1947, was a regal machine. Glossy dark blue paintwork and polished burgundy leather interior. A prize for the money, but apparently, more than Alistair could comfortably afford. It ran well, a monument to quiet, unfailing reliability. More than that, though, it was a conservative statement quite appropriate for Aberdare Road and certainly a respectable icon in the Woolworth manager's car park. So life continued happily for our family.

I paused, looking at Annetta. *H*ow serious she seemed as if any of this personal undocumented, unsubstantiated, anecdotal history could mean shit. Okay, possibly not shit to anyone except Annetta and me. So, I reluctantly continued.

CHAPTER EIGHTEEN

I was little Em-Jay, soon becoming bigger Em-Jay. Alistair often told me my wayward personality reflected my mother's independent spirit. I think it was at that time; I understood I had no love for him. During my school years at a strict all-boys institution, I found lessons and the process of learning tedious and painful. Painful? I was often chastised for unruly behavior. The punishment for unruliness was the cane. A four-foot length of flexible greenish bamboo about the thickness of a man's finger: this corrective tool was administered by schoolmasters, always wearing the traditional black gown and mortarboard. Their formal attire, similar to a judge's robe, perpetuated the belief in teacher omnipotence with or without a cane.

Either three or six strokes on each upturned palm, leaving three or six blue-black raised welts on each hand and rendering hands and fingers unusable for an hour or so.

Persistent or repetitive unruliness required sterner measures. The feared and always to be avoided *Six of the best.* Six on each hand, six across the unfortunate buttocks when doubled over. The pain was indescribable. The hiss of a cane through the air could be heard clearly in the expectant silence of a classroom. The righteous cane was also a public demonstration to illustrate the absolute power held by teachers over miserable students and to glorify the inevitable triumph of good over unruliness.

Let the agony wash through you, choke back hot tears brimming in your eyes if you can, for only a coward would show pain or weakness before one's peers and teachers. There was no shame in being caned; there was shame in crying. The worst I ever suffered at any time was three on each hand and three on the bottom.

Although the school was ostensibly an institution to promote academia and higher learning, it became evident that it was a secondary purpose at best. Perhaps that is why it was called a secondary school, as opposed to a grammar school. Children were graded and funneled into groups to learn blue-collar manual trades. Metalwork, carpentry, and plumbing were usually promoted above art, music, or literature.

"Use your Hands; Jesus was a carpenter, not a philosopher. He used his hands to glorify God; you think you're better than that boy?" A reasonable statement *IFF;* you were a Christian.

At least lively debate was encouraged between teaching staff and students. Freedom of expression was always held in high regard.

"But sir," *Always address the masters as sir.* "The great choirs in the cathedrals play music and sing to glorify God."

"And who do you think built the cathedrals and churches, eh? Men with their sleeves rolled up, tradesmen, not poets."

"But sir, architects and draftsman had to design and..."

"Sit down, boy. If I want to hear from you again, I will let you know. Until that time, be quiet and only speak when spoken to. Is that clear? I will not tolerate insolence or an irreverent attitude in my class; is *that* clear?"

"And, of course, it was very clear. And there were times I was merry, times when I cried and looked for shelter, never at home, though. I knew there would be little comfort or refuge for me there. There were times when this mattered to me, but most of the time, it did not.

As a teenager, my great loves were motorcycles, blues, and jazz, passions enduring to this day. My earliest ambition at that time was to own a motorcycle. Both my parents, fearful of awful accidents, offered to loan me the money to buy a good used example, provided I wore a crash helmet. They believed in the absolute protective power of a helmet; it was, to them, an angelic amulet that would deflect any misfortune on a motorcycle. A crash helmet was, in reality, a cranial condom to contain any brains from spilling onto the road in the event of a bad accident. I found a heavy old, Matchless 350 single in excellent condition, and that was the beginning of my great enduring love for motorcycles. The Matchless was my first bike and one of many I would own in quick succession.

True to my word, I wore a crash helmet, but only during winter months. In the summer, I did not. Eventually, I fulfilled my obligation and even managed to repay my parents from the miserable wages I earned as a stupid trainee auto mechanic. Life as a stupid trainee auto mechanic was as boring to me as school was. Not as painful, though. Two friends, also with motorcycles and as bored as I, plotted to join the merchant marine. High adventure and a wage packet. I joined the marine plotters, and within two months, the three of us had signed on for six months as galley help and deckhands.

A tragedy that affected my life and haunts me to this day prevented one of my two co-conspirators from fulfilling his destiny as a sailor."

"But that's another story, sweetheart." I said, "One to be told much later."

She smiled dreamily with eyes half-closed and shrugged her shoulders.

"If you saying, dearest. But, if you thinking I do not remember, you will be wrong."

"I neglected to inform my parents about my plans. A week before I embarked on the first voyage, I confessed. For some reason, I was expecting a grand argument and a plethora of reasons not to join the Navy.

Mother was in shock. Alistair thought for a few minutes before congratulating me. Both parents were dismayed by the thought of their only baby sailing the high seas but accepted my inevitable transition from boy to man. Mother could only remember the miserable ferry crossing to Liverpool, convincing herself that I would freeze to death in foreign waters.

It was not to be. I flourished at sea; a sailor's life was, for me, the perfect antidote to life as a stupid trainee auto mechanic. After the initial six months, I happily signed up for three more years, determined to visit every port and sail every navigable sea. During that time, I discovered the astonishing visions concealed within a small black opium pipe. Only possible off-watch in the confines of a dark corner of the engine room. This temporary distraction greatly pleased me and prompted me to inquire about other, more potent material.

With opium, I lived in dreams for a while; the dreams gave me hope for the future. My new sweet dreaming would eventually be reconciled with a much darker reality—the daily grind of living. When I was a stupid trainee auto mechanic, had I that simple magic pipe, then; it would have dissuaded me from pursuing a life at sea. At school, it would have reduced the vindictive thrashings to laughable insignificant encounters.

My three years of mandatory service were fulfilled. A sweet Spanish lady in Buenos Aires temporarily detained me. This delightful distraction was problematic. I missed my return passage to Ireland. Eventually, I returned from Argentina, working my passage on an old Russian freighter as far as France.

A week marooned in Burloigne, then across the channel to England again. I intended to pursue a career as a sailor at that time. Too many of life's distractions in the waterfront boarding houses and bars; conspired to prevent me from obtaining necessary formal discharge papers in a timely manner.

I signed on for six months working a fishing trawler. Four months of backbreaking, dangerous labor on the bitter wintry North Sea waters convinced me never to return to the sea.

That's about it, beautiful lady, the genesis of a wandering British biker, and his subsequent bad behavior. Wow, did I just say all that without an attorney?"

"No, my foolish and darling Em-Jay. That was a wonderful story and history, but much more to say, yes? Much more to tell me. Tonight or tomorrow, you say me."

"Yes, but that story, those experiences are no more than anyone would tell—nothing special there, darling. There are many amazing lives with stories untold or waiting to be told. In every life, there are a million experiences every day that are woven into the fabric of those lives, and within that fabric are the memories of stories needing to be told."

"Dios Mio Em-Jay. Are you a prophet, politician, or evangelist? This is a good wine, better than I thought, have more, and you can tell me the history of the world, dance, or sing a song for me."

"Yeah, sorry, darling. You're right; it is good wine, but I'm Just trying to say there are so many stories more interesting than mine worth listening to."

"Perhaps, but I have not interest Em-Jay, only this story of you. Please tell more for me."

"I will, but not now, honey. I need time to think up more lies. Tomorrow, I promise, no fingers crossed. You remind me, though."

And so we continued into the bright hours with daylight at our disposal. We talked late into the afternoon, at times seriously, at times laughing. We kissed and held, exploring with our hands and tongues until, with a surge of wanting, we fucked, with her leaning naked across the patio table. I buried my face in the hair beneath her arms and between her legs, drawing in her sweet, dark woman's musk smell. Dense black hair formed a perfect triangle between her legs. Her magic triangle was a gift I could not resist, for I knew what lay just beneath.

There are times appropriate for fuck, without eloquence or social graces, just the basic needs and expression of reproductive satisfaction. There are special times appropriate for making sweet love. This was fucking time. After we parted, tired and spent, we sat again naked on the swing. Within the hour, the afternoon had returned into evening, and I knew this was the right time, perhaps the only time to tell about Aunt Jen.

"Walk with me, darling, please, now as we are."

So, we walked through into the desert that waited for us quietly.

"Let me get my shoes, and for you too. There are sharp stickers out here."

"No, there is nothing but soft sand, nothing that will hurt us."

"Okay then, look, I will come with you, against my better judgment, though."

So we walked naked without shoes, an astonishing sensual encounter with the breeze and approaching darkness. I felt the evening about my body, the warmth of the coming night coiling around my ankles and between my legs. We held each other again, and this time in the desert, sands made love. The sand covered Annetta, covered me, drawing and pulling on our bodies until we became part of the ground beneath us, sinking into the sand. Songs of the Small night dwellers joined in harmony with the occasional moaning wind whispering and laughing with us, feeling our nakedness playfully.

We were willing willful children of our great nurturing mother earth. Time had filled the darkening sky with stars, and a crescent moon before us gave good reason to return to the patio. We stood, at last, silent and amazed. Hand in hand, we walked slowly to the gate, gazing into a star-bright picture of eternity. We were no more than dust with nothing promised or delivered, just hopeful babies without understanding. I wiped tears from my face as we walked silently through the gate.

Under stinging waters of the shower, we found resurrection and were eventually cleaned and comforted by hot water jets that left a thin carpet of sand beneath our feet.

We sat without speaking, emotionally drained by the evening. I smiled at her and raised my glass in salute for what more could I do

"Soon, my darling, you will agree with me. There is magic for us in the desert."

I nodded slowly, thinking she was probably correct.

"There is magic in heroin, Annetta; I have seen a magic cat God at my door after a little powder."

"Tell now to me, darling, please."

"I have injected heroin three times, morphine one time. I don't use the needle anymore, and I don't use morphine because heroin is much sharper and easier to get. I still smoke heroin occasionally. I enjoy opium to smoke and cocaine to snort. That is the extent of my current drug use. A little whiskey and wine, but I don't count that. So, my first experience with smack was with a few folks at Pat's place.

I watched three people get high after talking with them for a while. One of the girls came with a new syringe and needle, loaded it with a small dose of Mexican number four, and showed me how to tie off and feel for a vein. No problem with the needle, just a little sting, but the effect was immediate. I understood then why people use. The effects lasted about five hours; I stayed the night and crashed on the floor."

"And this is your God experience?"

"No, that was the second time at my place in this house. Same stuff from Pat, except I was alone. When he found out about the first time, he was pissed. He lectured me about using and told me as a friend that he would not see me hooked and wouldn't let me have any more powder. When I think about that, the more I think he was right. Look, I will show you where I saw God."

We walked to the front door; Heavy, leaded colored glass inserts in the top half. In front of that, a black security screen door.

"So, after I had injected, everything became very quiet. Gradually the hall and front room became filled with light. Beautiful glowing colors moved slowly everywhere in the room, and with every change of color came a sound, an audible sensation perfectly matched to the visual experience. I think there must have been a light shining through the glass in the door. That was incredible, a lovely experience; I don't know how long it lasted, but suddenly there was a noise at the door. Through the glass, I could see a shape, probably the height of an average man. I opened the front door very slowly and very much afraid. I was looking into the face of a large cat clinging to the screen, staring straight at me. It told me to calm myself and listen carefully. Large golden eyes and the mouth slightly open, it looked surprised."

"Listen up, dumb ass; I'm here to help, not to hurt."

"I couldn't place the accent, East Coast, New York, Boston perhaps, but it spoke clearly in English. I listened for a long time, but now I can't remember what it said. The more it spoke, the less afraid I became.

The whole scenario was like a chapter from *Alice in Wonderland*. I do remember it was a two-way conversation, not just the cat speaking. After some time, it told me to close the door slowly. With the front door closed, the outline of the cat on the screen gradually broke apart and vanished, but the wonderful colors remained, moving all around the room."

"Then this was your God talking? A cat?"

"Just a little more, my beauty. I felt very tired and decided to sleep for a while. Even though the door was closed and there should have been no light, the bedroom was bright with moving colored shapes. Gradually the light faded, and a strong wind started to blow. How was that possible, tell me? Anyway, I pulled the bedspread over my head, and went into a deep sleep, didn't surface till about nine in the morning. There were no wind or colored lights, but the house was a wreck. Stuff was thrown everywhere; every room was a mess." It took me nearly two days to clean the place. Sounds strange to tell now, but at the time, it was a profoundly disturbing experience, enough that I stopped using the needle."

"That was not God, my darling; that was a Devil cat, angry because the house was dirty and want you to clean. Just think you talked with God, but you forget what God tells you?" She laughed loudly.

"I sorry, my darling Em-Jay. I laugh because I am thinking of you under the sheets with a hurricane blowing over you in the bedroom. And God is calling you dumb ass. Probably because of your drug using? But the heroin Em-Jay darling, the smoke is the same as the needle, stop this please before it becomes too strong, then not possible to stopping, eh? You making me frightened, my darling."

This woman had marked my house with the imprint of her vitality; the sound of her laughter would remain long after she had left. Within the hour, we went to bed, not as we had done before but now tired and relaxed, soothed by the feelings of the evening. We held each other, neither of us remembering or caring when we fell asleep.

Annetta was the first to leave the bed that morning, making coffee and toast, then threatening me with breakfast. During the working week, breakfast was never an option. My body was programmed to get out of bed, shower, dress, and perhaps have a quick coffee before tracking the roads to work. Annetta's presence added a new delightful dimension to my life. Another was breakfast. We sat in the bright morning, finishing our toast and coffee. This Saturday morning felt like a vacation, and I suppose, in a way, it was. It was early enough that we could take the train to Los Angles and walk the streets as tourists. Take the car to the station, about a half-hour drive, then off we would go.

And we did. The day felt quite different for me, with neither car nor bike. In the city center, there was no loss of convenience without a vehicle; in fact, the freedom from parking and driving through heavy traffic was more than enjoyable. We were on the homebound train at five-thirty, having stopped for lunch and coffee. About seven-thirty when we arrived home. Annetta had her shrimp and seafood thing left from Friday, which, combined with pasta, would be more than enough for dinner.

We sat at the patio table eating crab meat and scallops, something else, and Alfredo sauce with pasta. This, washed down with the inevitable red wine, was as good a meal as I have ever had. "Should be served with white wine, darling. That is the proper way."

I nodded my agreement to give the impression that I actually cared. I would have poured kerosene. The food was so good, and I was hungry. "So true, my dearest. I will have white wine here waiting for you next week. In the meantime, I will have another glass of red, inappropriate though it may be."

We chatted about the day, drank our improper wine, and finished a fine meal. I cleared the table, stacked dishes in the sink, and returned to Annetta sitting on the swing. Every time I sit here on the patio, either at the table or on the swing, I find a new reason for wanting to be here. My very good reason that evening was Annetta.

"So, my darling Em-Jay, is your stomach full and happy?"

"As it has ever been, babe. Since the wine is no longer appropriate for such fine food and I have no champagne, I'll get a whiskey. For you?" She shook her head, laughing.

"No, thank you, darling, for thinking of me. I will have another glass of wine with you, though. It is, as you say, not appropriate, so I hope when it greets the pasta in my stomach, it will not cause explosions."

"Trick is to drink sufficient wine that the pasta is overwhelmed and unable to respond. Be back in a moment." I don't drink that much whiskey, but the scotch I do drink is excellent. Half a bottle of black label remaining would ensure an enjoyable evening. I returned with the whiskey and glass to find Annetta sitting at the table, grinning.

"Hello, darling Em-Jay. I think the table is for easy, yes?"
"Easy?"
"Yes, easy darling, to finish the story of yesterday that you promise to me. Not heroin cat stories, though. Here at this table, you not looking into the desert and thinking of your beautiful Annetta who loves you, then forget the story words, yes?"

"I have no answer for that, honey; you are correct, and I will stay at the table with you. But, as you are sitting with me and are such a vision of loveliness, I am distracted and may have to cover you with a large blanket or plastic bag. Anyway, there's not very much left to tell now." I drank whiskey and thought of years past and the years passing before continuing.

"So, after the Navy back to Old England again. Meanwhile, while I was playing sailor, Mother and Alistair bought a house in the London suburb of Hendon. All very new and clean, close to the airport and within easy reach of the Woolworth store that dad was now general manager off. Three bedrooms, a small front garden, and a large walled back garden with a small detached garage. A very attractive dwelling, all brick construction, as were most of the houses in that area. I stayed with them for three weeks before moving closer to work and the city. I had no marketable skills except for some experience as a stupid trainee auto mechanic. But to my credit, I was hardworking, loyal, and honest, values I have since called into question.

My first job was driving a forklift and moving scrap metal for processing. The job was miserable and smelled bad, but fair wages almost redeemed it. I was working in a field driving an antique diesel forklift. Happily navigating around a mountain of scrap, I nearly collided with an old BSA motorcycle hidden behind overgrown vegetation and trees.

The motorcycle was an ex-English Army issue, still in. Original dispatch riders trim—a scruffy old flathead workhorse from 1942. Everything was finished with flat olive-drab paint. Obviously, it had been sitting unused for several years. I was delighted. With a little work, this could be my humble utilitarian transport until I saved enough money to buy a car. At the company office, I negotiated the sale—no sale to negotiate because it was inventoried as scrap. "Just take it Em-Jay," and of course, I did. New battery, oil, and fuel. So, wind in the tires, clean plug, and points, then after a few other adjustments, I was ready.

There were advantages to owning a motorbike—being cheap to run and maintain were good reasons. Another primary reason was that I loved riding them. I had savored the excitement and reveled in the mystique of riding large motorbikes before my time in the Navy and would do so again.

There is nothing to do but think when running long distances on a big motorcycle. This lumbering old beast had several unique features; the headlight, for instance, was a wonderful device. A metal shield with small adjustable slits covered the glass allowing minimal light to escape with the slits closed. Thus any marauding German troops would not be alerted to the rider's presence. An elite team of war department designers must have hatched this device. True, no recalcitrant Nazis would be alerted to a nighttime rider, but the rider would not be able to see the enemy either. Worse, a rider would not be able to see the road unless a full moon prevailed. At that point, he would be in full view of the enemy, a tricky situation, to be sure.

The old bike performed well enough during the two years I owned it. A ponderous old creature, but the fact that it still worked at all after the many years of enforced retirement was quite astonishing. Regretfully it met its demise on a slick, wet road in West London.

The ancient rear tire suddenly deflated as I rounded a sweeping bend in the West End Lane. Fortunately for me, oncoming traffic was far enough away that my injuries were relatively minor.

Memories of the incident are clear in my mind to this day. I remember the reflections from the road as light rain polished the black surface, and car headlights danced briefly with neon signs from the stores.

Suddenly everything changed, and with a crazy slow-motion excursion came the sound of breaking glass and people shouting in the distance. Bike and rider flew across the road, mounted the curb, and over the sidewalk, coming to rest after partially demolishing a chest-high ornamental brick wall surrounding the West Hampstead police station.

Several astonished but helpful police officers extracted me from the rubble and, after dusting me off and wiping away a small amount of blood from my face, stood me on my feet. As I was able to remain vertical for more than thirty seconds, the sergeant gave the command to load me into a police car and drive me to the local hospital.

My major injuries were four broken fingers on my right hand and significant bruising to my chest and legs. All in all not too bad, though.

I fared better than the bike, which was damaged to the extent that repair was impractical. As for the police station wall, it was rebuilt with the addition of several short-reinforcing buttresses.

I was never charged with any offense or billed for the damage I had caused.

Anyway, that's my bike story, darling, one of many. That old pile was responsible for my further education. So, time for another whiskey.

Do tell me, why are you interested in this old history stuff? Let's talk about you for a change. Much more interesting." Annetta laughed as she poured me a drink, filled her glass, and raised it in salute.

"To my darling Em-Jay and his childhood story yet to come, of course, I interested my darling. Here is you at another time, another Em-Jay for me to love."

"In the face of such flattery, I'll finish, then we can move on to something sexual, preferably in bed."

"Ha! As you know, the bed is only for us sleeping, eh? Tell the time you were sad, remember on the swing after we walk. What is that story?"

I did remember, and it was a miserably depressing time for me. I can't say how old I was, about seven or eight, probably. Both parents worked full-time. They would leave in the morning before school and return in the evening about four hours after school finished. I wore a key to the front door on a piece of string around my neck, a badge of poverty, and shared with several other children in my class. I was branded with many others in the school as a *latchkey kid*. In the summer, it wasn't so bad with the extended daylight hours. The cold winter months made life miserable. Winter rain was a terrible enemy. I had to walk about a mile each way, so I could sometimes sit in wet clothes all day. Many times I did so. Going home, there was a good chance it would rain again.

The house on Aberdare Road was my home for several years, at least, until I joined the Navy. The exterior of the building was a sedate and quite imposing old, slightly crumbling structure, as were most of the houses in the street. The basement floor, two bedrooms, kitchen, and bathroom we were renting required redecorating, and many other minor problems needed attention. I had the smaller of the two bedrooms and hated it.

This room was dark and depressing, full of shadows and sudden, indistinct scratching and tapping noises. I was convinced a malevolent spirit haunted it, angry at me for intruding. It was worse at night. I could never tell my parents about my fears. My only recourse was to pray to Jesus for help, pull the sheet and heavy army blanket over my head, and keep very quiet. I even took an old milk bottle to bed with me in case I had to pee in the night. I was too frightened to leave the bed and face the demons waiting in the blackness. I knew in the darkest corners of the room; something watched me—something with sharp pointed teeth, wicked and angry. Eventually, I would sleep. So I told my story to Annetta as promised and almost avoided further interrogation.

"For a civilized country, your England was cruel to children then. I listen to you, Em-Jay, and I also am made sad. I thinking you are feeling good to tell these things like a program of therapy, yes?"

"There is poverty and hunger in the US and every other country if you look for it.

I never thought of myself as mistreated or anyone being cruel to me. Just part of growing up, although the terror I felt in my bedroom at night is with me to this day. Still, hate to be alone at night, and I still listen hard for little noises. Remember, though, times change, and these stories are from a long time ago. The later years when I was about twelve years or so, were better, or at least until Aunt Jen came. As for telling these stories, it makes no difference to me one way or the other."

When I crashed the old motorbike, I stayed with my parents while I healed and never returned to the scrap yard. Alistair made me study and hounded me to do something with the brain he said I had. Oddly enough, I discovered I had an excellent aptitude for learning; now, I was no longer in school. Perhaps the cane of Damocles no longer hanging over my head took some of the pressure off.

So, thanks to my parent's support, I became a full-time mechanical engineering student. I owe mom and dad an enormous debt of gratitude for their help. Mom and dad were dirt poor to start and dug themselves out of poverty to lead a comfortable middle-class life. I remembered the poor times and decided to do better so my kids if I ever have any, will never need a latchkey around their necks. A rope perhaps, but never a latchkey."

"This was good to me to listen, especially about the rope around the little necks. I know you better now, darling, thank you, now Aunt Jen, that story?"

" Okay, I do have one more story to tell you; love, this one I have never told anyone and doubt I will ever repeat it. This haunts me and always has, so perhaps telling you *will* make a difference. More to the point, though, I have drunk enough good whiskey to tell the story now. Maybe even learn something from the telling."

Annetta, head in her hands, said nothing. Annetta, the beautiful, imperturbable lady I loved, gazed out at me across the table as I began.

" Late July, just a few weeks before my fourteenth birthday Aunt Jeanine moved in with us, staying for a few months. She slept in my bed. I slept on the floor.

I was told Jeanine was Alistair's sister, although Alistair would never discuss the situation or talk about his family. Mid-thirties, I think, with a slight Scottish accent. She transformed my dark bedroom with her chatter and laughing. No more lurking demons. I would leave for school, say goodbye to Jenine and see her again when I returned. She always called me Bob, never by my birth name, even when she spoke about me to Mother or Alistair. I was always young Bob or Bobbie. Anyway, on Monday, about four-thirty. I arrived home from school; Aunt Jen was in the kitchen; it would be at least two hours before Alistair and Mum returned from work.

"I made mushroom soup, but before you can eat, you must have a bath."

I was a little surprised by that. My bath-time was Tuesday and Thursday, but no matter, I followed her dutifully to the little bathroom. Aunt Jen ran the hot water until the old enameled tub was about half-filled. Cold water followed with Aunt Jen testing the temperature frequently with her hand. "In you get, then, lad, before the water gets too cold."

I stared at her "will you be waiting outside then?"

"No, I want you naked so I can examine you carefully. No need to be embarrassed or ashamed. Nothing you have that I haven't seen before. In you get now."

And so in I got. My heart was beating loud enough to be heard in the street. My face was bright red, shamed by my nakedness, and scrutinized by my Aunt Jen. Immersed as I was within a bubble of humiliation, my Aunt washed me thoroughly, probing my bottom with her fingers and squeezing my penis, laughing as it hardened beneath her fingers, and all the while a running commentary on my growing body and how she would show me her naked body soon, and how I would wash her all over.

"All very well for you, my darling. I hope you enjoyed the soup. You know, of course, this slutty prostituta Auntie of yours was a pedophile, a molester of children, yes?"

"I knew it was wrong at the time, but she was magic. I was not sophisticated or street smart, just a kid interested in model airplane engines, not female body parts. At the time, I hadn't even ejaculated yet. Aunt Jen taught me how to masturbate and would insist I did so in front of her.

Many times she would pull my hand away, replacing it with hers. Sometimes with her mouth. She often hurt me and was quite rough; I had to whisper how much I was enjoying it and how good it was. I liked it much better when we were in bed. She showed me how to have sex with girls and how women respond. She gave me much more than a crash course in sex; she held me through the nights when I was afraid. Thinking back to that weird part of my life, I should have been happy. I was not. She was very pretty, though; I thought she was beautiful. Slim, with long blond hair and dark eyes. I fell in love with her.

"Ah, and a great humanitarian then, and what happened to la puttana? Did she join a convent, become a nun? I do not like this story of yours, darling; there is something wrong."

"Just a story, love, only words. Aunt Jen left suddenly, never said goodbye, packed, and left while I was at school. Just after Christmas, I was fourteen then. That relationship changed me; I could never enjoy a normal friendship with any girl my age. No innocents or wonder was left for me, and this experience was a great secret; I couldn't tell anyone or talk about it to friends at school. I had become a different person. Neither Alistair nor my mum would talk about her. They would not talk about her at all, another enduring family mystery they created. Who was my real Father? What happened to Aunt Jen? I often wondered if they knew about us. Perhaps arranged the whole thing."

"Well, Em-Jay dearest, Now you have said this story to me, it has no more important to you. Let it go; you are free from it now.

Suddenly Kisses from Annetta, whiskey from the glass, and the evening was good again.

"Walk in the desert with me, darling Em-Jay."

"No, no desert walking this evening. Too much magic out there for me. I will sit on the swing with you, though."

Laughing, she took my hand, and we found our place on the swing. With glasses in hand, we sat quietly for a time. I broke the silence after a few minutes.

"Have you ever been to Ruben's house?"

"Yes, two times, one to helping Dot with a party. I help her with cooking. Two, I stay overnight when Dot and Ruben were away. I stay to watch the little daughter Alice."

"Yeah, I know their girl. I took her for a bike ride recently. Annetta, I didn't say anything to Ruben or Dot, but I think she's very sick."

"Why? Why you think that?"

"Just something I feel. Her eyes are sunken, looks as if she hasn't slept for a month. The poor kid looked like a little meth addict. Really heartbreaking. No healthy child should look like that." She nodded slowly, considering my words.

"I see Ruben when you came to me. Dot or Alice a year perhaps ago, so I don't know. She seemed good then. Ruben says me everything is good with the family. Alice is the only baby. Dot no more babies can have."

"Ruben tells me everything is fine as well, but he always says that. I still have this bad feeling; Alice is a nice kid; there's such a happy air of innocence about her. I like her; I hope there's nothing wrong. Dot and Ruben aren't stupid. I'm sure they would take her to doctors if they thought there might be a problem." So we left the conversation with nothing resolved, both of us hoping Alice was okay.

Our weekend continued with laughing, loving, drinking, and thinking. These delightful activities were punctuated by eating fine Annetta Italian food. Sunday afternoon, she rode with me to Pat's place, having decided to leave her two cases and most of their contents in the bedroom. Philippe was the only one in attendance when we arrived. Pat was out on business, so I stole a beer from the unguarded fridge, chatted with Philippe, and watched Annetta feverishly clean the living room and work her way to the kitchen. She stood by an open fridge staring at empty shelves and shaking her head.

She asked Philippe if Pat entertained the entire Turkish army while she was away. Why Turkish? I didn't know and didn't ask. Presumably, Turks were considered voracious eaters—time for me to head home. Annetta was sure we would spend the next weekend together; she said she would call to confirm.

My week at work passed uneventfully, except I was given a new project, one that I had some passing interest in. So, the boredom that was slowly engulfing me dissipated for a while.

There was no boredom at home. Every evening I found some meaningful distraction before bed. Recently Annetta was a fine distraction at weekends.

CHAPTER NINETEEN

The little neighborhood is quiet, which is one good reason for my moving here. I have lived in several major cities in Europe and the US and presently spend at least eight hours per day working in one. I find any possible advantage of convenience offset by the dubious street attractions and attendant clamor. I much prefer a tranquil environment. Not for everyone, I realize, but for me, the breath of life is found whispering in quiet places.

Wednesday evening, when Alan rang the doorbell. Alan is a firefighter working for the Los Angeles County fire department. We first met about five years ago when he and his wife bought a vacant house on the other side of the street, six houses from mine. My interest was aroused by the new motorcycle he sometimes rode. We shared a common interest and naturally fell into casual conversation. Another commonality we shared was our age—both of us were in our mid-thirties.

This neighborhood supports many elderly folks. I am surrounded on all sides by antique citizens. A goodly cross-section of ancient men and women, some drooling, some tottering about unsteadily with vacant watery eyes and hollow bones. There were times when I viewed them as an entirely different species identified by the faint odor of mothballs and formaldehyde. Some are interesting, with remarkable life experiences and history to share. Others are boring, brimming with regret and self-pity, crushed by the accumulation of their squandered years with no tolerance for the younger ones. I think beneath their collective frailty may exist an unquenchable rage at the common disease that will eventually afflict us all.

As a group, they are quiet, avoiding noisy gatherings and violent demonstrations. Most believe it unnecessary to share their personal taste in music with every resident on the street or broadcast it publicly at several decibels above the pain threshold. There are many younger tribes whose members believe their music and personal opinions of everything are important enough they must always be shared and promoted with evangelical fervor, so the world around them may be converted. It occurred to me that within thirty-five years or so, I would join rank with other ancient ones. Perhaps engage fellow shufflers and wobblies with incessant accounts of my dysfunctional intestinal activity and expound upon various prostate anomalies. I think I will do well as an old coot or perhaps a belligerent shut-in when the time is right. When I am called, I will go, of course, willingly or not.

Let us never forget the unthinkable, the awful demon running at our heels. Never look behind, for the ones now immortal and strong, daring all and confronting adversity with a sharp blade and agile whit, will also become old and smelly with the passing of the seasons. As it has always been and always will be.

Suddenly I was there. The ornamental cane I found myself holding saved me from falling as I adjusted to a sudden shift in a twisted doo-dah mental continuum. Oldness was suddenly upon me, covering me like a dirty thread-worn blanket, bringing for my amusement arthritic limbs and leprous age spots on my hands and face. Glancing wildly about a large green room that I found myself tottering about in, I saw the *restroom* sign with an arrow pointing to nirvana. There were strollers and wheelchairs piloted slowly by other ancient ones, and the faint smell of odor-masking antiseptic spray hung in the air. Plastic benches and padded chairs indicated I might be in the dining room. Trying to engage others in conversation proved a futile endeavor. Although I spoke loudly and shouted twice, there was no response. It was as if I did not exist.

At the far left corner of the room, double doors opened suddenly, admitting two white-uniformed nurses or helpers. A young woman held a small handbell and rang it vigorously, a pleasant tinkling sound.

"Here we are again, boys and girls" Her voice carried lightly but purposefully in the room. "Evening meal time, so please take your places at the tables. Jose will serve the food today." Jose, a burly Latino fellow decorated with colorful tattoos, smiled and chatted with the old ones. While Jose seated the venerable residents, I tottered over to face the pretty bell-ringer woman. Like the others, she ignored me when I introduced myself. If not willing to listen to me, perhaps she would acknowledge a hand on her arm. I felt nothing as I squeezed her free hand. Nothing as I felt for the bell she held. Here was a woman, insubstantial yet very real to me. Drastic measures were required if my presence here was to be recognized.

A lucky accident, perhaps? The clatter of my cane was loudly heard, echoing in the room as it dropped to the parquet floor. To save myself from falling, I reached with both hands to grasp her bosom and squeezed happily. Nothing beneath my fingers as I fell through her form with arms flailing. I had returned to my house, standing, holding the front door open for Alan as he entered the living room.

From slow beginnings, Alan and I formed a firm friendship. He and his wife, Mary, would often come to the house, and I was a frequent visitor to theirs. Mary and Annetta had become good friends during the short time they had known each other, sharing many interests, including art and writing. Mary aspired to a full-time writing career, having her first novel published a few months ago.

An obvious advantage of having a friend like Alan is that his house is within walking or even crawling distance should unhealthy amounts of booze, or other materials be ingested at either residence. We sat for about an hour, drank two beers, and talked. His visit was to invite me to a party Saturday afternoon. A friend of a friend's twelve-year-old son would celebrate his thirteenth year.

"Mostly, adults with some kids, family stuff, no need to stay long. I'll drive; the house is about twenty miles from here." It sounded like a perfect distraction for Annetta, Something different for her instead of drinking wine and sitting on the swing.

She would not come with me on Thursday.

"Too much working at Pat darling."

Friday, it would be then. As Friday evening approached, I realized just how seriously Annetta regarded her *cook-clean* agreement with Pat.

"I tell him I will clean and cooking, so I will. I tell him, and it is my word, so of course, darling, I am bound to do this and with a happy heart. Wouldn't you?"

No reply from me, but I thought about it seriously. I was impressed, another facet of her personality that I was only now beginning to appreciate.

Friday at Pat's place, talking and joking as we usually did. I noticed how clean the front room was and remarked to Pat about it.

"Yeah, the Mexican gyp...Nah, sorry, I must watch me fuckin mouth in front of her husband." Then grinning, he continued, "Mexican woman, not gyp, she is about the best. She looks after this place an all the shit in it like it was her own. Dead honest too. You got a good woman there, brother. Treat her right." He stared at me before continuing, "Hey! Check out the kitchen, limey."

His kitchen gleamed with an unholy luster. The fridge was cleaned and stocked with provisions and cooked dishes. The cupboard that once contained straws and paper towels was filled with canned goods. The walls looked like they had been repainted, but Pat told me Annetta had cleaned or washed every surface. I shook my head, amazed by the restoration.

"Yeah, with Philippe fixin' the outside, your gyp doing the inside, I could retire with no problem."

He was probably right.

We stopped at the supermarket for weekend food and at a liquor store for drink. Annetta reminded me of the white wine I had forgotten about. Two bottles of Pinot Gris that she was familiar with and, at a price that ensured it would not be used for cooking. Once again, we were on the patio with red wine in hand. Alan and Mary appeared just as we were deciding on the evening meal. They refused offers of food, but when Annetta suggested a delivered pizza, we were all suddenly in agreement. Beer and Pizza evening, a conventional evening enjoyed by ordinary folk with no magic or vanishing white rocks lurking over the gate.

"How is it your patio is so peaceful?" Mary asked. "At our place, there is always noise, but here it's so quiet." Allan nodded,

"I find the more I drink, the quieter everything gets. Everything's very quiet when I'm asleep."

"Perhaps for you, but there's nothing quiet about your snoring." Mary laughed and shook her head.

"You're right, though, Mary," I said. "I love sitting here in this place. This house is so quiet, not just the patio. One of the reasons I bought it."

And so the evening continued with happy chatter and good humor. Alan explained about the party again for Annetta's benefit.

"Quiet is in the land and very good. For to find it, you have to look most hard." We all turned to Annetta, considering her statement. Alan was the first to speak.

"I think I understand what she means. The silence around us now comes from the ground, the desert. Not the neighborhood, the altitude, or anything else. I think there are quiet places, and this is one of em. Except for the growling and rumbling out in the desert. I think there are good and bad places too." Annetta smiled

"Yes, if a house is not on quiet land, it will never be quiet or with peace. Always a bad house. There is a good and bad ground, Alan; yes, I agree."

I sat without comment, believing *bad ground* was land with high property taxes. Before sharing my insight, I suddenly remembered the first time I came to Pat's place and how I was struck by the almost eerie silence before he opened the door. Did I have to concern myself with quiet places now? An added complication was confusing a previously simple understanding of real estate. I decided to wait before voicing my experience at Pat's house.

"Growling and rumbling, buddy? Don't think I ever heard that before."

"Not all the time Em-Jay, sometimes, though, when we're quiet. It sounds like a huge animal. You never heard this before?" I shook my head. "Never have."

So the discussion continued. Annetta, Mary, and Alan were knees deep in fanciful *new age* opinion, arguing as if there was a factual basis for anything they discussed. The pizza delivery guy unknowingly restored balance to the proceedings, and we all leaped upon the plump young pizza. Once in a while, a great greasy, fattening, unhealthy dinner is the perfect antidote to bullshit if washed down with beer. Caution is always needed as the same antidote will, at times, promote more bullshit quite unexpectedly.

And so we ate, devouring the cheesy foodstuff at the table. We all managed to sit on the swing after eating, three of us having graduated from beer to wine, with me drinking whiskey. Another hour or so locked in happy, animated conversation before Alan and Mary left, Annetta promising to call Mary if Alan's snoring kept us awake.

"So darling em-Jay, you think Mary is attractive? She grinned at me, putting a finger to her lips.

I shook my head, trying to decipher the meaning behind her question and the finger on her lips. Perhaps a secret Italian signal, so secret that it meant nothing to me unless she guessed, saw my growing interest in Mary.

"Hadn't thought about it, I lied. She's certainly a good-looking woman. Clever, too, by all accounts, a pretty good writer. The only thing for me is that she likes to be in charge. The boss lady. Perhaps she'll write a story about us."

"Mmm, perhaps about you, she is good to looking at. She married, though. Otherwise, I may try to seducing her to my bed. And. I see you look at her, feel her with your eyes, so perhaps you bring her to your bed, eh."

I stared in astonishment; it was some time before I spoke. *This must be a failure in translation.*

"Say again slowly, my little Italian nutcase; you want Mary in bed with you?"

"Yes, she is beautiful, yes?"

"Well yeah, but she's a woman; you want her in bed with you. For sex?"

"No, my dearest fool, I want her in bed, so we are cooking together and burning down the bedroom. Yes, of course, If I not with you and she not with Alan, then yes. For us loving each other."

"You are a lesbian then? I mean, how many women have you been with? You never told me about this."

"Ah Em-Jay, I think perhaps five girls. *N*o, I am not a lesbian. I love, I love men more than women. There is a big difference emotionally and with sex. But is love, yes? I love you. Is love for everybody, yes? We are creatures thrown here in this world and allowed to live. Do we living because a group of peoples tells us it is right to do this, and another group tells us no? And which is right or good? The ones shouting and making more noise? The ones who have more guns? No, I think to fuck that, eh? Let go to bed now, darling fool Em-Jay."

And so we did; my head was spinning through the whiskey and wine, trying to rationalize or even understand her arguments. I tried to imagine Annetta lesbianing with Mary, but it just didn't work for me. Mary would be the dominant one, naked on top of a naked Annetta, directing the action, I supposed. Who would do the laundry, I wondered? Who would make the coffee? Of more concern was Annetta's latest revelation, leaving me wondering how much more was to be revealed.

"What do you make of Alan and his growling sounds."

"I think Alan is more sensitive than you or sexy Mary. The noise he hearing is real, as the beloved white rock is real for you."

"Okay then, but what makes the noises he hears? Is there some animal out there? Could it be an echo from his snoring?" Annetta glared at me but couldn't suppress her laughter.

"The only animal here is *you*, my darling." And so the question remained unanswered but not forgotten.

Five the following evening was the time arranged for Alan to meet us at the house. From there, he would take us to the party. The following day passed quickly enough, *too quickly* as it always seemed to in Annetta's company.

Alan and Mary appeared with the SUV, and we were soon loaded and on the road. Less than half an hour driving before we were parked outside a large fenced front yard. Many people were wandering and talking, some jabbering and babbling, apparently without intent or purpose. There were creatures of all ages, laughing and frowning, some drooling, some gagging to the music. It was Mexican rancho music that filtered over the gathering, completing a cheerful ambiance to the proceedings. We were greeted enthusiastically by the wife of the house owner and ushered to the back of the house, where there were several long tables and chairs. I would guess about thirty adults and children filled the front and back areas.

As the evening progressed, so the happy music increased in volume; farting, babbling, and dancing erupted spontaneously as more liquor was poured. A bull-riding machine was set up by a drunken vendor, and children were encouraged, perhaps threatened to participate in the portable madness. A few robust adults tried their hands; the machine had a speed adjustment set to accommodate such brave folks. None were able to stay mounted for more than a minute or so. A large inflated mat broke their fall when they were ejected. Alan and I tried this unhealthy activity, and both of us failed ignominiously. A knot of noisy drunken young adults, probably ten or more, were gathered outside a sliding glass door leading into the kitchen.

The nosiest among this crowd was the homeowner. A large burly Latino fellow wallpapered with fresh, colorful tattoos. He introduced himself to me as Cisco; his friends called him Chico. Here was the friend of a friend holding the party for his thirteen-year-old son. For a few moments, I stood in shock. This was not Cisco. Before me was Jose, a tattooed Mexican gangster nurse in the green dining room I had recently visited. Nothing was simple for me anymore.

Pouring a large glass of tequila, Cisco offered me the bottle and waited for me before drinking himself. I found a plastic cup at a nearby table and poured a big shot, hoping I hadn't violated an old drunken Latino custom by not drinking from the bottle. Apparently not, for we were both holding plastic party cups now.

We raised our glasses in a friendly salute. Oh, but this was good liquor, the experience not diminished by the plastic cup. Although not an expert, I knew for sure this was an exceptional tequila. The grin on my face must have resonated with Cisco, and we shook hands. After the second shot, Cisco was now my Bueno Amigo insisting I call him Chico and rolling on his feet like a sailor in a storm.

He leaned precariously against the nearest table, grinning happily at me. I was about to pull a chair for him and pour another shot when he spotted a dog behind the glass door. A brown and white pit bull slightly bigger than Rubens's dogs stood against the door, tail wagging dementedly. "Es-me perro man, es Joey. He pulled the door open, and Joey barreled into the yard, a happy boy jumping and greeting visitors. Cisco told me he had the dog for about five months. He's a smart mother, man; I teach him tricks; he learns quicker than my brother. We both laughed as Cisco pulled a chair from the table.

"Eh, Joey up" Joey turned, ran to the chair, jumped up, and sat. I was impressed and told Cisco so.

"Yeah, that is some smart pit, Chico. He sat on the chair with only your voice command, no hand movements at all."

"Yeah, all by voice. This is one clever fucker, man; look here." He disappeared through the door, from which the dog Joey had recently emerged. Joey dog and I found ourselves part of a small expectant crowd of spectators. I nodded to Alan as he joined the gathering. "Wait for the dog show, buddy; just about to continue."

Cisco weaved his way uncertainly through the door, navigating past unseen obstacles and holding a saucer with a lump of hamburger meat.

"Watch this man."

He told Joey to sit. Joey sat dutifully as Cisco placed the meat before him. Joey turned his head away from the saucer and stared into space as if he was offended by the food. After a minute or so, Cisco winked at me.

"Now watch. *Take it, Joe.*"

Within a few seconds, the meat had evaporated, with Joey licking his face, waiting for more. "Eh, Joey up," again; the dog jumped on the chair and sat, waiting expectantly. It occurred to me that Cisco had spent considerable time with his dog, training him. By this time, the crowd had increased, with several children chatting excitedly about the coming attraction. Neither Annetta nor Mary was in the gathering. I was sure Cisco would repeat the highlights of the performance for them if he were sober enough to remain standing.

"Okay, Joey, you're goin to die; you been a very bad dog, so I'm goin have to shoot you."

Cisco opened his shirt and, with an exaggerated flourish, withdrew a heavy short-barreled pistol from the waistband of his pants. He pulled back the hammer of the gun slowly until the unmistakable double click-clack of a revolver that cocked and locked into place sounded loud. He must have rehearsed this performance many times with slow, exaggerated movements. Many in the crowd had seen this before, showing no surprise, although a few gasped and whispered comments when the revolver appeared.

"Die, Joey" There were a few seconds of absolute silence after a small cloud of dust blew out from Joey's head, and he fell unmoving from the chair. The sound of the pistol rolled and crashed, booming around the garden as children screamed and people ran for the gate. Cisco dropped the gun as he knelt sobbing beside his dog. Alan retrieved the weapon emptying four live cartridges into his pocket. Joey lay unmoving as blood continued to ooze thickly from his head into the dirt. The Joey and Cisco show was over.

Alan steered me hurriedly to the front yard where Mary, Annetta, and another girl previously locked in animated discussion were now standing, amazed by the sudden activity.

"We gotta go *now*! " The women moved from the table as Alan opened his phone. We were on the road for only a few seconds; it seemed before the first of three police cars passed us. Alan had called the troops, who responded quickly with lights and sirens announcing their presence. The women, unaware of the drama that played out behind them, seeing nothing, but hearing the gunshot, filled the car with questions.

"Can't talk now?" Alan said, grinning, "I'm driving. Em-Jay will fill you in on all the details."

"Since when can't you talk because you're driving? I understand you can't talk when you're snoring but driving? That's a new one." Mary shook her head, laughing.

I was probably as drunk as Cisco. Alan, to his credit, only had a beer since he was driving. I tried to paint an accurate verbal picture for the girls, stumbling over a few words and promising to continue when we reached home.

"I'm still in shock. I was right next to the poor little bastard when Cisco shot him. For sure, this was a kid's birthday party to remember."

By the time we reached the house, my head had cleared sufficiently to discuss the dog show reasonably. We congregated on the patio with a little wine and rehashed events at the party. This most eventful evening was one I would not forget. Alan said Cisco was "just an idiot Mexican gangster, full of macho bluster with no brains."

"Perhaps he was, but I rather liked him, gangster or not. Obviously, he had performed this move with his dog many times."

"Yeah, but Em-Jay, the last thing anyone would do is to pull a gun at a party, in a crowd, and with kids present. Why not a friggin toy gun for this great clown and dog show? Think about it; he could have used a banana, drawing a lot of laughs. Not to mention the fact he was too shit-faced drunk to stand, let alone understand his gun was loaded with live rounds. Stupid fucker should go to jail for that alone—another five years for being a cholo gangster."

"Another two years for being Mexican,"

I said, thinking Pat would have certainly approved of my comment. Alan shook his head, frowning but saying nothing. Mary and Annetta glowered at me, indicating my brilliant whit was neither funny nor appreciated. *Probably beyond their comprehension,* I thought

"Perhaps our friends Ruben, Dot, and little Philippe should be in Jail then." She said, pointedly frowning at me. I shook my head, knowing I was in error.

"Okay, okay, sorry, just joking, smile Annetta, just a little British humor."

"Is good he, not British then," Annetta said sharply, looking at me. "That should be at least four years of hard laboring."

"And suppose he was unfortunate enough to be Italian?" I replied.

"Police give him fifty dollar and say *Grazie della sua pazienza e comprensione.*" There are times when pursuing an argument with a lady is an exercise in futility.

Alan laughed at Annetta's comments.

"Look, Em-Jay, like him or not, he managed to shoot his dog, could just as easily have shot someone in the crowd, a little kid maybe."

Alan was right; no argument, but no matter how dumb he was, I still liked him. His tequila was also a redeeming feature, although I made no mention of that.

"Will he go to jail for a long time?" Annetta asked. Alan shook his head.

"Probably not. It was a genuine accident, according to Em-Jay, and from what I saw. Probation and a lecture, maybe if he has a clean record. By the look of him, though, he could well be a convicted felon; in that case, brandishing and being in possession of a handgun should get him jail time. If punishment is the objective, then it has already been administered. He obviously loved his dog and was heartbroken when it died. I'm sure we'll hear about it soon. A good lawyer would help."

I thought about Joey and Cisco. How would he explain the situation to the police? There were too many witnesses for him to deny it ever happened. A good excuse then, "I was pointing the gun intending to shoot a fly on the chair when out of the blue, the dog jumped up."

"I was holding the gun when Joey grabbed it and shot himself in the head. He had been depressed for some time."

None of that stupidity would fly. Cisco was surrounded by witnesses who would tell about the final departure of a good little dog. I felt terrible for Cisco, even worse for poor dead Joey, although his going was quick and almost certainly painless. And so the evening drew to a close. Alan and Mary made their way home, with Alan offering his profuse apologies for the interesting but violent end to the party.

Mary and Annetta both claimed to have enjoyed the party up to the time of their enforced departure. I'm sure Alan and I felt the same. I stayed at the table talking with Annetta until we both felt tired enough to sleep. I lasted about an hour before realizing sleep was impossible for me and left the bed. To the swing I went, sitting as was now my custom, gazing out into the cold black midnight at stars and trees. I felt sick again, with a bad cold or flu perhaps, aching joints, and very tired. The feel of September was in the air with a sulfurous smell of distant rain. This was another night for unkind reminiscing and returning briefly to my youth in England.

CHAPTER TWENTY

Motorcycles were again the focal point in this cruel twist of fate. These dark memories must have been triggered by the sad events at this evening's strange party. Sixteen years old, recent holder of a new motorcycle license, and now the new owner of a battered but very fast Vincent Rapide. My friend Mike Miller was with me riding a Norton International, of which he was justifiably proud. Mike was small in stature with a big heart. The delicate film star's good looks and outgoing, happy personality amply compensated for his lack of bulk. Our friendship began in school and now revolved around a mutual love for motorcycles and pretty girls. We were recently preparing for a six-month haul in the merchant navy. This would probably be our last run together before we embarked on our first voyage.

We left early Friday morning, navigating damp overgrown country roads soon after leaving London's city sprawl. We would ride to the small town of Chertsey with no purpose to the trip other than the joy and thrill of running the big bikes. Within two hours or so, we arrived at the banks of a large reservoir. We sat for about an hour, shaking out the stiffness, discussing our ride, and watching dragonflies skimming the smooth gray water. Leaving the bikes for several hours, we explored the old town and abbey, eventually settling for a while at a small café for a late lunch. Having eaten, we decided to head home after filling the tanks. A little after four now, already wintry skies streaked with gray bought the promise of rain.

Mike stuffed his woolen watch cap in his jacket pocket, long blond hair swept by the wind and looking to me like a happy Viking warrior. He grinned at me as we headed home. My bike was much faster in a straight line. His Norton was an agile dancer flicking effortlessly through curves and sharp bends. The tortoise and hare were on the road again and pointed to home. The hare led comfortably along the straight highway until we approached the first bend. Mike breaking late, passed me easily, laughing as he did so, his hair spilling like golden ribbons, streaming behind him. The crackle of the exhaust, an uneven cadence harsh, then muted as he changed gears. That is the song of the highway, and that is the memory I have of him that will always be with me.

A downhill run now, with the narrow road overgrown by trees on each side, forming a high leafy tunnel overhead. I was catching the Norton as we fast approached the next tight bend. Mike was through the turn and accelerating hard while I was heavy on the brakes. My bike protested by twitching and sliding before bringing me unsteadily through the turn and onto the straight again. Just before the next corner, the leafy canopy above me was suddenly illuminated by a brilliant incandescent light. There was no rain yet, but I felt water drive hard into my face. Stung by sharp fragments, I rolled almost to a stop trying to understand what I had felt. Slowly rounding the bend, I saw an orange glow and small showers of sparks from a fire on the side of the highway.

Mike Miller had left the road and ridden hard into the jaws of a steel assassin waiting patiently for him. The half-lowered shovel of a yellow county earthmover parked off the side of the highway, now in silhouette from the burning Norton.

There was nothing for me to do; no help or demonstrations of grief would make a difference. Mike Miller was dead. There was blood on my face and in my eyes, or perhaps it was oil or fuel. Perhaps tears. I felt the fierce heat from the fire on my face as I came closer. My voice trembled, and I asked him to go with me, shouted at him to leave this place with me, although I knew he would never hear my words. My face was burning as light and heat from his funeral pyre shone in the black paint and sparkled in the polished aluminum engine covers of my bike. I Waited for a few moments more to wish him well on his journey before I left him alone like trash on the highway, riding on as if I never knew him, as if I never loved him, not stopping again or looking back.

Two days later came the newspaper accounts telling of a motorcycle rider involved in a fatal accident. A county JCB parked with no lights was thought to have contributed to the accident. Excessive speed was also cited as probable cause. Police were examining evidence, and the investigation was ongoing

"Hey, Em-Jay, you heard about Mike Miller?"

"Em-Jay, did you hear Miller is dead? He Died in an accident Friday or Saturday. Weren't you going into the navy together?"

Questions kept coming up with no answers from me. I had no answers to give or reasons to explain my treachery or why I abandoned him. I Sold my bike to a local dealer, with traces of blood and oil on the paint.

A week later, I was sailing alone on the hard north sea waters to another place. Another place on a map and another place in my mind.

"And what became of investigations? Police wanting you to talking?"

My answer choked off as Annetta asked me the questions. These were the most reasonable questions I was ready to answer, except I was now in bed next to my darling instead of drifting on the swing. I made no reply but left the bed. Turning on the light, I watched Annetta Cover, her eyes squinting and complaining. For a few seconds, I stood, adjusting slowly to my new surroundings.

"Sorry, honey, I was sure I was alone on the swing."

"No, my darling, you were here with me. You were dreaming, then sat up and tell me another old story."

Turning off the light again, I returned to bed and now shivering slightly, trying to accept this situation and reconcile the dark wave of confusion washing over me. I knew I should be back on the swing; for me, there was no doubting my senses at all. As I lay my head back on the pillow, Annetta reached for me and held me tightly, giving a frightened child comfort in her arms as I fell into a deep, dreamless sleep.

Three weeks before, I saw Annetta again, at least in a meaningful way. Two or three times at Pat's place, one time when we went for lunch between her schedules. I did see Ruben, though, Sunday at about two in the afternoon, a bright afternoon pleading for a motorcycle ride. I called Pat, but neither he nor Reg could join me. I was tempted to call Alan, but remembering the dogfighter's aversion to unfamiliar company, I thought better of it. Late September, with clear skies and a warm breeze in my face, encouraged me to continue. Southern California was on its best behavior.

CHAPTER
TWENTY-ONE

Ruben, Dot, and Alice were finishing lunch when I arrived. Refusing offers of food, I did accept a beer. Alice giggled "I know you've come all this way just to take me for a ride Em-Jay."

"Sorry, sugar, I don't have the bike with me."

Her face was a picture of confusion.

"Ooh Em-Jay, you lie. I saw you from the window. He came on the Harley, didn't he, dad?" Ruben grinned, shaking his head.

"Never saw him arrive, sweetie."

Alice ran to the door. "I see the bike Em-Jay. Now you have to take me for a ride for lying."

"Ruben frowned, "Enough, Alice."

And Dot flooding the dining room with buckets of parental angst and feigned disbelief at her only daughter's belligerent attitude and rudeness in front of a visitor.

"Okay, Alice, you caught me. I will take you for a ride if your mom and dad say yes. But, one other condition, your room must pass inspection."

A short gasp from Alice as she scampered away to correct the disaster that was undoubtedly masquerading as a teenager's bedroom. Ruben grinned as Dot hugged me.

"Sorry, Em-Jay. You've only just arrived, and already Alice is badgering you for a ride."

"No problem, plenty of time to relax while she cleans her room. It should take about two days at least. You are the inspector, mom."

I sat chatting with Dot as Ruben left to clean the dogs. I liked Dot, a few years younger than Ruben, with short curly black hair. Classic Latina looks with a few extra pounds that sat well with her. A happy, personable woman, outgoing and friendly.

"Alice has serious medical problems. We knew something was the matter with her for a while. Test results came Thursday." Dot poked her head around the door to foil any eavesdropping.

"Hospital said she has Crohn's disease; we knew something was wrong; she'd lost so much weight. I'm sure you noticed something."

She stared at me as I nodded, and then she continued.

"Always seems tired. They don't think she will need surgery soon. She'll have to be monitored closely, though. Thankfully they say it's not immediately life-threatening." I listened to a detailed description of this nasty condition from Dot.

"Never heard of it before. She can be cured, though?" Dot shook her head.

"Cured, no, but the symptoms can be managed. Not one of those things where she will suddenly fall over dead."

"So sorry, Dot. I wish I could say or do something to help. I was going to take her to Aunties again; she said she liked that last time, but as she's already eaten here at the house, she's probably not hungry. Just a coffee, perhaps? Are there any diet restrictions?"

"Not yet Em-Jay, a little and often, doctors will soon give their recommendations. What she does eat passes through quickly. And yes, she loved Aunties and kept talking about the ride and breakfast for days" I nodded, saddened by the sad health news.

"How is Ruben taking this?" I asked. She shook her head and sighed.

"Well, not too bad, I suppose. Just living from day to day at the moment, that's about all we can do at this time."

I chatted with Dot for a few more minutes before walking across the yard to talk with Ruben. Nothing had changed with the dogs, as far as I could see. Red Sue was now chained with her neighbors. There were no signs of her previous fight. Ruben seemed quieter than usual. The ebullient back-slapping man I had come to know now frowned, more than smiled. He brightened a little when discussing the dogs but lacked enthusiasm for the subject. He showed me a litter of six pups, just two weeks old, that brought a huge smile to his face as he outlined the many fine qualities of their breeding.

"Nothing else to show you, brother, just the same ole shit."

The irony of that statement became apparent as he finished scooping the *same ole shit* dropping in the *same ole* large plastic bag.

"Philippe's day with Pat today; otherwise, he would be doing this job. Think I'll hire him away again. Pat lucked out with that kid."

"Yeah, with Annetta, too. I got the best deal, though."

Ruben nodded in agreement and told me he was pleased things were working out between us. We talked about Alice for a while, with nothing substantive from either of us to contribute. I told him about the recent party and the sad demise of the dog, Joey. He shook his head in disbelief,

"There are some people in this world not able to drink tequila, just incompetent to handle firearms and unfit to own Bulldogs. Born that way, I guess."

About that time, Alice, the girl in question, trotted through the yard, grinning.

"Hey, Em-Jay, I cleaned my room, as I said. Can we go now?"

"Did mom check it?"

"Yeah, she said it was perfect."

"Perfect?" Ruben asked, staring hard at Alice.

"Okay, dad, maybe not *exactly* perfect, but she did say my big mess was now a smaller mess. So, that's close to perfect. Can we go now?"

I took her to *Aunties burgers and sandwich* again, her choice. All very adult, with waves of sophistication almost overwhelming Alice again. There was a real waitress who would listen and take her order. She smiled shyly, ordering just French fries and a milkshake. We talked for a while, with Alice telling me about her medical condition. She looked better to me now than the last time we were in the restaurant. Although her eyes were still shadowed, the pinched pained expression no longer clouded her face.

"Sometimes, it hurts real bad; I can't stand for a few minutes until the pain goes away. Usually, I'm okay, though."

There was nothing for me to say, just nodding and listening to her sorry story. She asked about Annetta, *Nettie,* as she called her.

"Dad says Nettie is your girlfriend. Will you get married? She is very pretty. I like her a lot. She's nice and stayed here with me once."

"Don't know if we will marry Alice; that's a very big step for both of us. I haven't spoken to her about it."

"If you are shy about asking her Em-Jay, I can ask her for you. I think it would be good if you and Nettie were married."

"No need for you to ask her, but thanks anyway. Let me think about it, sweetie; If we decide to get married, I promise you will be the first to know."

Thankfully the conversation turned to school and the excellent progress she was making despite her medical problems. By the time we had finished eating, then cruising for an hour on the bike, it was past five pm when we returned. I stayed chatting with Ruben and Dot for about two hours before heading back to the desert.

Two messages were waiting for me when I arrived home. One from Annetta saying how much she missed me, missed being at the house, and the good times we had. She said she hoped to come next Friday and stay for the weekend again. The other was from Ruben, thanking me profusely for spending time with Alice. I called him the following day, spoke to Dot and told her what a good afternoon I had. I thanked her for letting me take Alice to Aunties again. Dot laughed, saying Alice hadn't stopped talking about the ride or the fries. Ruben was with the dogs, so we never spoke that morning.

Annetta decided to come by train, encouraged by our trip to the city a few weeks ago. I met her at the Amtrak station on Friday evening at about seven. There I was at the station, leaning against a light pole waiting with other loiters. A heavy-set young fellow strolled past me.

"Do you think the train is late?"

He stared at me quickly with a guarded expression. Perhaps he thought I was a gay man trying to proposition him or a hoodlum preparing to take his wallet.

"You think the train is late, pal?"

Louder, this time in case he was slightly deaf. He just stared at me, backing away slowly with a quick shrug. He was probably a mental patient, perhaps a recent escapee from some criminal institution. It was too late for me to stop now.

"Hey, sorry to inconvenience you, just your opinion, whether or not the train is late. I know you must be busy with some great work. You're obviously an artist, composer, musician, or perhaps an architect. Believe me; I do not wish to waste your precious time or engage you in some esoteric discussion of ancient mysteries, just a simple opinion as to whether the accursed train is or is not late. You know, the train; it's that long thing carrying passengers. "

He pointed to his mouth, nodding and grinning, moving further away. Perhaps he was exercising his right to remain silent. This should have been such a simple personal interaction between two people, a brief smile, a nod, a whispered "*good day*." This quick acknowledgment of our common humanity must occur a million times each hour. Here on this busy station platform, I had picked the only child-molesting loony from the crowd. At that moment, a distant horn announced the imminent arrival of the train, forestalling any further commentary from either of us.

And there it was, grinding and grunting, squealing loudly as it stopped. The long snake of a train was soon disgorging passengers from its belly. Many riders with bags and cases were staring hard at the platform spectators hoping for recognition. The waiting ones on the platform were now walking purposefully alongside the carriages hoping to see a familiar face. Annetta was carrying a small suitcase, walking across the platform with quick, elegant strides.

Dressed in a dark blue skirt and blazer, she was the epitome of casual European fashion. Her persona of Italian sophistication suddenly evaporated when she saw me. Both arms held wide; her case dropped to the ground as she skipped towards me.

"Em-Jay, Em-Jay darling, look, I come on the train for first time in this country.

She attracted the attention of several people as she danced into my arms. I saw several smiling faces as we hugged and kissed.

"Dios mio Em-Jay darling, my case, I drop my little case on the floor."

There was no case to be seen, but a middle-aged woman approached us from the crowd accompanied by the asylum escapee. His handler smiled broadly at us and then, turning to the mute thug, spoke quickly to him in an unknown language. With an extravagant sweeping gesture, he bowed, handing the case to Annetta.

"I am very pleased to meeting you. I am Marta Ameliachenkov. My brother Yuri here is from Ukraine, as I am. He came to this country yesterday. He cannot speak yet any word of your language, but he will soon learn as I have."

So, the mystery was solved. With a few simple words, the child molesting criminal idiot, asylum escapee, and worse, was raised again to standards of comfortable normality. For a few minutes, we chatted with Marta while Yuri smiled and nodded. She said her brother would stay with her while training in the US. We were told Yuri was a professional boxer with an unbeaten record in Ukraine. Eight matches since turning professional, eight wins, six by knockout. Marta wrote her number on the back of an old business card and said to call and arrange to watch Yuri train. Hands were shaken, and we promised to call. My favorite sport is boxing, so I had a genuine interest in watching Yuri spar and train. I wished I was able to pronounce his last name.

An uneventful half-hour drive home for me. Just delighted to be with Annetta again. The car was filled with chatter, passing the time most pleasantly. It was too late now for Annetta to cook, so we stopped to eat in town. A good choice. The *Texas steer and beer steakhouse*. I had never eaten there before, although it was prominently situated on the main boulevard. Inside was much bigger than the front door and entrance suggested—a great barn of a place, with rough red Mexican pottery tile on the floor. Walls were hung predictably with plastic longhorn cattle skulls and coiled rope. These were augmented by bits and pieces of genuine old Texas branding irons, railroad spikes, and so forth.

Most interesting to me were the many photographs of old towns and their long-departed inhabitants. Waitresses flitted between tables, white wide-brimmed cowboy hats, tight blue jeans, and checkered shirts. The short-riding boots they wore must have been hell on their feet, poor things. Buss-boys and other helpers did not suffer that indignity. I liked the atmosphere and the warm, attentive service. More so, the food. We both enjoyed a steak and thick-seasoned fries, mushrooms, and onions. The empty plates before us bore testimony to the excellence of our meals and also to the emptiness of our stomachs.

Our conversations turned to mutual friends, and I told Annetta about Alice and her unfortunate stomach condition.

"She really likes you, Nettie. She told me you stayed with her and said we should get married."

Annetta laughed when I mentioned her nickname, Nettie—frowned when I told of the girl's medical problems and shook her head at the thought of marriage. That was a subject I hoped to postpone indefinitely.

At the far end of the room, two young women were eating and talking while restraining a small child about three years old. The little fellow would wait for a moment's inattention from his keepers, then seizing the opportunity, totter through the dining room. A huge smile on his chubby little face as he stopped at various tables gazing at the eaters before running again when one of the women approached. He was soon captured and returned to his table, reluctantly sitting on a small chair. This catch-and-release program was repeated three or four times. The reactions of other diners were interesting. Annetta clapped her hands, smiling and laughing with him. A few smiled and talked to him. Others ignored him, pretending they never saw him. A few showed annoyance scowling at the two women when he escaped.

"Look, isn't that just typical—children themselves with no idea how to raise a child? No parental control at all. Let him loose to annoy others because they're too lazy to teach him. Imagine the little horror when he grows, running the streets and joining gangs. I shudder to think when he's eighteen or so, in jail for sure".

He made no noise, happily toddling about and celebrating his brief freedom with other diners. It was his vitality and the happiness shining from his face that was so attractive. Perhaps the response when I engaged him with my eyes endeared him to me. Either way, I liked the little fellow, as did Annetta. We watched him, silently cheering for him when he escaped, laughing when he avoided capture—a grand diversion as we ate.

The two women left before we did. As the younger of the two passed our table, she smiled at Annetta.

"Thank you for being so patient. He can be annoying sometimes." Annetta shook her head.

"No, *thank you*. All children should be smiling and happy. If we are not so blind and forgetting how important we think we are, we learn much from happy children."

She may be right, I thought. I stood at the small reception desk, waiting to pay. About seven feet above the floor, fixed to the wall at the back of the desk was a dark wood frame covered with glass. This shallow display case held rusted strands of various antique barbed wire samples. I asked the cashier about this, remarking on the curiously elevated placement of the display.

"The owners had to do that," she said, shaking her head. "Originally, the display was on the wall where the photos are, you see? She pointed to the opposite wall.

"Someone managed to prick their poor little finger on a piece of wire, never had a glass covering it then as it has now. The instant lawsuit, only in California, eh? Cost us six thousand dollars for a prick. The prick who sued and the legal prick who helped him. Now the display is out of sight and unreachable."

She grinned, and I paid, shaking my head, saddened by her prick story.

We changed our tomorrow plan. Originally Annetta was to inventory cupboards and fridge, make a list, and I would stagger into town to buy groceries and food as instructed. I simplified her task—nothing in the fridge but three bottles of beer and a prehistoric sandwich. The cupboards held a roll of kitchen Paper towels, a teapot, and a disassembled Harley clutch. Inventory is accomplished immediately from memory. Nothing left to do now but enjoy the evening and listen to a lecture on poorly maintained refrigerators and incompetent household management.

CHAPTER
TWENTY-TWO

Annetta saw our needs were many; her list was extensive and had grown considerably from the last time she stayed with me. She insisted on accompanying me to the stores. Nothing left from the meal last night, and no food in the house meant we would have breakfast at a fast-food joint. This was okay for me, but only just. I was now conditioned to associate fine home-cooked Italian food with the delightful Italian Annetta. Anyway, into town, we drove, settling at the nearest Carrows restaurant, in my opinion, as good as fast food gets. So, with a goodly pile of traditional greasy breakfast stuff and strong coffee before us, we bent our heads to the trough.

One important topic to be discussed was the disappearing white rock. With or without her help and input, I had to bring a satisfactory conclusion to the mystery or get drunk and forget the damn thing. Drunk, I may get, but the bell cannot be un-rung. The white rock mystery would soon be solved. Sunday, about six in the chilly afternoon. I drove Annetta to the station. Pat or Phillipe would meet her at the other end. Only a handful of people are waiting for the train with no distractions or eccentric characters to bring any diversion. I knew I would experience a great emptiness when I returned home; this emotional vacuum had now become a predictable condition when Annetta left. It was as if something had been turned off in the house. This evening was no different. There was a message from Alan threatening to come over and drink beer. Another from Ruben inviting me to a birthday party on Saturday. No dog stuff, just food and beer to celebrate Dot's birthday with a few close friends. A function Annetta and I could attend, perhaps. Alan made good on his threat, bringing Mary and six bottles of scotch ale. A little too cold for comfort on the patio tonight. We sat in the dining room and idled away the time beneath inconsequential talk. Three happy hours, though, and a great antidote to my self-induced depression.

About ten minutes after they left, Annetta called. Not able to make it next weekend. She would have to work Saturday and Sunday, an unexpected substitute for two vacationing girls. I arranged to visit, perhaps spend a lunch hour in her company while she worked. And so my working week continued uneventfully. A few days lost in trivial pursuit and punctuated by a little smack bought me to Thursday afternoon. A late lunch and a ten-minute drive saw me outside the sizable *Airport hotel restaurant*. A large busy dining room, American food, and an expansive menu. Annetta was trotting happily with several plates of food balanced on a small tray. With the tray momentarily perched on one hand, she waved to me without breaking stride. I know if our situation were reversed, the tray and everything on it would be decorating the nice carpet. Annetta was the professional and looked delightful in her short waitressy skirt and frilly white blouse. Many customers at the tables followed her eagerly with their eyes. During the time I watched her, she was raped two times, stripped to her underwear, and forced to perform many sexual acts at the tables she waited upon. An older woman dining alone beckoned Annetta to her table.

She stood when Annetta arrived and reached for her thick braid, pulling her head back before kissing her mouth forcefully. They remained with mouths together for a long time, exploring each other and probing with their tounges. The other woman, slim with short silver hair, was aggressively feeling beneath Annetta's blouse. That, of course, is a patron's expectation and every waitress's destiny to please her customers at all times.

Annetta smiled through it all, pretending not to notice. "I come with food for us and sit with you, darling; I have lunch with you." A large plate of barbecued pork ribs, beans, and fries for me. A shrimp salad for her. The food was delicious, and the delightful company enhanced the meal. We spent most of our time together, eating and telling about how much we missed each other. "I will coming with you next Friday, darling Em-Jay; I miss you very much."

Saturday morning, the day of the Dot birthday, I went to my bank in town, where I have a small account at a long-established rural institution. Inside there is a pleasing atmosphere of quiet, somber elegance with a thick dark green carpet and a large grandfather clock, sounding slow in dignified harmony with the light oak furniture and brass fittings. I remember a time when customers mattered in this place. At least, attentive service and a smiling cashier behind every station gave that impression: no bulletproof screens here and no lumbering security guards on patrol. Opening hours were extended from four hours to a full day Saturday and four hours Sunday. *"For the convenience of our loyal customers,"* the notice read. About two years ago, the bank was absorbed by a national conglomerate. No longer was opening hours extended for customers' convenience.

The grand social experiment was drawn to a close. No more open Sundays, no more full day Saturday. And so, that which was once a bank had become a box. Gone were most of the smiling cashiers, the girls who knew my name, the ones who would greet me with a wave or nod. Gone was my sense of self-importance, leaving me with the nameless ones, relegated to join their extended shuffling lines. Here the residue of loyal customers muttered darkly in their discontent.

Waiting behind me was a young black girl. Just black enough to be categorized as such, but without the deep glossy finish. A few minutes had passed before she spoke. "Well, you free tomorrow, then?" I turned and smiled. "Who me? She nodded, passing a hand quickly beneath her chin.

"Maybe. What did you have in mind?" Not bad looking, mid-twenties, perhaps with a huge smile.

"Okay then," she continued, "have to be after two. Gotta finish up here first, then pick the car up. You come to my place."

I thought about that. Was she a hooker, I wondered?

"Can't-do, have to be at a birthday party later. Tomorrow would be better." Something was wrong; I felt cold liquid dripping down my face, past my ear, and splashing onto my shoulder.

A few seconds later, as I felt my hair, I realized there was a small stream of hypocrisy and betrayal running from a tiny open fizure at the top of my head. Was I willing to compromise my relationship with Annetta for the chance of a sexual encounter with this unknown woman behind me? She continued the conversation.

"Yeah, babe, that fine wid me then, I be waiting."

As the fluid of deceit soaked into my shirt, I realized the girl was talking into a small device inserted into her ear. I had intended to insert a small reproductive device into her vagina. However, she walked to the counter and, having concluded her banking business disappeared forever through the exit doors, still talking. Fate had intervened, saved me from myself, and I never even knew her name.

Ten minutes later, I was homeward bound, the hard wind biting at me, reminding me to listen for the coming winter. I remembered my recent encounter at the bank. Thinking about that, I wondered why I would do such a thing. What was wrong with me? Was I worse than a thief, priest, or politician? At least as bad I supposed and, actually, dripping with treachery and deceit. Annetta was a loving woman, sensual, intelligent, and possessed of so many other desirable qualities a lady, any man, would be proud to have as a wife or companion. And yet, I would have endangered that relationship, embarked on a sexual encounter with an unknown woman because I found her to be superficially attractive. Is this the male human condition, or am I just an asshole?... Probably, but the magic triangle is an amazingly potent geometrical device amply demonstrated and recorded as such since the beginning of time. It perpetuates the continuing conflict between cock and conscience.

In my living room is a white, long-haired sheepskin rug, about six feet square. It was on this rug kneeling naked at my feet, the black girl from the bank was waiting, and in perfect ebony on white contrast. I quickly knelt behind her, feeling and fondling each plump rounded globe before parting them gently and entering her vagina. I saw both cheeks as swollen black plums, given to me, a gift from a vegetable and fruit worshiping tribal leader. I was tempted to apply oil or cream and massage it in deeply to reveal the glossy black finish beneath.

And the loud jingle jangle of her tribal triangle called to me clearly from the rug where she lay.

That would work. Better would be a lemon-scented furniture polish. Apply liberally; wait for a few seconds before buffing to a fine luster. Satisfaction was assured and enhanced by the faint scent of citrus and lemon. Later, during the course of our lust, I penetrated her other place. Both were offered without reservation and readily available to me. Both felt tight, warm, and satisfying. Either bought grunts of pleasure from me and little squeals from her. Sex at its very best, for sure. The scenario may not have played well in a Louisiana courtroom.

"Did intercourse take place, mister Oconnell ?"

"Yes, your honor."

"Did anal sex occur? If so, was it consensual?"

"Yes, your honor, and it was consensual."

"Am I to understand that knowing full well sodomy is forbidden in this great state, you persisted with this anal intrusion?"

"I did, your honor."

"The woman with whom you indulged yourself sexually, she was a Negress?"

"Yes, your honor, I pleasured Shantell Washington, a black girl, entered her vagina, and penetrated her anus. I prayed to the Lord for help, your honor, but I am ashamed to admit that my penis had become ridged and altogether disobedient. For a little time, my cock seemed possessed, a servant of the Devil, an unwilling, misguided tool of Satan.

Knowing I was seriously in error but unable to avoid the inevitable penetration, I instructed Shantell to recite the Lord's prayer during the carnal proceedings. This seemed appropriate at the time, for she had cast herself down upon her knees before me."

"Am I to understand, then, that your preferred sexual partners are black rather than Caucasian?"

"Oh no, your honor, sir, I much prefer Chinese ladies. They are tighter, smaller, and easier to move around. Also, they make much less noise."

"Thank you, Mister Oconnell. Now, to return to the Washington woman, did she follow your instruction to recite the lord's prayer?"

"She did, sir; yes, as soon as I was properly and securely inserted, she began the prayer with a loud, enthusiastic voice. When she had finished, she straightway began another supplication to the Lord. First was Psalm 23, and then psalm 19. She was obviously educated and from a good devout family, as she was able to recite the biblical verses faultlessly. Toward the end of psalm 15, her voice was no longer fully coherent. Soon after, I withdrew my wayward member and quickly procured a can of lemon-scented furniture polish. I then polished the cheeks of her bottom to a fine glossy finish. My reasoning for this unusual procedure was to alleviate any possible feelings she may have of a white man's superiority in the relationship. She may have thought I was taking advantage of a simple black girl. We would eventually go our separate ways, me with satisfaction, she with shine.

"Mister O'Connell, You are obviously a principled and pious man of honor. The court thanks you, and I thank you for your candor. Despite the bestial nature of your behavior, this case is dismissed. You are free to leave at once."

"Ms. Shantell Washington, please see me in my chambers before you leave."

That is not what happened, of course. What happened was that I shaved, splashed some aftershave on my face, glanced at the white rug, and left on the bike for Rubens's place. About three miles from the house, the rain came. Not a heavy storm, but the sky was overcast with no promise of relief. Another half mile or so convinced me to return to the house and take the car. I was getting wet, cold I already was, and would soon be a lot colder. I should have known better and checked the obvious before leaving. Too busy enjoying anal sex with gleaming, highly polished black girls, I suppose. Ah, the bane of an overactive fertile imagination.

The Dot party was uneventful, about fifteen attendees happily confined inside the house. There were no introductions. It was assumed, I supposed, that we all knew one another. A few people I recognized from the dog match some months ago. Pat came later with Barbra, his girlfriend, a happy, outgoing woman with long brown hair. One of several, he told me, laughing, this one plays guitar and sings. The first time I had seen him in the company of a woman at any social gathering. "Reg? "Nah, has to work." He said, shaking his head. "Poor bastard hates the fuckin job, soon be outa there," Ruben told me that Alice was more accepting of her miserable condition and seemed to be improving.

Alice babbled happily, flitting from guest to guest with a tray of Dot-made tamales and casadias. The perfect little hostess. Great food, good company, and just a little booze. The rain would not let up for any outdoor activity, but I did walk quickly through the wet, accompanied by a fellow I met at the previous dog match. We braved water to visit with the dogs. The pups Ruben showed me during my last visit were now thirteen weeks old, and some had to be separated. Even at that young age, they would fight hard with each other.

When we returned, Dot told me Annetta had called, wishing her a happy birthday, and love to me. So the little party drew to a close. I gave Dot a small gift card from a large boutique dress store for and on behalf of Annetta and me. This released many thanking's and appreciative cooing from Dot and loud commentary from Pat, suggesting to Ruben that he better keep an eye on his woman. I would have expected no less. Within half-hour Huggings, hand shakings, and cheek kissing's all terminated in an uneventful drive home. Hypnotic metronome slap of the wiper blades for the first half-hour waiting until the rain stopped, and then came the night and slick wet roads.

The house was waiting dejectedly for me as I came through the door. In silence, unhappy Annetta was not with me but not resentful.

I sat in the living room for some time before realizing I was sick again. Cold soaked into me, causing me to shiver involuntarily.

An early night long overdue, two Advil, and a small shot of whiskey in warm milk. Into bed, I crawled, drawing the blankets around me, comforted by warmth and feelings of security. I was insulated from reality until daylight.

Daytime was with me, suddenly intruding with uncompromising brightness settling over the bedroom, reminding me to close the blinds before sleeping—nearly nine when I rolled from the bed, sickness still with me, shivering but no headache.

"Shake it off, lad, only a touch of Ebola, a few deep breaths, and a bite to eat. Here's half an Asprin if you think you need it. You'll feel much better soon."

Sadly I realized I would not "feel much better soon" or recover from anything contagious. I felt the beginning of withdrawal, and the fix for that was a little more heroin. Tear a small sheet of baking foil, fold it in half, sprinkle a little H in the crease, heat slowly from the flame of a cigarette lighter, and draw in the smoke through a large straw. Suddenly much better, the itching on my face and stomach would soon stop, and my hands would steady.

My preferred way to smoke was to hand-roll a cigarette with tobacco and powder; wasteful but satisfying. A pipe would also work well, although I never tried that. So, shower, have coffee, and, if weather permitting, ride into town for a small breakfast. The weather gave reluctant permission, late October, and although skies were Grey, the rain had stopped. Not yet cold enough to discourage an hour or so on the bike.

Avenue O has a sinister reputation, widely considered by local inhabitants to be haunted by ghosts of travelers killed in frequent accidents along its length. Rough wooden crosses mark a tragedy on both sides of the road. Flowers and photographs of the victims promote a dismal aspect of the area and enhance the miserable reputation. The road is wide and straight. There are frequent small hills marked with double yellow lines and often posted "no overtaking" signs. Reasonably so, as vision is obscured before the crests of these rises. Every six months or so, the county levels and maintains soft shoulders, removing any homemade markers. Within two months, residents will have replaced these memorials. Avenue O was my daily route of choice, into town and usually to work. So it was today. Within the hour, I had finished a breakfast of good greasiness, filling my stomach with satisfaction. The day was before me, cold and bright, precisely the right conditions to explore the white rock mystery. Today this enigma would be solved, and Annetta informed of the results. All trickery and subterfuge laid bare in the face of rational scientific analysis.

Approaching the crest of the last hill before home, cruising happily at sixty, I was suddenly confronted by a small car on the wrong side of the road. The idiot, vegetable, buffoon driver was trying to pass a truck without regard to any approaching traffic. Probably high on drugs. Flight or fight? I saw the oncoming vehicle exhibit signs of panic. Suddenly swerving, braking, then accelerating in a futile attempt to pass the truck before we met. Instinctively I shut the throttle and cranked the bike onto the soft shoulder—a poor choice perhaps, but probably better than meeting the masturbating monkey driver head-on.

There were loud noises. All around me were gunshots, sirens, and people shouting as if I were at a fast-food restaurant in the ghetto. Sand and soil were violently blown into my face, a good, logical result of my evasive maneuver. My front wheel was suddenly buried in two feet of sand, stopping the bike instantly and throwing me forcefully beyond the ditch and onto the hard desert ground. Try that in a car sometime.

The great weight pressing between my shoulders was no longer there, to be replaced suddenly by slight friendly pressure. I stood very slowly, shaking and confused. My bike lay against the trunk of an old cottonwood tree, obviously placed in that exact position to arrest further unexpected motion from an intrusive biker. I stared for a few seconds before reaching the tank and shutting the fuel valve off. Salvation was all around me. Brushing dirt from my clothes with shaking hands confirmed arms and hands were functional. The fact that I was standing indicated that my legs and feet worked.

So far, so good. My head hurt, as did my back and chest, but there was no blood. Scrambling from the ditch to the side of the road gave me hope that I was not seriously hurt. I was shaking and confused, though. I walked a few unsteady paces, then squatted by the roadside for a while, trying to clear my head. There was no sign of the car I encountered and no other traffic as far as I could see. I planned to get home, enlist Alan and Mary for help, borrow or rent a truck and recover the bike.

The getting home part involved a five-mile walk in the direction I was now headed. I was able to walk without pain at the moment, although I knew tomorrow morning I would hurt like hell all over. Reaching the crest of the hill, I rested for a moment looking behind me to the place of the accident. In the distance, there were flashing lights. Two vehicles in the desert beyond the road, both at odd angles, suggesting they had encountered each other at speed. Flashing lights were from a red fire truck parked on the shoulder.

Was this activity from my recent encounter with the fool in the small car? It had to be; that would account for the noises I heard. Obviously, both vehicles, having left the road, were obscured by small trees and vegetation, therefore invisible to me from the road. Okay, now, I retrace my steps, lose the half-mile gained, and involve myself with the crash participants or continue in the home direction. Not the best choice, perhaps, but I decided to continue walking. At least I would be gaining some ground, and any passing motorist would probably stop if I waved. Downhill Walking was getting easier. The movement and activity were stretching muscles and exercising joints. I walked until the road flattened, and the view beyond the hill disappeared.

An old Ford truck slowed in response to my raised thumb a few minutes later. Not just any old Ford truck. There was an antique gem of a pickup truck. About nineteen-fifty or a couple of years earlier, perhaps. Faded red paint but otherwise in excellent condition. Perfect timing, I climbed aboard as the elderly driver reached across the seat and opened the door. Before I could sit, he had to lift a small black and white cat from the passenger's seat to his lap. He nodded to me, saying nothing for the entirety of our ten-minute journey. He pulled over at a small convenience store, leaving me with a five-minute walk to the house. I thanked him profusely as he closed the door.

The craggy, lantern-jawed old bastard, this unshaven hollow desert creature, as old and rugged as the distant hills, nodded slowly to me, touching the brim of his stained fedora hat.

"Change course now, sonny, for only a fool like you would choose to ride such a road of grave misfortune, but Fairweather to ye lad, you be home in a few minutes."

I stared after the old truck as he drove away, dizzy and confused, wondering what he was talking about. A heavy Scottish accent, my stepfather's voice. Childhood memories returned suddenly, and I stopped on the street, staring into the distance, trying to suppress the flood of feelings that threatened to overwhelm me. The house was as I had left it. Why wouldn't it be? In the bathroom, I stared into the mirror as a wild-haired ragged stranger returned my gaze.

A hot shower rinsed away the dirt and brought comfort to my bruised body. I changed into clean clothes, scooped up the old ones on the floor, and threw them in a pile by the washing machine. As I turned, I saw the ghost of Kerry Rice wagging a manicured finger at me. Suddenly I felt very tired and disregarding the sound of a distant telephone made for the bedroom. Choosing to ignore the repetitive phone summons, I crawled into my unmade bed, falling quickly into a deep, welcoming sleep.

A couple of hours later, I rolled from the bed, making myself ready to confront the inevitable post-crash reality—first, a police report to satisfy the insurance company.

"Yeah, I'll take the details now, but please come to the station and fill out the form. ...Avenue O, where on Avenue O?... Okay, two vehicles?... What time did this accident occur?... Okay, please hold.

Sir? We have no report of an accident in that area. If the motorcycle is still at the scene, would it be visible from the road?... Okay, please hold... Sir? A patrol unit will check the area soon.

And so the wheels were set in motion. I verified my phone number and address, thanked the disembodied voice at the receiver's end, and ended the call. Insurance company next. They took details as I told them and, as expected, asked for a police report. All well and good so far. Bike recovery time. I decided to revisit the scene, perhaps take a few photographs and assess the damage myself. I remembered closing the fuel valve but couldn't recall much after that. For sure, I did remember the gnarled, crusty old Scottish driver, blue bib overalls, and brown fedora hat. More so, the silent drive home. I was very grateful for his help and the ride in his gnarled, crusty old truck.

I got into the car with a camera and notebook, heavy boots, and a jacket. After my return to the accident scene, I intended to go to the police station, make a report, and have a copy available for the insurance company. As I reached the end of my short drive and turned onto the road, I saw a nice Harley motorcycle parked by the curb. A black hard-tail shovelhead bored out to 80 cubic inches. How did I know the engine capacity? It was my bike sitting there, my bike without dent or damage, unmarked paintwork, fresh and clean. Not even a yeast infection to concern me. It was a long time before I left the car and walked to the waiting bike. The paint was splashed and streaked with light road dirt, exactly as one might expect from riding along a wet road. There was a difference, though, something about the machine. It looked bigger somehow; there was something about it that had changed. Something with the front end and tank.

Everything was functional, though, and the number plate confirmed my ownership of this machine. I started the engine, rode to the end of the street, turned and coasted into the driveway, then parked in the garage. This overwhelming mystery pressed heavily on me, and there was no feeling of joy at the magical return of my bike. I sat in the kitchen, returning to the garage two or three times to stare at the big bike, half expecting it to vanish before my eyes. Here was a desperate situation, sudden redemption from a huge disaster only to be confronted by the onset of madness. I couldn't accept the evidence before me.

Today was Sunday. I will not go to work tomorrow. What I would do now would be to continue with my plan to investigate the accident scene. Hopefully, my Toyota would be at the end of the drive where I had left it. With luck, it would still be a car and not a huge rotting vegetable. My car was still a car, but unfortunately, it did possess many unpleasant characteristics of a rotting vegetable. A slow drive to an area where I thought my excursion into the desert had occurred. The old cottonwood tree, my landmark for reference, was in plain sight. Nothing in the vicinity would indicate recent activity. The ground, soft with the recent rain, showed no footprints. I explored the area for a hundred yards or so, taking many photographs. Leaving the car, I crossed the road, walking to the place where I believed both vehicles had crashed. Again no sign of anything unusual, no tire tracks or debris. After half an hour of fruitless exploration, I returned to the car driving to the crest of the hill.

Stopping for a few seconds, I looked back to the place where a few hours ago, I stood watching two vehicles and emergency responders tending to an accident. An accident I was involved in. None of this made sense, another white rock scenario on a much larger scale. I would call Alan or Mary and check if either had a report of an accident on Avenue O. Always possible that Alan had responded and was part of the red fire truck crew. I called Alan, but no response. It was at that moment I remembered my intention to debunk the white rock thing. Another early night for me, and then Monday afternoon...White rock.

CHAPTER
TWENTY-THREE

Monday morning, out of bed, a few minutes after eight. The priority, check the garage for the bike. The bike was as I had left it. Next call work. I had no remorse when I called in to explain my impending absence. No feelings of guilt, having left the bed about three hours later than usual. I deserved it. I was sick after all, certainly ill enough to miss work for a day. Also, there was a white rock in the backyard waiting patiently for me.

One acre of desert land is enclosed by a six-foot industrial chain-link fence, forming an irregular rectangle. My house sits at one end, positioned within the rectangle, to give a reasonable front garden and a considerable backlot. About fifty yards from the covered patio, a four-foot chain-link fence spans the width of the yard. Beyond this fence is uneven desert sand and scrub, upon which sits a large tool shed. Before the fence is short grass extending back to the patio and my beloved swing.

The fence supports many climbing roses and honeysuckle vines along its length. A small gate allows access to the sand and shed. On the house side, I have grass and a swing on the other, desert sand, and a shed. I intended to document the behavior of the white rock and record its position, size, weight, and temperature. To that end, I bagged all the necessary equipment for the great rock investigation. Having secured the physical data, I would then call upon Alan as a witness. A small tape recorder and digital camera were already secured in my pockets.

About two in the afternoon, when I walked to the gate, still feeling sick but determined to finish this long, overdue investigation before another fix. Looking over the gate and, as expected, no white rock to be seen. First, two photographs are to be taken from the desert side. Step back a few paces, then two more photographs from the grassy side. Now open the gate again and into the desert. The gate won't open. A simple frame with a chain-link covering, two crude hinges, and a hasp to keep closed. It won't open. This lightweight, flimsy, bastard gate thing, the same gate through which I had passed so many times, was now stuck.

Grasping the top rail with both hands, pulling, pushing, and shaking made no difference. A well-placed front kick in the same area went unnoticed—a ridiculous situation. With the latch lifted, the gate would swing open with a single finger push, but not today. I walked back to the garage for a few simple tools to fix a simple gate.

Loosen the hinge bolt clamps, lift the stinking gate from the two hinges, and throw it on the grass with a good measure of disgust. No, wrong mindset. I would examine the gate and fence, determine the nature of the problem, and fix it accordingly. At least the car and bike were unmoved, still where I had parked them.

And now, back to the gate with a few tools to fix it. My small bag with test gear was on the floor by the fence where I had left it. The gate was open, swinging freely as I pushed it. The examination was quick but thorough because there was very little to examine. Thinking and head-scratching consumed more time than gate appraisal. I concluded that because of my sickness, I had never actually tried to open the damn thing in the first place. That reasoning brought no comfort; I knew very well it refused to open when I tried. So, what now?

Move on, darling fool Em-Jay, finish what you started, then get to bed early with a goodly shot of whiskey.

I lifted the latch and pushed, closed the latch, and pulled. With the latch lifted, the gate swung easily in either direction as it had always done. With the latch closed, it did not move. Leaving the handful of tools on the grass, I shouldered the bag of test gear and walked through into the desert, closing the gate behind me. A white rock mystery was now a gate and rock mystery. Perhaps I should paint the miserable gate white. Better paint the rock and gate red. My watch showed three twelve; the weather was overcast, cold, and miserable. Another hour and it would be too dark to see. I walked on slowly, past the dark, indistinct bulk of the tool shed and into the sand and scrub beyond.

What the hell was I doing? I was wandering without direction or purpose. *Turn back now and photograph the white rock and gate. That is your reason for being here, the very reason you packed the test gear. Get a grip, and pull yourself toward yourself. Concentrate on the task at hand, or go back, go to bed, and try the following day again.*

A few unnecessary images of the tool shed. A few views of the mountain range ahead…And then I knew fear, a cold shock that caused me to turn and walk quickly back to the gate.

Of course, there could be no mountains ahead, just the chain link defining my property boundaries beyond which my neighbor's backyards. The mystery unfolded again as it had done before. A distant mountain range exists only behind the gate. A white rock that I never saw when passing through the desert was sitting before me. A familiar belligerent marker that now radiated terrible, malevolent purpose in the misty half-light. All imaginary, I had walked to the shed a thousand times with no mountain range or white rock in sight. And then came the doubting, perhaps I never saw the mountains in the distance. The white rock Annetta moved from its original parking place, placing it by the gate to show me. I then lifted it and replaced it where it now lay. Perhaps there was no mystery after all.

There was not. There was no mystery here, For the sand was moving beneath my feet, rolling and sliding. I was shipboard again and happily because the seas were my friends. The worst time, at least for me, was in calm waters, when the ocean swell would move the ship in a predictable slow rolling motion. Rough weather, with screaming winds and waves crashing and roaring across the decks, was expected and accepted as part of sailors working life. The ship's movement in those conditions was a dance of joy, the Fandango celebrating the triumph of living over the acceptance of secure, oppressive mediocrity.

Logic I know well. Natural sciences, geometry, and physics comfort me in times of doubt, like a baby at the breast, but in the face of my present situation, I wanted to run. So intent was I to pass safely beyond the gate that I never photographed the rock just a few feet before me. I cried out like a fool, knowing something wicked and destructive was at my heel. I was pleading frantically to any spirit of the night to please restore a degree of normality in my life again. I, despiser of everything normal or conventional, asking an unseen deity for help. So for all my physics, geometry, and reliance on everything logical, here I was, crying out in the darkness. Walking on grass again with the patio in sight, my courage returned. There was something behind me, the sound of a great ocean, perhaps a friend, maybe an enemy, that could or would not follow me beyond the fence.

In the secure cocoon of my warm living room, I stood with a cup of hot milk and whiskey. The floor beneath me seemed to roll as if I were still on deck. This feeling subsided after a few minutes as my drink slowly fulfilled the promise of comfort and sleep. I thought of these things, considered my irrational panic, unable to reconcile these fears with this whiskey-induced bravado. I would wait for the morning and venture out again with daylight on my side. I would, for sure, confront any lurking demons; this was my backyard and my property. Any angel or goblin on my land would be required to seek permission and, without such, face the possibility of eviction. There would be rent to negotiate and, among other things, lease conditions and boundaries.

Another shot of Black Label, and I was ready to confront Satan himself and drive him into the ground like a polished tent peg. Good scotch whiskey vanquished my fear of the unknown, the devil, bad cooking, and the department of motor vehicles. I was no longer afraid of the unseen and readied myself for bed.

Seven-thirty, little noises, small animal sounds but no bright daylight in sight yet. I made coffee in the half-light, then sat, preparing myself for the rapidly approaching daytime. Call work, eggs and bacon, more coffee, and through the gate to confront any waiting dragons.

And so my morning unfolded quietly. No living person was available at the office to take my call. I left a message detailing the symptoms of my sickness and promised to call later. Scrambled eggs and potatoes, there was no bacon, but there was toast. Coffee strengthened my purpose. Complete the unfulfilled investigation. With a full stomach and bolstered ambition, I made for the gate. A small notebook and pencil, a camera over my shoulder, replaced the bag with test and measuring gear. These items I would use later if my initial foray gave sufficient reason.

First, a few images of the white rock, referencing its position from the gate. Next, I took a few more pictures of the distant mountains, using the shed as my primary reference. The quality of light was different now, an unpleasant brownish haze all around me. No overbearing sense of terror, though, unlike the previous evening. I retraced my footprints in the sand as far as the shed and leaned against the door. I wanted to deny the obvious and ignore the evidence of my senses, but I was forced to accept the unwelcome existence of a new reality. I was intruding, a stranger, in my own house and grounds where I felt no welcome. I continued walking for a few minutes, then stopped looking around me: no chain-link fence or shed and no gate or distance outline of the house. Annettas's words returned to me with a sobering finality.

"Don't wander too far, Em-Jay. Easy to get lost out here."

She knew, knew exactly what this place was, hinted at the dangers and possibilities, and never tried to correct me when I dismissed her observations. I sat on the sandy ground again, looked around me, and wondered. There was a time when I wandered to the back fence, many times to the shed. Just ordinary experiences with everything in its proper place and nicely grounded. Nothing had changed; the one common denominator, it seemed, was Annetta. If I could experience these curious changes and shifts from normality, perhaps, others would be able to.

Small groups at first, friends and neighbors by special invitation. Bring your chairs and tables. Ice chests, beer, and wine are welcome.

Italian food would be available courtesy of Annetta. Alternative reality weekends with live music and catered food. The possibility of an emergent business opportunity could not be ignored, guided bus tours with scripted commentary from a babbling scantily dressed female college student. Many strategically placed portable toilets, of course. How big was this place, I wondered. What would be found by digging beneath the surface? And what lay beyond the mountain range? Perhaps I had indeed found diamonds in my backyard or desert demons, as Annetta mentioned earlier.

Oh, here I was, stranded in this mysterious desert land, without any reasonable expectation of salvation—a wandering vagrant in a sandy metaphysical wasteland. Should harm befall me, a good lawyer would make much of the fact that it is easily accessible through a small garden gate. No warning notices posted, no barriers, or fat security guards. I felt confident that if I pursued a claim for damages against myself, I would prevail in a court of law. Would it be possible to ride the bike into this place, I wondered? I would certainly try, but here I was, sitting on the sand gazing around me, a little frightened now, and considering my next move.

Return to the gate to my starting place. That would at least show me familiarity was where I reasonably expected it to be—having regained the house a quick meal, then out again to explore further. Turning my back to the place where I was recently sitting, I began to retrace my steps. My fear was making me nervous and jumpy. From the corners of my eyes, I caught movement, something dark sliding quickly out of sight when I turned my head.

The Madness collected and coalesced around me. Dark, soft dripping clouds of crazy thinking rolled and drifted. I shouted—a sudden "HEY" as loud as I could. The noise was without substance, a grunt instead of a scream, dull and lifeless to my ears. Was I the first human in this barren, otherworldly landscape? If I pissed on the sand beneath me, would my urine carry the first trace of humanity ever recorded in that spot?

Again I was aware of motion, a dull milky white creature about the size of a large cat, too fast for me to see details, as it repeatedly moved from my sight. And then a dark shadowy form, much larger and threatening, about the size and shape of an adult human male. Again it was impossible to examine this thing as it continually defied my attempts to focus on it. The large shadow form was frightening; the white slinking thing was absolutely terrifying.

If Annetta was with me, If she would come and share the blanket of neurosis that sheltered me, just for a while, so that we may experience the emptiness all around and perhaps take comfort from each other. Otherworldly, maybe, but there was sand, sky, and air. No stainless steel, titanium, or plastic, just the basic familiar terrestrial building blocks. It was getting dark now, and I felt an urgent need to return. To tell the truth, I was very afraid.

So, while Em-Jay was feeling the urgency and needed to return, similar to the unmistakable internal pressures and desperation accompanying an unexpected bowel movement, with no available restroom in sight, he retraced his footsteps as best he could.

CHAPTER
TWENTY-FOUR

A few years earlier, pretty little Marisol Uribe sat in her cluttered kitchen, staring fixedly at a small photograph of her brother hanging on the brown peeling wall before her. She was no more than a schoolgirl when she first entered the US on a six-month counterfeit visitor visa. This illegitimate document allowed her to visit members of her Salvadorian family, already resident in New York.

1977 was a bad year for the Bronx, a bad year for New York as a city. None of this concerned Marisol. She was with her older brother, her only brother, and his wife, living back to back in a one-room flat on the second floor of a crumbling old art-deco brick building. The Melrose area around 154th was almost habitable by comparison to other areas in the South Bronx. By comparison to her Salvadorian shack, it was a promise fulfilled.

Marisol remembered her beautiful mother remembered a robust and loving woman, not the pitiful skeletal creature ravaged by disease. A tumor grew quickly in her neck, causing her left eye to bulge from the socket. This condition remained until her death.

Less than three weeks after her mother's death, her father insisted she share his bed. "A man needs special comfort; a good daughter should provide for such needs. I teach you how a girl should please a man."

So began her nightly torment. For two years, she assumed the role of her mother, cleaning, cooking, washing clothes, and most reluctantly fulfilling her father's needs. Time passed slowly in the wretched dirt floor hovel that was home to Marisol. The grinding poverty, the only life she knew, now threatened to take her youth and destroy any hope for her future.

But there was a way out. Her friend Enrique would give her passage on his small fishing boat for a few hours before the Mexican customs patrol boats would have reason to challenge them. Desperate and dangerous acts for sure, but those words defined Marisol's broken family and most residents of the coastal Pueblo. And so for her, another night of misery, with her drunken Father snorting and grunting from a ragged black sleep. His dutiful daughter slipped unnoticed from the bed, returning after a few minutes with a heavy rock, cold in her hands, and held high above her head.

Her friend Monserrat, two years older than Marisol, once told her that *"there is much money waiting for you under your skirts."* And, as she had done many times before, she slipped her hand beneath her skirt and two fingers between Marisol's legs, probing for the place that always caused a small cry from her friend. Since her mother's passing, these furtive encounters with Monserat were the only times Marisol took comfort from another's embrace. "You are a beautiful girl; many men will pay happily to do what I am doing to you now." Marisol would soon exploit the wisdom of those words.

It was a circuitous route from El Salvador to New York City. It would be four months of cheap motels, cars, trucks, and stolen wallets before she saw Manhattan.

It was another circuitous route from the cold West Side New York City streets to a loving husband in the Morrisania area, a detective working the forty-second precinct. Beginning in the eighties, the Bronx was not a place of choice for most people. For her, the one redeeming feature of living in the Melrose area was a continual Hispanic influx. The colorful Latin cultures almost replaced the old Irish dominance as years passed.

"Colorful" most of the older residents did not want nor were prepared to accept. The gradual "white flight" and subsequent urban decay were well established. For Marisol, music, dancing, and drugs had become a daily panacea for the crushing boredom and loneliness, apparently a requirement for a New York City police officer's wife.

There was an unexpected distraction in her life, though. About a month after Christmas, walking home from the market, she heard a sharp cry, faint but insistent. A small alley to her right, leading to a neglected, overgrown park, was the source of the noise. A few yards from the turning, A dumpster sat, a communal convenience between two small stores whose back doors opened on either side of the container. The sound seemed to come from inside the dumpster. She tapped on the lid, and immediately, a cry came in response—the pitiful sound of a small animal in pain. Pushing open the lid with some difficulty, enough that it leaned against the wall behind, Marisol peered into the foul-smelling darkness.

A small face, obscured by paper and other rubbish, large yellow eyes frightened but defiant returned her gaze. A kitten, probably no more than two months old, cried again. She shook her head. Only in America would someone throw away a perfectly good cat. A heroic rescue attempt, with Marisol, nearly joining the cat in the trash. Concealed in a paper bag beneath her coat, she avoided the *super* and installed the little black and white creature in the apartment. The small furry fellow was happy and promptly availed himself of food, drink, and an old dirt-filled baking tray restroom.

Despite her contrary expectations, Reg was surprisingly agreeable when he saw the little furball kitten. His opinion was, The scent of a cat in the apartment would surely discourage frequent visits from rodents. And so, life continued uneventfully for Marisol and her baby Nikki. Ignoring Reg's cautions to keep the cat a secret, she shared her little Nikki with a few of her friends in the apartment block. Another distraction in her life took the form of a handsome Cuban guitar player. Ronaldo Gonsales met Marisol shopping at the grocery market. A mutual attraction and a convenient one when Marisol learned that Ronaldo lived alone in the next apartment block. It was two weeks since their first meeting, and this Thursday morning, Ronaldo decided he could wait no longer. Splashing plenty of aftershave on his face, on his armpits, and around his genitals, he mounted the stairs and rapped on the door of Marisol's apartment.

Within twenty minutes, they were both naked beneath a sheet on the bed. Ronaldo prepared to roughly penetrate his beautiful bulging Salvadorian woman and roll her around the apartment until she begged for mercy. Marisol had accustomed herself to the powerful *Old Spice* odor now permeating her love nest and prepared to amaze her partner with her many loving skills. The cat Nikki sat at the foot of the bed, shook his head, and licked a paw.

It may have been a combination of *Brylcreem* hair cream *and Old Spice* aftershave adversely affecting Ronaldo. Perhaps the aftershave splashed in such quantities around his scrotum seeped into his reproductive system, rendering it useless. A sudden fear of failing to satisfy this statuesque beauty may also have contributed. Whatever it was, it caused his once-proud member to hang deflated and worthless for the intended purpose. He assured Marisol that his cock was usually as stiff and proud as the flagpole outside the presidential palace. She was not impressed. Reaching for the small, defeated, deflated sausage skin, she pulled, rubbed, twisted, and flicked the end with her finger, encircled it with her tongue, and blew on it. There was no response to her ministrations.

"Your little dick is dead," she snapped, angry and frustrated. "It will probably fall off soon; perhaps God will give you another that works."

"Rub it," he implored, "it will soon return and punish you in every hole."

"And how do you suppose I can rub a piece of string or a strip of bacon?" she replied harshly. Rolling from the bed and crossing herself, she pulled on her underwear, quite overwhelmed by disappointment.

Anger and shame consumed Ronaldo. "You have cursed me, evil witch, you and your cat from hell. You have taken my manhood."

Jumping from the bed, he strode to the window, then pulling it full open, he returned to the bed. Seizing the unfortunate cat by both rear legs, he swung it in a full circle before hurling it through the open window. The cat shrieked, and Marisol screamed in anguish and fury as Nikki sailed in a graceful arc through the window and continued his flight gliding past the rusting fire escape before hanging momentarily above the alley below.

Rushing into the kitchen, Marisol returned with a small cast iron fry pan. She never saw her brave little feline astronaut make his final descent, but she did deliver a stunning whack to the side of Ronaldo's greasy head, sending him to the floor. Such was the noise coming from the normally peaceful apartment that Mickey, the superintendent, called the police before entering with his passkey. A small crowd of spectators, mostly friends of Marisol, had gathered outside the door, offering assistance should it be needed.

An astonishing sight confronted the aging super and the assembly behind him. A fine raven-haired woman dressed only in her revealing, lacy underwear was standing over a naked Cuban musician, beating him repeatedly with a skillet. She was still screaming insults at her cowering victim as Mickey approached. Taking her firmly by the waist, he pulled the frying pan from her grasp and manhandled Marisol away from Ronaldo. In his gentle, consoling voice, he tried to calm the volatile situation.

"Now, missy, if you will kindly shut the fuck up for a moment and tell me what in the name of all the saints is going on here."

"This stinking Cubano Bastardo, this worthless limp dick shithead, threw my little cat outa the window."

"She's a whore and an evil witch. Her and her piss ignorant *puta* cat, I curse them both."

Two strides and Micky stood over Ronaldo, Marisol firmly in his grasp.

"Shut the fuck up, bucko. Get yer clothes an get out."

The cops are coming for yer in a minute.

A sharp kick to the ribs emphasized the urgency of his message and caused a cry from Ronaldo, a ripple of approval, and a smattering of applause among the spectators.

Ronaldo scrambled for his clothes, blood trickling from a significant tear in his ear. Mickey bravely restrained Marisol, standing behind her and cupping a prominent breast in each hand. By the time Ronaldo staggered down the stairs, her bra had become unhooked and fallen to the floor. Meanwhile, Ronaldo, bespeckled with blood, dirty and disheveled, stopped in the street for a few moments to consider his misfortune. He was ruined, unable to inflate even a stupid Salvadorian whore, then beaten and mocked in front of her neighbors. He cursed God in his misery. As he did so came the first motion, a stirring, and then an unmistakable throbbing indicating the onset of an enormous but belated erection.

"Why you do this to me? Why do you make my member useless for any activity other than squirting water? I should have directed my supplications to the old bum in the doorway. No more from you, Almighty miserable Father of the worthless sleeping penis."

And God, hearing Ronaldo's sad complaint grew angry, speaking to Ronaldo from a tremendous roaring wind.

"*Okay, you ungrateful grease ball, consider this. You were attempting fornication out of wedlock. That's not so bad, but committing adultery at the same time. That don't fly. Remember this day, sinner, for your punishment will continue for a full six months. You will be mocked and reviled in the Latino community, shunned by women of all ages, and driven from any whore house door. You will forever be known as bacon balls, the incapable. Not only that but as a reminder of this day, the very day when you were stupid enough to blaspheme, complain and address your heavenly father so rudely, you will be chastised appropriately. So! Fuck you.*"

God seldom revealed himself to people in New York City in those days, but when he did, that was the manner with which he spoke to sinners on the south side of the Bronx. For he knew most of them were not normal people. Ronaldo shook his head as a great wind howled around him and knew in his heart it was too late to apologize, too late for forgiveness.

Back at the apartment, Marisol shifted nervously from one foot to the other.

"He never touched me, I swear. He threw Nikki out the window because of his limp cock. You can ask Micky the *super*."

Reg stared in disbelief, wrinkling his nose at the smell of cheap cologne billowing from the bedroom as he listened to his wife bleating and babbling. There was nothing for him to say. For sure, this would be the final straw that ended his marriage. No reply would ease his pain or lessen his sadness. He could, however, address a great injustice to the cat.

Ronaldo, walking slowly and in great pain, was staring at the ground when the police cruiser stopped several yards before him. Reg stepped purposefully from the car and showed his badge.

"Got a few questions for you." Ronaldo nodded and continued to stare at his feet, blood oozing from his ear and pooling on his shoulder.

"Why did you toss the cat out the window?"

"It was an accident, man. I never meant to hurt the fuckin cat, but she kept on about my dick, not being hard enough to do her properly."

"Who kept on, the cat? You were screwing a cat?"

"Eh? Oh, no."

"No, No man, I never did the cat. I swear, I mean the Salvadorian whore in the apartment. She wanted it bad. I tell her to rub my cock an wait for a little bit, but she laughed at me, said my dick was soft like a strip of bacon. So, fuck that, I am a proud man, so I throw her fuckin cat out the fuckin window. Any man would do the same. It was an accident."

Reg nodded. "Yeah, I hear yuh. We get a lot of accidents with cats flying outa windows. Accident an accident, though, something that can't be helped, eh." Ronaldo nodded.

"Yeah, an accident. Stupid whore made me do it, hit me with a pan after, an broke me ear. And it was only a cat, just a dumb fuckin cat."

"Okay, pal, got a few more questions, then you can go. I want your name, address, age, last birthday, date of birth country of origin."

At the end of every question, before Ronaldo could respond, Reg drove his fist hard into Ronaldo's stomach. By the date of birth question, Ronaldo was on his knees, gasping and vomiting.

"Okay, you're free to go."

Pulling him to his feet, Reg stared at him for a few seconds, then stepped quickly to his left

"This one is for the cat." A hard roundhouse punch to the liver sat Ronaldo back on the pavement again, gasping for breath as waves of agony washed over him.

"Enjoy the evening; looks a little like rain, eh?"

As the agony eventually subsided, a strong wind suddenly blew around him again, and he heard a familiar sonorous voice intoning

"Thou shalt not covet thy neighbor's wife. Thou shalt not commit adultery or throw innocent cats up in the air, eh, asshole. Read the book sometime."

Laughter, then silence again as the wind subsided. Indeed, God does work in mysterious ways. And we know he does, for as the cat Nikki plunged into the alley below, a sudden wind caught him, blowing him close enough to a small elm tree allowing him to break his fall, cling onto the trunk and scramble to safety below. Marisol never saw the cat Nikki, Bacon Balls Gonsales, or Reg Brown again.

Her soon-to-be ex-husband, Detective Investigator second class Reginald Brown sat on the corner of his bed in a shabby two-bedroom apartment a few blocks from the forty-second precinct office. Four years since he married Marisol and a little more than a year since he became aware of the sign. A glowing neon sign with large red letters, forming the words *"NASTY BITCH "* clearly defined, hung from her neck. Reg shook his head, inwardly cursing himself for a fool. A seasoned detective, one of NYPD's finest, and he, of all people, never saw the sign nor listened to his friend's warnings.

He saw the sign now as he had done for nearly a year. It was visible to anyone for several yards. Thankfully a quick divorce was pending. Hopefully, the last act in their disastrous marriage he would have to participate in. There was nothing left in their joint bank account; she had successfully drained their savings, funneling most of the cash to her lawyer. He gave silent thanks that she was unaware of a blue canvas bag on the top shelf in Ted Banning's locker. Nor was she aware of the motorcycle in Ted Banning's garage.

It was no surprise when he learned Marisol was much more than a client of Marty's. He briefly considered a visit to Lieberman's office, making a formal complaint to the old man and then an informal complaint to Marty on the end of his fist. Upon reflection, he decided against any action. They deserved each other; Marty would soon have to bear the cost of her drug habits and the inevitable medical bills. He would eventually realize his fine prize was an empty duplicitous shell and would soon see the sign, the same one he could see: Marisol and Marty, a match made in the Bronx, certainly not in heaven. Reg continued to sit on the edge of the bed, staring morosely at the wall in front of him, lost in thought.

He remembered the good times, the first nine months or so before booze and drugs poisoned the relationship. He also understood his part in the problem the long hours at the station office after his promotion, weekends, and late-night calls requiring his attention. If nothing else, Reg Brown was a reasonably honest, dedicated cop. Unfortunately, Marisol cared little for honesty or dedication. She had grown to dislike most things about the South Bronx now and nurtured an unreasonable dislike of the Morrisania area and, with it, the forty-second precinct. Harsh winters were killing her, summer heat and the relentless humidity also played their part. Above all, she hated the restrictive second-floor apartment on 153rd, the perpetually-malfunctioning air conditioning, and so many lonely evenings when Reg was working.

Marisol could not remember or had chosen to ignore her bitter Salvadorian childhood. Being undocumented, hungry, and homeless in New York was infinitely better than her previous life. She had quickly adapted to life in the US. Youth and charisma, long raven black hair, and an insolent curvaceous body were her passports to easy, upper west side city living.

She was in the South Bronx now, with the street gangs and crumbling infrastructure, a dystopian vision that her husband could not see. In truth, Reg was affected by the deteriorating situation around him. A brief encounter with four members of the *"Savage Skulls"* left him with a permanent reminder of a baseball bat every time he saw his reflection. Missing teeth were quickly replaced, but the deep disfiguring scar from chin to nose remained.

Reg stood in the squad room, gazed about him, remembering the people at the forty-second. Special friends, rookies, whores, and junkies. The hardened street gangsters were no more than children when he hauled them in. This was his life in New York City. It would resume after a little while in Los Angeles. He left the old Fairlane in the street outside the apartment and left a short note for the *super* to give to Marisol.

"Keys are under the passenger's seat. The rent is paid for a month; congratulations. Have a nice life."

He shook hands with Mickey wishing him well and

"Please give the note to Marisol when she returns." Mickey glanced at the note.

"That I will, sir. Soon as the little lady returns, I will happily give her the letter."

He remembered the Cuban whacking incident clearly and nurtured a fond hope that someday, Marisol would require further restraint.

Reg knew she hated the car and everything about it, but since she had no car of her own, she may grow to love it. Perhaps Marty would buy her one. He smiled to himself and nodded absentmindedly as he walked down the street.

Detective Reg would ride his newly liberated motorcycle to LA. Nine thousand dollars in a blue canvas bag would see him with motel money, food, and gas. He allowed two weeks on the road to LA, another week to find a suitable apartment, and a day or so in interview time at LAPD offices. And so, early Monday morning, July fifteenth, Reg Brown wheeled his bike into the street. The engine running, first gear selected, clutch feathered, and then a high arm salute to his dear friend, officer Ted Banning. Time to go now, leaving the early morning mist, smells, and sounds from the east river. A large loop passing the old forty-second station for the last time, a fond farewell before joining Interstate 87 north and pointing his new life towards LA.

Reg had a detailed plan. On the road by 6 am in a motel or boarding house by 7 pm. He would be able to survive fast-food dining for a week or so. No night riding, half-day Sunday for laundry. Depending on his progress, he would visit places of interest and national monuments along the way. Everything went very well; he did somewhat deviate from his plan as he was often distracted by the tremendous natural beauty and sheer size of the country he rode through. A journey of a lifetime, and he never brought a camera.

Seven days out. He left Las Vegas in the morning, deciding to stay at Death Valley overnight. All would have been well had he not taken the wrong road and arrived at Shoshone by way of Highway 127. No problem, turn off 127, then into Death Valley. Only a couple of hours wasted. Wasted was the wrong word, he thought. No time on this journey was wasted. He may not have wasted his time, but he did waste his gas. The tank was dry as he pulled to the side of the road, just past the sign at the Death Valley National Monument entrance. Highway 127 is a deserted two-lane road; there are few vehicles, no gas, and no water. All the miles he had traveled, and now he was marooned like a fool by the side of a California desert road. Midday now with the blinding sun full in a cloudless sky. He pulled his jacket from the bike, making an ineffectual attempt at a sunshade.

He heard the engine way out in the distance, a thousand miles, it seemed. When Reg pulled himself from sleeping and stood by his bike, there was a shadow on the road, shimmering in the distance bringing temporary hope. As he stared, the sound of the engine became louder. Only it was two shadows and the sound of two big engines. Both bikes pulled to the side of the road a few feet from Reg. Both riders stared at him for a long time, it seemed, before shutting their motors down. Neither rider wore colors or any recognizable club insignia. Both were unkempt and bore the unmistakable imprint of sun, wind, and road dirt. The rider nearest to Reg stepped from his machine and inclined his head.

"This ain't a fuckin bus stop and there ain't no fuckin train in sight, so either you're stuck or waiting for the ranger," Reg grinned,

"Yeah, I'm stuck. I took a wrong turn and ran out of gas."

"Nearest gas pump is twenty miles in either direction; which way you headed?" Reg shook his head.

"I was planning on spending the night in Death Valley, look at the sights in the morning, but I'll think I'll pass. Just carry on to LA."

Reg eyed the bikers, mentally assigning them numbers. Number one was the talker, large and intimidating. About six-three, two hundred and thirty pounds or so. Shoulder-length brown hair and piercing gray eyes. Number two, the quiet one, Hispanic looking with long black hair pulled back and tied in a ponytail. Neither was particularly friendly, and he noted number one never smiled when he spoke. He put some physical distance between them and felt the comfort of his small thirty-eight pistol holstered in the waistband of his pants.

"You're pointed in the wrong direction for LA. That's the way we're goin'. The gas station is at the big truck stop in Baker, about twenty miles down the road." He pointed in that direction. "Neither of us got enough fuel to get three of us to Baker. Here's what we goin to do. Since you're goin to owe us big time, we start with introductions. I'm Pat Winslow." Pointing to number two

"This here's Ruben Castillo."

Reg extended his hand, "Reg Brown, glad to know you.

Pat spoke. "Got any money?'

Reg nodded, "Yeah, a little, about fifty bucks, probably."

"Thirty should do. Ruben and I will get gas, bring a gallon or so back with us in a can, but we have to buy a can first. We get you goin an meet back at the gas stop, fill the tanks, eat, an on the road again."

Reg nodded, handing two twenties to Pat. He started to thank them, but Pat cut him short.

"Yeah, no problem. See you in a few." He turned on his heel walking back to the bike. Both Harleys sounded their unmistakable chorus; both tires spat dirt and gravel as they joined the road again. Reg shook his head, sitting back down by his bike. He wondered briefly if he would ever see his money again.

Listening to the fading roar of the exhaust from the big engines, he knew then that they would do exactly what Pat said they would do. For bikers, this was the code of the road, and he felt a little ashamed for thinking otherwise. Within two hours, they were at the truck stop diner ordering food. Over coffee, Pat asked what Reg would do in LA.

"You looking for pussy, goin to Hollywood to be a movie star or what?" Reg started to tell about his failed marriage when Pat interrupted.

"You sound as if you're from back east, for sure not from around here."

"Right, New York is where I'm from."

Pat nodded, "shit, you're a long way from home then. How long you been in California? Now I ain't prying into your business, just interested."

"No problem, brother. I arrived in California today. Came in from Vegas this morning."

Pat shook his head. "So, you live in Vegas, then?"

"No, man, like I said, I'm from New York City. Left there seven days ago, Arrived in Vegas yesterday but screwed up this morning; otherwise, I'd be in Death Valley now."

Ruben stared at Reg.

"You come from New York on that scooter then?" he asked in disbelief.

Reg nodded. "Yeah, I left the Bronx last week, an here I am."

Pat shook his head.

"Tell me it ain't so. You rode a fuckin hard tail Pan Head from the Bronx? You are one righteous mother fucker then. Better get you to a doctor, stop them kidneys from bleeding."

Ruben grinned

"An stop his arse from bleeding. Pat's right. You are one tough hombre, eh."

Reg laughed. "The bike is all I have in this world; my brothers left the Bronx to find work in So Cal." He told his story, told of the failed marriage and Marisol's affair with Marty, how all his money was filtered to Marty. He described how he hid the Harley in his friend's garage and took off, leaving Marisol with the old Fairlane.

"So where you stayin' then?" Reg shook his head.

"First, get to LA, then a motel. I need a couple of days to find my way around and make an appointment for an interview."

"Then you got money for a motel, for food, and you got a sweet Pan Head. Think about this. I just rented a place with the option to buy. The house is secluded and an easy run to the freeway. Ruben is looking for a place in the country. He ain't found it yet, but while he looks, he's staying with me. We got three bedrooms; I got one, Ruben, wife, and kid got the other, so we got one spare. Yours if you want it. Don't have to be forever, but it would be a decent starting place for you. Have a look, follow us down, spend the night, and decide in daylight. I never shared a house with a fuckin cop before."

Ruben grinned. "Come on, Reg, good company, and the beers cold."

CHAPTER
TWENTY-FIVE

Reg stayed the night and never left for five months. During that time, Pat landed a decent machinist job at Disneyland. Ruben bought a large house in the hills. Reg started work with the LAPD, not as he wished but on a six-month probationary period. Even though the hiring freeze was over, he could not transfer directly to his former NYPD rank. No matter what, he was working and building a new career. He found a decent two-bedroom apartment in Chatsworth, closer to the city, with more room and less questionable traffic passing through the house. Although he still rode the bike, he now owned a clean, used Ford f 150 long-bed truck. Life was good again.

The passing years brought changes. As six years rolled quickly past his door, Reg slowly became disenchanted with his position at LAPD. He was promoted twice and was now a senior officer in a newly formed anti-gang task force. Most of his time was now spent undercover, gathering information from small-time street players and concentrating on local supply houses. Narcotics were freely available, most distributed by local street gangs.

Five experienced officers known as *the bomb squad* would select a target deep in unfriendly territory. Early in the morning, they would conduct a surprise raid: property seizure, arrests, and destruction of drugs. The goal was the intervention, disruption, pursuit, and in the process, promote a neighborhood environment within which gangs could not easily flourish—all noble causes designed to improve the quality of life in poorer inner-city neighborhoods. An ideal Reg wholeheartedly subscribed to. But, he was beginning to hate undercover to the extent that he decided to leave LAPD and start a career in real estate. He also had a new girlfriend. An Italian girl, renting a room at Pat's house, as he had done before her.

She was the best yet. Not only a great woman excelling in all good girlfriend qualities but also an enjoyable companion and an excellent cook asking for little and giving much.

She was, he thought, *the exact opposite of Marisol*. And she was, but he was almost resigned to the failure of the new romance. Never finding quality time to enjoy themselves together, always an undercurrent of uncertainty and tension. The life of an inner-city police detective was not at all conducive to serious or extended romantic attachments. "*When I leave the department, everything will improve,*" He told himself repeatedly. And so it did.

Pat found a new prototype machinist position, having been fired from "*the happiest place on earth*" for threatening a supervisor with great bodily harm. He started to grow a beard, adding to his already intimidating appearance.

Ruben and his small family rolled the imaginary dice and bought a large modern house sitting on an acre of hilly unfenced land at a remote picturesque location. His dog breeding program flourished, and he was able to earn and save enough from matching the dogs and selling a few pups to pay the mortgage promptly. For him, a unique lifestyle and a way of life he lovingly embraced, unfortunately, without the full support of his wife and daughter.

"Daddy, why can't we be like normal people, a normal family without all the dogs?" Ruben realized that the dogs were not a secure steady income, but it was a start. A means to establish a world-class strain of fighting Bulldogs and make a name for himself.

Pat's new machinist job was almost ideal. Close to home, mentally challenging, and with decent pay. Working hours were reasonable and did not intrude into his pharmaceutical enterprise. He had found a new friend at work. A kindred spirit, a committed biker with no pretentious veneer. Em-Jay was another new hire, a badly needed mechanical engineer who was knowledgeable and easy to work with. Socially he was a good fit and not given to unnecessary yapping. Pat was convinced Em-Jay would be a reliable and trustworthy friend. Although he was English, he could easily be forgiven for that unintentional indiscretion.

The household was more than satisfactory. Annetta was low-keyed; she was mainly at the university or working. True to her word, she maintained, cooked, cleaned, and did so happily. The only downside to their arrangement was the obvious and burgeoning attraction between her and Em-Jay. He saw this as a potential disaster and an unnecessary complication in his life, simmering now but soon to reach boiling point.

The three of em were adults, fuck em, let em sort their own business.

Pat gave a room in the house to a Mexican kid Philippe, another newbie at work. Ruben's old bedroom was many levels above a corner in a local garage previously occupied by the boy. Pat watched in amazement as Philippe danced around the room, then ran and hugged him, promising "to always work hard."

Monday, October 7th. The *bomb squad* moved forward with another mission. Van Nuys, on the outskirts of LA. They were going to a known gangland residence at the end of Blythe Street. The Mexicans delivered eight kilos of cocaine the previous day. The blow was paid for in cash; the two sellers, now under surveillance, were leaving that day, meeting separately at the airport. The boys were left at the house to fulfill pre-paid orders, then cut and package the remaining powder for street sales.

The bomb squad would arrive at seven am: two unmarked cars, two unmarked vans. Local Sherif would cordon off any streets necessary for preventing entrance or exit. Two squad officers would enter through the front door, one through a side window, and two positioned at the back to detain possible escapees. Four sleeping occupants would be rudely awakened and transported to a local county holding cell. Four squad members would process and photograph the cocaine as material evidence before moving it to a secure location. Three officers would remain at the house to intercept potential buyers, answer and trace any phone calls. A Hazmat team would investigate the property for dangerous or restricted contaminants. At that time, county health officials may recommend evacuating any surrounding residences. And so the process would continue, gathering momentum like a boulder rolling downhill.

The plan was a good one and, in the ordinary course of human endeavor, a reliable one. But, it was not foolproof, for it was impossible to account for all the vagaries and unexpected responses from those encountering sudden early-morning intervention. Pat Winslow was at the house under cover of darkness. About 6/20 am, in time for coffee and before the bomb squad arrived. He took possession of one key, paid nineteen thousand dollars in cash, and stuffed the package in his coat pocket before complaining about the shitty coffee. Suddenly Francoise (crazy Frenchie) came through the back door grim-faced, whispering harshly to those in the room. "Amigos, we got pigs, or East LA soldiers maybe, some cars. I go by the tree." He disappeared through the back door, shotgun in hand, crouching low as he ran and kneeling quickly beneath the old tree. From his concealed vantage point, he surveyed the few yards to the back of the house and a short section of the street. There was just enough misty gray morning light to see the outline of an intruder.

Pat came jogging through the back door on his way to the alley, as the cop positioned by the fence yelled. "Police! Get down on the ground. Do not move." Pat lay face down as the officer approached, handgun drawn. It was then Francoise concealed behind the old tree trunk, squeezed the trigger, sending a twelve-gauge deer slug into the back of the arresting officer, killing him instantly. "Vamoose homie, rapido amigo." Pat scrambled to his feet, glanced at the fallen cop, then ran into the back alley and to the safety of the street.

Crazy Frenchie dropped the shotgun by the body on the ground and ran back into the house. At best, he would grab a kilo while confusion and noise distracted the cops, then follow in Pat's footsteps into the alley. At worse, he would find the blow moved, in which case he would run for the alley anyway. A detective, alerted by the gunshot, was now waiting in the shadows behind the door. As Frenchie made his entrance, he was stopped, searched for weapons, and questioned. Nothing he had to say was of any consequence, and his replies were not recorded. The detective recognized Frenchie immediately as an active gang member and wanted as a *person of interest* in a recent and ongoing homicide investigation.

Holding both arms before him as he often had before, he waited for the inevitable handcuffs and a quick recitation of his rights. He received neither. Detective John Alvarado fired two bullets into his chest and two into his face; in doing so, he possibly violated his civil liberties and fundamental human rights. For sure, he was treated most unfairly, and he died without the reassuring company of a freshly lubricated lawyer.

Had this drama played out in Japan, Frenchie would have lost face and, as culturally expected, endured great irrevocable humiliation. This was Los Angels County, though, and Frenchy's loss of face included an eye, teeth, patches of charred skin, and many bone fragments. Within a few minutes, Frenchie had been tried, convicted, and executed; the judicial proceedings were unorthodox but most efficient and rightly so. For several years Frenchie had been rude to his mother, badly behaved, and very naughty. An old Colt revolver with no identifying numbers was found in Frenchie's hand when his body was examined, providing an excellent and well-publicized reason for detective Alverado to have fired his weapon in self-defense.

Pat sat, leaning back in the small Ford pickup truck, driving slowly before quickly merging with the Monday morning commuter traffic flow. He stopped at a fast food place on Sepulveda Boulevard. Over more shitty coffee with hands still shaking, he considered his most fortunate position.

This morning came the boogyman he had avoided for so long—arrest or involvement in a shooting. Perhaps stopped, searched, and found in possession of contraband—all these things he had avoided and was apparently still immune to. Time was his friend on this occasion, but for how long, he wondered. He never knew the *bomb squad* was early. Never knew the Sheriff was late, never understood how he had escaped with a kilo of high-quality cocaine.

He finished breakfast, downed another cup of shitty coffee, and drove to work. He was early, but it didn't matter. Time was his friend but only for today. Later in the evening, Pat would reconstruct the morning's events and come to realize that he was entirely responsible for the sudden and unnecessary death of a good friend and fine police officer.

Tuesday afternoon, after a great wave of publicity flowed out from all local news outlets, he left work early. Returning to his empty house, he stood in silence for several minutes, then threw himself on his bed and cried, sobbing as he revisited many fond memories from the earlier times.

There was an extensive inquiry, hand-wringing, yucking, scratching, and beard pulling. As a result of this, public angst procedural changes were implemented. The *bomb squad* was renamed. It would continue to function as *The special crime intervention detail*. With a replacement member, enhanced communications hardware, and improved cooperation with outside agencies, the unit continued as before.

Friday at 11/am, many curious onlookers lined both sides of the streets as the grand procession moved slowly towards the Forest Lawn funeral home where all preparations were in place. A very nice service with a flag-draped coffin borne slowly by Six ranking officers attired in formal uniform. The chief delivered a moving speech, extolling many virtues of their fallen officer, so brutally murdered in the line of duty. The crowd was estimated to be more than one thousand. Those who knew Reg and loved him stood with those who knew him and didn't love him but thought it necessary to attend the proceedings lest they were thought of in an unfavorable light.

Notable attendees were the mayor, the flatulent and puffy LA supervisor, with representatives from his flatulent puffy, and inefficient departmental offices. The remaining *bomb squad* operatives and five NYPD detectives from the old 42nd precinct squad were in attendance.

In fact, detective first-class Edward Banning was assigned a position as a pallbearer. There was sufficient television and newspaper coverage to ensure the public would be adequately informed, and a large photograph of the deceased was always within view of the cameras.

"They shoot poor Reggie down. They Lay him six feet under the ground; they laid him away."

Of course, the wretched Em-Jay knew nothing of these matters, isolated as he was in another reality and within a strange place not of his choosing. So he continued wandering, bemused and a little frightened as darkness approached.

CHAPTER
TWENTY-SIX

In truth, I was a little scared now. I continued walking towards the shed, or at least where I believed the shed to have been. I remembered fragments of distant dreams in which seemingly endless walking inside a busy railway station, riding many escalators, and climbing many flights of stairs. Competing with crowds of passengers eventually brought me to a street-level exit somewhere in London, with no direction, money, or means to return home. Was this place a dream, then? If it was, how would I know? The dull, lifeless, rather humid atmosphere I had experienced since my arrival was transformed by a sudden wind sounding mournfully around me. With a shock, I remembered this same wind gusting around us when Annetta and I walked together in this place some time ago, and with that memory came hope and a feeling of peace.

I sat again on the sandy ground beneath me and closed my eyes, listening to the wind and feeling the surrounding space. There was no fear now; I knew I could travel in this place without harm. With eyes closed, I stood, then opening my eyes, saw the fence and gate in front of me, exactly where I would expect them to be. In front of me, so at least my sense of direction was intact.

Through the gate, I went, relieved and very happy. Almost like a homecoming, it seemed, then closing the gate, walking quickly across the grass past the swing and through the sliding doors. I sat for a long time, letting the silence wash over me before falling asleep on the couch. I woke to bright daylight; I was cold and stiff, but no sign of my previous sickness, although I knew it would return. Brew coffee, shit, shower, then review my recent life experiences. All these actions were performed in quick succession, leaving me to call work and listen to messages on the answering machine. There were many messages from work, all wishing me well and a speedy recovery. Pat, Reg, and Ruben called, *"sorry to hear about the accident; anything they could do, just call."* The insurance company called twice, asking me to return their calls.

I never remembered telling anyone about the accident except the police and insurance. Annetta had left a message saying she would be here Friday evening as arranged. Coming by train again, if I didn't feel well enough to meet her, Mary said she would. I sat in the kitchen, digesting the great confusing mess of telephone rhetoric, and then realized I did not know what day it was—no idea of the day, date, or time. No matter, I would soon rearrange all pieces in their correct order. It was Friday, October twenty-first.

My genius watch displayed all this information at no charge. It also told the time, eleven fourteen. Then came the sudden shock; Dot's birthday was Saturday, and the accident was Sunday, early afternoon. Had I wandered behind the fence for a week? Not possible, surely. Head clearing time.

I walked past the swing to the fence, not even bothering to check for white rock. I collected a few tools by the gate, left on the grass at the time of my investigation. Still confused by the missing days, I returned to the house, intending to replace the tools in the garage.

I sat on the garage floor, staring at the bike. The fuel tank was pushed back with a substantial disfiguring dent on the right side. Front forks were twisted and bent beyond repair. Here was the same pristine machine I had gazed upon on Monday morning, the same motorbike I had started and ridden to the end of the street that previous afternoon. I had no answer for this bizarre occurrence. Here was a deepening mystery that presented a different set of conditions every time I looked in the garage.

I reluctantly called the insurance company. They were aware of the crash on Avenue O, aware that the bike was at my house, and told me an estimator would evaluate the remains either later today or tomorrow morning. Full coverage would thankfully reimburse me for eighty percent of the repair cost and some out-of-pocket expenses. Apparently, they had a copy of the police report and had mailed it to me. All well and good, but a situation so totally different from my experience after the accident that I remained in a state of confusion and disbelief.

I called work. Good wishes filled the air, hurry backs, and get well soons were all around me. Pat would be back on Monday, having taken a few days' leave. Nothing that couldn't wait until Monday, then. Later I would call or go to Allan and Mary's. I was certainly well enough to meet Annetta at the station. It was red wine time, and the call of the swing was loud. I sat, mentally regurgitating the time I spent beyond the gate. Through the gate, walked about half a mile past the shed, stopped, turned, and walked back to the gate. So, an hour at most, not four days. During that time, I was not particularly hungry and not thirsty. So, what the hell happened? How could I account for the missing four days?

No magic. I was sick, went through the gate, farted around for a couple of hours, came home, and went to bed. Then fell into a deep sleep, as sick folk, with or without heroin, often do. A reasonable explanation and a good attempt but, too many gaps, too many blank spaces, and unanswered questions. Okay, what then? Only one thing to do under the circumstances. Bust out the ole crack pipe. Well, I don't smoke crack, and no opium for me, because if I were picking Annetta up at the station, I would at least like to see the station. What then? Obviously, scrambled eggs, toast, and bacon. There was no bacon, but there were a few spuds and certainly enough coffee. Done deal. A late lunch, call Annetta, check-in with Allan and Mary. All these things were accomplished in that order.

Annetta sounded subdued, almost depressed, a quality to her voice that I hadn't heard before, one I found a little disturbing. Alan and

Mary were delighted to see me. Very concerned about the accident and my subsequent disappearance. Alan, with the help of a friend, took his truck, borrowed a trailer, winched the wreck on, and brought it to the garage.

"Got a little confession Em-Jay. We looked everywhere for you and called all the local hospitals, but nothing. I didn't want to leave the bike outside, so I jumped the back gate and came in through your backdoors. A little fire department magic. I'm glad you don't have a pit bull."

"Magic, for sure, if you cleaned the kitchen and bathroom while you were there? Seriously, many thanks, Alan. You are a very good friend."

I told them what I could remember about the oncoming truck. Mary said that "Apparently, the truck was not at fault, just cruising along. A small Ford tried passing over double yellow lines, saw me, and lost control."

"Yeah, Em-Jay was so ugly the car driver just panicked. Said so in the police report."

Mary shook her head and glared at Alan. And so the conversation continued. My problem was not being able to explain the missing days from Monday to Thursday. Eventually, I took my leave, thanking them for all their help and promising to come over or call later that evening when Annetta was at the house.

"Show Em-Jay, our new house guest."

"Can't see him; he's probably out in the back garden." Mary grinned, "got ourselves a little cat, cute black and white, not very old, found him a couple of nights ago by the side of the house. I think he's here for good. I really love the little guy, such personality." Suddenly remembering the cat Felipe found at Pat's house, I grinned as I remembered the conversation. "What's his name?" I asked Mary.

"Alan calls him Gyp, short for gypsy, seems to suit him."

The train was right on time. And Anneta was walking from the train, slim and straight with her huge grin. She did not dance into my arms; this time, she walked to me, throwing her arms around my waist and kissing my lips—a kiss from a beautiful but subdued lady. We walked to the car, holding hands and speaking in generalities.

"Shall we stop to eat?" I asked, "I know this sounds strange, but I only returned to the house this morning. By the time I caught up with the world, it was time to leave for the station."

She nodded, "So you tell me on the phone, darling. You must have much to say me, yes?"

"Much darling, none of it worth a damn. Anyway, you're here now, and that's important. How about we stop at the big steakhouse on the main street, eh?" We sat again, watching cowgirl waitresses with tight Jeans and white Stetson hats flit between tables.

"You look much better doing that, sweetheart." She smiled weakly and nodded.

"Thank you, darling; I never realized how much work these girls do that job."

"What the hell's the matter, sweetie? Talk to me. Tell me what the problem is."

She shook her head, "I sorry, darling fool Em-Jay. Just such a shock for me, for all of us, yes?"

I was about to reply when the food came, the same as last time, pepper steak and a grand assortment of veg.

"I talk with you Em-Jay dearest, after we eating, Okay?

And so the feasting began; the steak was flavorful and so easy in the mouth, a meal to remember. Waitresses hovered, chatted at times, and performed waitressy stuff. Annetta smiled and nodded with no connection to the evening at all. Food came and went. No dessert. Coffee was essential, though.

"Now, talk baby, *what is the* matter?" She shook her head. "I know I feel this thing more than you, darling; my feeling was much more than you because of we were so much closer, yes? This hurt all of us, me most, I think, as much as Pat."

I stared at her for some time, trying to comprehend at least a small fragment of her reply. Shaking my head, I gazed into her eyes,

"Honey?" *A short pause for dramatic effect,* "what on earth are you talking about? For sure, I have no idea."

"What are you thinking, Em-Jay? Are you a blob? I speaking of Reggie, of course."

I don't believe I am a blob, not knowing what one is and never having been called one before, but perhaps I am.

"Okay, what about Reggie then?"

Her turn to stare. "You know about Reggie, don't you then?"

"No, what about Reg? I've been missing for a few days, and I thought you knew that."

"Reg is dead Em-Jay, shot and killed. Pat tell me he is there but doesn't know it, Reg, who got killed. How you don't know this?" She told the details of the Reg murder, clutching and squeezing her hands as she spoke. I listened in shock, without interrupting, remembering the few times we were together. Remembering the time he came to the house.

"Okay, darling Em-Jay, we have been sad; now is time for happy, eh? Your turn to tell me but on the swing with wine, yes?

So yes, it was. Like it was before but different now without Reg. I never called Mary or Alan, wanting time to digest the sad story Annetta told me and wanting some alone time with her. The evening passed with Annetta as shocked as I had been when I showed her the battered bike. I told her my experience with the bike, how it was crashed, and then became uncrashed, then crashed again. I told her about my travels beyond the gate, how hours turned into days, and my lost week.

"What is that place, Annetta? What else is out there besides the mountains and sand?"

"I say to you quickly, darling Em-Jay, I say what I know." A huge familiar smile, missing since she walked from the train.

"I tell you before, but you never listen to me."

"Another glass of wine then, my beauty, and I promise to give full attention."

"Okay, Em-Jay, the important thing for you to do is we go tomorrow to a big bookseller or library. Okay, then after that, you look closely at the directions, and you understand much better, much clearly, when I tell you yes?"

"Why, of course, my darling, I wouldn't have it any other way. What are we looking for at the bookstore?"

"We looking at Chino, at old Chinese medical and healing."

"Yes, of course we are. I am so glad I asked. Should we also research prehistoric Neapolitan mattresses?"

"You may do so, my darling fool Em-Jay, but I would advise against such an unnecessary undertaking. Now, here is this evening's choice, call Alan and Mary, more wine, a short walk in the desert, or all of these things."

"A little cold for the desert walk, I think; how about ten minutes on the swing, wine, a short walk to the bedroom, and cuddle."

We did. The wine helped dissipate the depressive feeling draped over us like a thick dirty blanket. It was impossible to ignore the tragedy of Reg's untimely death. So, we sat on the swing, talking about Reg and Pat. I wondered if Reg had discovered his prisoner was Pat, would he have arrested or released him? Annetta and I were both convinced Reg would have released him and let him slip away. He would surely have some very harsh words to say to him the next day. But, all this speculation was irrelevant now. Had I been working, I might have taken the time and gone to his funeral. That was something we could still do: Ruben, Pat, Philipe, Annetta, and I. Visit the grave and remember him in our own way. Annetta nodded half-heartedly when I made that suggestion to her.

We both slept well; the wine usually helps. Next morning up and ready to descend on places of books, after breakfast in town, of course. The prevailing atmosphere between us was much happier now. I drove along Avenue O, visiting the scene of the bike disaster. Around the Cottonwood tree, obvious signs of recent activity, bark from the tree on the ground, and furrows in the soft soil. Exactly, as I would have expected, there was sure nothing there when I photographed that place earlier. Well, no matter. I would have the film processed and examine it to my satisfaction. Good breakfast at a large Mexican restaurant, two empty stomachs introduced to an overflowing buffet, the perfect partnership, and a delightful Saturday social occasion. Bookstore time, and Annetta, like a scent hound, pounced upon the alternative medicine shelves. She found a large illustrated volume of Chinese acupuncture methods and history. The damn thing cost nearly thirty dollars.

"Is good study material for you, darling."

I nodded and paid.

Later, on the kitchen table, I paged through the book, Annetta nodding and pointing to a reproduction of a male body with lines and points covering it. She traced a broad line on the chart with her finger, one of many.

"Here is meridians Em-Jay; they are the channel carrying the life force or chi. It is necessary that all the meridians are unobstructed."

I gazed at the chart for some time, and gradually it made sense *if* one believed in a flowing life force.

Annetta expounded on the positioning of points along these meridians and told of their importance and how they responded to pressure or the introduction of tiny silver needles. A fascinating overview of healing with acupuncture, and I told her so.

"Okay, babe, so well and good, but how is this relevant to the desert after the gate?"

"Because my darling, there are the same meridians that cover our planet. Channels that mark the flow of enormous energy pulsing continually, like arteries. Sometimes hectic, other times not so much, but always working. Your peaceful little house sits next to a meridian line. Through the gate, there is an enormous energy field. The reason Indians call this sacred ground. That is why your perception of time and present reality changes so much. All perfectly natural and very exciting, eh?"

I would have called bullshit to the theory, but I could not deny my bizarre experiences during the last few days. I sat in silence for a long time.

"I will go again, this time not to evaluate anything, just to explore."

She laughed. "There is nothing for you to evaluate, my darling. You have no instruments capable of interpreting anything out there. If you wanting fun, take a compass or a watch. You can explore a little but be very cautious, yes? It is possible to be carried away." She paused, shaking her head before continuing.

"Think of the ground around you like is a fast-flowing river. If you fall, we may never see you again. You may never come back to me. I have hope and wishing you will not do this; It's so easy to get lost out there, darling fool Em-Jay."

I thought about her analogy to acupuncture, thought about my backyard as a turbulent sea of energy, and shook my head. There was more to the story than that. How was it possible to build the house in the first place, then? How was it? I never encountered anything. I found no strange or abnormal qualities when I bought the home. It was about that time that Alan and Mary rang the doorbell.

The following two hours were lost to animated babbling about my accident and subsequent disappearance. Beer and wine contributed significantly to the quality of the discussion. It was Mary who decided we should eat breakfast together in the morning. I-Hop about nine; a majority call decided it. After our friends had left the table, pointing themselves to their home across the street, I returned to my confusion with the meridian line running through the house.

"No, darling, I said *next* to the house, not running through. These lines are enormous channels, not little wires like the electricity people have. If you remember the mountain range you saw in the distance, yes?"

I nodded, remembering clearly the *invisible* mountains I saw before me. "that is an intersection point where two lines are crossing. There are layers of alternative realities everywhere; in places along the meridians, the overflow of energy allows easy travel back and forth between them. The ancient dwellers knew these things and build temples and pyramids to use the energy for healing and travel." The little lecture continued, with me just beginning to realize how all-encompassing Annetta's knowledge was, from art and literature to acupuncture. A very remarkable lady. And so to the bed where I hoped she would demonstrate more facets of her education; happily, she did so with dignity, grace, and charm.

Although her mood had lightened, there was something wrong with our relationship. No longer the happy, spontaneous fooling between two lovers. A darker, more serious aspect, subtle signals but enough for me to decide; I would wait for her to call me before I called her, an unnecessary and immature decision, I thought. Undoubtedly the shock of Reg's death played a significant role; it had driven a wedge between us. Understandably so, I suppose. Another point of contention was my continuing use of heroin. Never a problem before, but now an issue between us that would soon have to be resolved.

We met with Alan and Mary at the I-Hop. We had conflicting agendas that morning, so we took two cars. Mary wanted to go shopping; I intended to visit the Harley store to arrange for bike fixing. Good greasy breakfast with a heavy cloak of cheesy and cholesterol overall. The iconic American feast. Happy babbling filled the air with happy children squealing and gurgling. Annetta wanted to accompany Mary and commit several acts of shopping. Alan rolled his eyes. I nodded and smiled as the seemingly unstoppable wave of estrogen threatened to engulf us all.

By contrast, the little Harley dealership was a welcoming place with testosterone in every corner. A sufficient antidote to my recent excessive estrogen exposure. It was a small motorcycle chapel on a side road off the main boulevard. There were several Harley worshipers, all beardy, growling, and chuffing as they were given to do. The rotund hairy owner Henry, nodded sagely as he listened to my description of the damage.

"Yeah, well, we fixed worse, I suspect. You wan me to pick er up?"

"Yeah, please, perfect; what's a good day for you."

"Weel, Mondays are busy fo me, full o fuckin customers. Tell you what, If I show up today at about six? That good fo you?"

"Perfect, thanks a lot." He nodded and grinned.

"Okay, man, when we get the bike, Il price parts, and labor and call you with the cost."

I showed my license, which he copied, gave him my phone number, and shook hands. That, for me, was an easy transaction, made easier perhaps because of the oppressive and unmistakable smell of MaryJane.

At about five-thirty, two tattoo-encrusted Harley guys arrived with a trailer. The bike was loaded quickly, a receipt was given, and they were on their way—a simple exchange, and now the waiting game. Annetta arrived at about six/pm loaded with several bags of stuff.

"Not much time left to catch the train, sweetie, should load up and head on out."

"Very good darling Em-Jay. Pat will coming to get me at the other end."

We said little on the way to the station, not much when we arrived. After we had kissed, she waved and boarded the train with no promises or plans to meet again. She would have to show at least one more time, I supposed; she had two small suitcases at the house.

After returning to the house, I stared at the place in the garage where the bike used to be. I stared at the place in the kitchen where Annetta used to be. I walked to the gate and stared at where the white rock used to be. It was too cold on the swing for more than a minute or so. Retreating to the kitchen, I drank whiskey at the table before going to bed. I will be up early tomorrow, an extra half-hour drive time in the car to get to work.

Traffic still invoked the miserable emotions of anger, frustration, and desperation, perfect conditioning to perform meaningless tasks at work. Many years ago, the difference between an idiot and a moron was explained to me. A moron can perform meaningless tasks under supervision—a prevailing mindset when I sat at my desk. Pat and I went to lunch. This was an excellent opportunity to revisit the poor Reg incident.

"Still, can't believe that was Reg. I heard the cop yell to lie down; I went to the ground, and next thing, a gunshot, and the cop went down. I had no idea whether he was alive or dead, no idea it was Reg. The guy with the gun yelled at me to go. I ran through the alley at the back, down the street, and away. That, my friend, is the nearest I ever come to gettin' busted. An, I never knew my brother Reg is layin dead just behind me. One totally fucked up situation. It could have gone either way, me dead, Reg shootin' me, not knowing who it was. I'm out, man—no more of that shit for me. I sell the last bag, an I'm done. Don't need the money; don't need no more dead friends. Now, one thing between you and me, Don't say nothing to anyone about me bein there. I know you don't talk about business, but this is serious, a totally different scene, okay?"

"Of course, I won't say anything; I don't know anything." Pat nodded, changing the conversation to my accident.

"Make sure the assholes put the frame on a flat plate or jig to check the frame aint bent. Sounds as if it's just a matter of replacing parts."

We sat silently for some time before leaving—no mention of Philipe, his cat, or Annetta. Tomorrow I will ask about them, Ruben, and his family as well. So my first working day since returning from my impromptu vacation closed uneventfully. I readied myself for the inevitable horror of the freeway. At home, there were a few messages. One from the insurance company asked me to call the estimator and arrange a visit, something I should have done a few days ago. One from Annetta saying how sorry she was and how she missed me and couldn't wait to come back soon. I would call the insurance in the morning and arrange a meeting with the estimator on Wednesday.

And so the trivia of my daily living continued, swirling around me like snowflakes, irritating and depressing. A little smack would probably help, coke perhaps. I needed company If I were to pursue those pleasures, a condition I had never found necessary before. A shot of good booze and some quiet time would have to suffice.

I called the appraiser in the morning and arranged to meet him at the Harley shop the next day, about two in the afternoon. So, no work for me Wednesday.

The insurance appraiser was, to all intents, a reasonable man. He knew the Harley shop owner, having estimated repairs with him before. Henry thought two weeks at the most, assuming no hidden nastiness emerged. Life continued, Work resumed, Pat and I chatted, talked about nothing, and never mentioned Reg again. There was a distance between us now, and I avoided his company when; possible.

Philippe hugged me without embarrassment, saying how sorry he was that mister Reg was killed. He shook his head and wiped his eyes with his shirt sleeve. A spontaneous, poignant gesture expressing more to me than all the recent public outpourings of grief on television. I resisted the temptation to call Annetta thinking to give her some breathing space and let her make her decisions without my influence. Thursday, I got a call at work from Alan, berating me for ignoring Annetta. Please to call her soon as possible. She had called Mary, telling of her history with Reg, how she wished I could understand, and not to tell me she called; because I might be angry, but how she hoped I would call her.

And, of course, I did that same evening. And of course, she came Friday, meeting me at the station in the evening.

"Oh, why you have your good girl staying here? She may shoot you. She may cut you; she may stomp you too. No telling what that girl may do."

Well, there are many reasons I have her staying here. I think I love her, I think she loves me, and we are good together. She is the sort of girl one can rely on in an emergency. Should I experience a sudden, powerful, and unexpected erection, she would quickly find a comfortable home for it. Fairly obvious, I would have thought.

CHAPTER
TWENTY-SEVEN

Annetta had returned. The Annetta of old, bubbling with happiness, overflowing with humor, and cutting sarcasm. How different from last Friday's meal at the steakhouse. We had adopted a simple routine when she came by train. I would meet her at the station; we would stop at the steakhouse and gorge ourselves before returning home. That is the nice thing about Friday for me, no pressure, no hurry. Monday will come, but during that time, two days are allotted to indulge in the simple acts of living.

My job is all-powerful. It tells me when to get up in the morning, when to arrive at work, how many hours I have to work when to leave work, and how many days I must work. It then decides when I may have a vacation and how long it will be. But, during those times, it pays me for my time and vacation. So, thank you, dear job; thank you, sweet work. I need you; I will do my best to keep you, although I despise you, despise myself for needing you.

I should have wealth without working; the government should subsidize me at every step as they do for others. Therefore, I am a free spirit and should not be burdened by trivial concerns or work-related matters. And when I die, I wish to be reincarnated as a wealthy Italian playboy, possibly a nice young Mormon with a nice shiny suit and tie, a nice plastic briefcase, a bicycle, and a friendly perpetual smile. I know

I am important enough that choices should be made readily available to me.

Unfortunately, important though I may be, I have sinned greatly and will probably return as a Jewish car salesman or a Lebanese bus driver. There is nothing I can do about such events, but *please, Lord*, give me a little headstart, just a modicum of common sense, so I don't screw up all over the place again. While we're on the subject, please don't make me a sniveling gay guy. If I have to be a whiny sniveler, well, so be it, but not gay with the lispy, faggoty gay accent. Just an average guy with a large penis, no erectile dysfunction, and a regular girlfriend, intelligent like Annetta but with bigger breasts. Not a mental patient; no recurring yeast infection or STD, please. No ADT either. Also, I would like to remain white, American, or European, not black, Mexican, or Jew. Although, if I were a Jew like Mark or Dave, that would be okay. Not from any third-world country, though. Since we are talking, please consider this to be a prayer. That being the case, I will try harder; if I do, please help me to quit the dope and the smoke. Thank you very much, sir.

Notwithstanding such introspective philosophy, I headed home with a full stomach courtesy of my job and a woman whose gastronomic desires were temporarily satiated. If all goes well, any carnal desires will be satiated later. At the house, we had to make adjustments to our usual routine. Too cold to sit on the patio, so we drank wine in the kitchen. Later on, we would sit on the swing for a few minutes wearing our coats.

As it happened, Alan and Mary appeared about ten minutes after we walked through the door. There is comfort in the familiarity between us; I am sure Annetta feels the same; I know Mary does, but that is another story. Babbling and grand verbal posturing filled the room. The more wine consumed, the greater the bullshit disguised as meaningful conversation. None of this mattered because we were with friends, enjoying the hour.

The following morning a call from Harley shop Henry. He could finish the job a week earlier if I agreed to a five-gallon fuel tank instead of the original three gallons. For me, a perfect choice, practical and aesthetically pleasing. Annetta made breakfast, and we discussed her relationship with Reg as we ate. A conversation she initiated.

I listened, she talked, and there was nothing resolved, nothing *to* resolve, but we ended the discussion without rancor or regret. She told me how Pat was devastated by the situation.

When I talked with him, it seemed he had absolved himself of any blame or wrongdoing. In his mind, he was not culpable or responsible in any way for the murder. Perhaps he was right, perhaps, perhaps, perhaps. Endless permutations of circumstances, infinite scenarios, but all leading to the sad passing of a good man. So endeth the first lesson, Reg is gone, and with his passing, an emptiness that will never be filled, relationships forever changed.

"*I went down to the depot; there's a sign up on the wall. Said there were good times here, but better on down the road.*"

So, there I sat on a chilly Sunday afternoon, absorbed in acupuncture study, with the renowned Professor De Fiore directing studies. The more I understood, the more I resolved to explore beyond the fence. And as Annetta suggested,

"for fun, take a compass and a watch."

One thing I would certainly do would be to ride the bike through the gate at the earliest opportunity, probably without Annetta knowing. I was sure she would strongly advise against such bravado.

Dot called an hour or so before I returned Annetta to the station. An invitation to a small gathering next Saturday afternoon. No dog stuff, just family, no reason other than the good company of special friends. Annetta promised we would be there; Pat, Dave, and Mark would show, we were told. And so to the station, we went, an animated chattering Annetta, an Em-Jay a little subdued because his sweetheart was leaving.

"I call when I am at Pat's, darling; I want to stay here with you soon. Perhaps I not study more, get a job in town, and we live together."

The train took her from my sight again, leaving me with the familiar lonesome feeling I would share with an empty house again.

Cold though it was, I sat on the swing, a big glass of black-label whiskey in my hand, thinking deeply about our conversation on the platform. I would dearly love Annetta to stay with me permanently, not at the cost of her study programs. I was draining my second glass when she called. Everything was good.

"Pat collect me, and I call from the house. Perhaps I not working Friday and come early."

It sounded good to me; the earlier, the better, as far as I was concerned. Work loomed largely as it always did on Monday morning. A two-hour commute in the car if I was lucky. There were distractions along the way—usually minor accidents in the carpool lane. I observed other drivers, sometimes angry and tense, fists beating the steering wheel or the dash console. This morning wasn't too bad except for the usual period of inactivity before the first major intersection. I thought of something Pat said a few weeks ago, answering my question if Reg would show up at Dot's birthday party.

"*Poor bastard has to work, hates the job, and wants outa there as soon as possible.*" I wanted to cry.

For me, it was not so much the job but the commute in a car. On the bike, the ride was tolerable, dangerous, but tolerable.

Ah, stop sniveling Em-Jay. The job pays you; you can afford a car to commute to the job and a motorcycle for recreational purposes *if* you have the time after you've finished work.

I thought about Reg for a long time. Hours rolled into days as they always do, and if it weren't for the smoke bringing the week to Thursday, I would have gone straight to Friday. That's the thing about smack; with the smoke, you can regulate the high, unlike the needle, when it's all and at once. You can control the high with smoke, but not the frequency. The need pulls you with such strength it is impossible to resist. Some users snort the powder, most quickly gravitating to the needle or smoke.

Either way, you're hooked; the smoke takes a little longer to kill you. The stuff lives inside you, a false lover, waiting with the sweetest promises and whispering how it will love and care for you forever. It hurts you, your bones and joints ache, and you feel old and cold. You are tired, with no appetite. The sweating and shaking come a little later. Tylenol won't help; the only thing to stop the sickness, itching, and shaking is smack. Now you're better, living again until the compulsion makes you reach for the IV or foil. Each time a little more, each time sooner than the last.

The other danger with opiates in any form is that the body develops immunity or resistance, so, for the same high more is needed. And so the cycle of destruction continues on two levels.

Your health deteriorates, bringing failing eyesight and hearing. No concentration and memory loss coupled with unreasonable anxiety and unreasonable fear of the world about you soon to follow. You kill yourself slowly for pleasure, although the pleasure soon becomes a hollow pain. On another level, the price for this suicidal experience is high. Like most products exchanged for money, the old maxim *you get what you pay for* is true.

With H, street shit is usually just that. Suppose you have deep pockets and can afford near pharmaceutical grade; so much the better. The journey will be easier, but you die just the same. My habit was modest, about two hundred dollars a week, perhaps another hundred for cocaine. I knew a girl who was spending that much every day. I also remember a time when I thought I was *cool and* had an edge with arcane knowledge. I was the man with the needle and spoon who knew it all, basking in the old mystique of the avant-garde writers and artists. The cruel reality was that my avant-garde persona was pronounced differently. *Self-deception and fool.*

How and why, I wondered, did Annetta continue to struggle through our relationship? Out of a sense of duty, worse out of pity:?

Thursday brought Annetta to the restaurant where she worked and where I picked her up that evening. She was in good spirits, the same happy girl from last week. No steakhouse for us this week; we ate at the place where she worked. I had eaten there before; good American food was served quickly. We discussed the possibility of her moving to my house. I made very clear to her my objections; she listened without comment and, in the end, reluctantly agreed to finish her doctorate first. Saturday morning Pat and Barbra, his musical girlfriend, would meet at my house, and together we would drive to Rubens's place. Meanwhile, I drove Annetta back to the house for an early weekend. She was her delightful sparkling self, dancing around the house and rearranging objects to her satisfaction.

Saturday morning came quickly, with Annetta leaving the bed at about seven. My hopes for a late morning were crushed. Annetta reminded me that Pat and company were coming, called me a blob, then threatened to pour water over me. So, in the face of such imminent violence, I left the comfort and shelter of the bed, showered, and made ready before sitting for breakfast. Pat, Barbera, and Felipe would arrive at about nine, planning to stop at a fast-food place for food. It was a good morning thus far, with Annetta cooking eggs and potatoes with thick garlic toast.

"Barbra tell me she brings guitar and violin with her for music later."

"Pat told me she plays guitar and sings; I didn't know she plays the violin, quite a talent."

"We see, darling. I playing the violin. I don't know if Barbera plays as well, eh" I stared at her for many seconds.

"You never told me, never said anything about playing the violin; what else is there to know about you then."

"Sorry, darling Em-Jay. I thought I tell you, never thought about it as important."

Our little gathering at Rubens was a pleasurable interlude. Much wordy babbling, happy nonsense, with conversation flowing without restraint. Inevitably the Reg story was retold with Ruben and Pat telling of their first meeting in Death Valley many years ago.

I managed to suck in a little cocaine during a quick visit to the bathroom. The problem with snorting powder is the dripping nose and constant sniffing. Better for me is the heroin to smoke. Much better for me would be neither, but I never did choose that option. With heroin, it was the needle or smoke, of course, although for me, I no longer used the I.V. for anything. Perhaps bubble gum would be a reasonable alternative. And so, back to the party.

Most of the tension had evaporated, with humorous anecdotes replacing much of the raw, ragged details of his last moments. His death was with us, though, looming large in the room when conversation faltered or stopped. Barbera started to play softly at Pat's suggestion; Annetta joined her on the violin, a tentative accompaniment, gradually increasing volume, and tempo.

Their music rolled and swelled as a near-perfect improvision on an old folk song, *Careless Love*. Barbera played the melody with Annetta following her at first before swinging and winding high above, then returning to the melody and repeating the sequence. It sounded like old New Orleans club music. Their version would have been perfect if accompanied by a harmonica. They wound the volume down simultaneously, Annetta stopping to let Barbera finish on a series of soft, plaintive chords. That music will always recall memories of Reg and always bring tears when it does.

Absolute silence in the room as the last notes died away. The spell was eventually broken by Alice jumping up and down with a short series of "oh's." Clapping furiously, her applause was soon joined by the rest of us. Their music continued by request; although request implies a choice, there was none on this occasion.

"Play or die." Said Pat, and of course, they both laughingly complied. The next song was a cover of an early Leonard Cohen number, *Hallelujah*. Barbera's husky vocal rendition, with the soulful violin of Annetta providing the accompaniment, ensured many tears, including mine, were shed before the song ended.

Dot broke out sandwiches and wine, agreeing with Ruben that this was one of the best times they could remember. For me, certainly one of the most emotive.

"We dedicate this meeting, this party to Reg then. Every November fifteen, we meet here again in his memory. And *Hallelujah* must be played or sung by someone."

The company wholeheartedly adopted my suggestion, and we all promised to return on that date. Eventually, our little party drew to a close with much of the usual blustering and warm cackling. Hands were shaken, and hugs administered, kisses were installed appropriately.

Pat and the company elected to go home despite our invitation to stay for the night.

Philippe insisted that he could play the accordion, but nobody took him seriously.

CHAPTER TWENTY-EIGHT

Annetta and I pulled on coats and sat on the swing, dissecting the evening and drinking wine. We both agreed Barbara was a talented gem of a girl and how lucky Pat was to have her. I was surprised to learn from Annetta they had known each other for about five years. Although I chose not to show my feelings, I was furious with Annetta. We have been dating for about five or six months now. During that time, she never mentioned her extraordinary talent with a violin, and I never even knew she had one, although she said she had told me.

First, I find out about her interest in women as sexual partners; then, she's a violin virtuoso. I wondered what else, an escaped mental patient, a covert agent for the Mossad, a serial killer perhaps. She probably had a second home in rural Mississippi mother of five black kids.

I could see her as she walked home slowly along the grassy trail by the river. On one side, a few old oaks and a scattering of younger pines; on the other, a rustic wooden fence. She leaned with her back against the fence for a while, eyes half-closed, at peace. A large black raven descended suddenly, struggling to maintain balance on the fence top rail, wings outstretched, hopping in an ungainly dance as it approached Annetta. She laughed at the antics and gasped when it jumped to her shoulder.

Grasping the strap of her dress in its beak, it lifted it from her shoulder. With its head against her cheek and a great curved beak by her ear, it began nodding its head as if talking. She lifted the other dress strap from her shoulder, pulling the garment below her waist. Then, unhooking her brassiere, she let it fall, exposing both breasts. Holding her forearm so the raven could perch, it hopped to her arm and took a nipple in its beak, pulling gently. It performed this action several times until the nipple was hard and erect.

Side to side, it went, stroking and pulling, then nuzzling each breast. Both nipples were now standing hard and full as the raven continued its astonishing ritual. As quickly as it had jumped on her arm, so it jumped to the ground, seeming to grow and elongate until a dark changeling or demon was standing before her. The creature was in the likeness of a slender black man, with a large silver ring in each ear and even Negroid features. He smiled suddenly, an exaggerated gesture to show flashing white pirate teeth. He was naked and aroused.

Taking Annetta's hand, he placed it firmly around his prominent member. Being the sort of girl she was, a humanitarian, willing to help anyone in need, she began to rub slowly, then sensing the urgency from his hardening penis, she increased her motion as the fellow gripped both her shoulders with claw-like solid fingers. Soon he was grunting as he ejaculated violently, spilling his seed on and around her. He dropped to his knees, pulling free her dress and panties as he did so.

He pulled her down beside him, as he had probably done to many women before her, effortlessly parting her legs with his hands. I heard a little cry as he entered into her roughly, and I knew he was fully inside and had reached his objective. Her hips rose to meet him as he pushed, and, after many minutes, when he had finished his labors, he withdrew. He stood looking down at her as she lay supine, long black hair in disarray, with her lips parted in a weak half-smile.

With no more to accomplish at that time, he shrank back into the form of a raven again, rising suddenly in ungainly flight to settle in the topmost branches of a nearby oak tree. Perhaps to wait for another passing woman in need. Annetta lay for some time before leaving her leafy bed. As she rose, a single black feather fell from the tree, twisting and turning to settle somewhere between her legs.

Of course, the feather may have come from a blackbird or an angry sparrow, an intoxicated parrot, perhaps. No, far too big for that; it was from the raven. This was the Delta region, after all. What the hell did I know or even care? How would you feel? Watching your wife or girlfriend naked from the waist up, rubbing and manipulating a stranger's substantial cock? Worse, enjoying it, biting her lower lip in anticipation, as she did with me. And, in Mississippi, of all places, in daylight, in the open air. Did I want a serious relationship with a woman like that? Unconcerned by such an act of betrayal with another partner.

I was thinking of her violin and the recent duet with Barbara again, wondering if they had ever played music together naked in a Mississippi Delta whore house. And once more, I felt an uncomfortable distance between us. Before going to bed, I drank another glass of wine, never asked about the music or the accursed violin, and swore I never would.

Breakfast at the I-Hop, Sunday morning at about ten. Before such dizzying heights of culinary excellence could be explored, Harley shop Henry called. The bike was ready, excellent. About a week early, it seemed. Annetta and I would have breakfast.

First, she would take me to the Harley shop; then, we would go our separate ways. I rode home on a gleaming Harley, black tank with gold pin-striping and hand-painted emblems on each side. A gem of a machine, better than before the crash, in my opinion. Annetta followed me to the gas station, where we filled a car and bike, then home. The bike handled well, with no sign of problems, steering was responsive, but I did show some restraint because of the new front tire.

Home in short order, I parked the bike by the curb, waiting for Annetta as she came into the drive. Walking to the car, opening the door for her, then staring back at the bike, suddenly all the confusion and doubt, all the emotions I experienced when the *uncrashed* bike first appeared, were returning to me again.

Here was the gleaming black motorcycle with a trace of road dirt, the same resplendent machine I had looked upon the day after the accident. *Something has changed.* I thought at the time, and of course, it had. A new five-gallon fuel tank, front wheel, forks, and tire.

We walked back into the house and sat in the kitchen for a while. Annetta was full of praise for the refurbished bike. "I'm calling Mary and Alan, so; they're coming to see." So she did, and they did, examining the cycle and praising the Harley Henry artistry. "Alan, if you were a *real* man, you would sit Mary on the back and take her for a squirt up the road."

Within half an hour, they were at the table again, extolling the handling and performance. Alan was the only person I ever let ride my bike. "Okay, guys, here's a thought. I'm taking Annetta home in a bit. Get your bike and come with us. We stop at the restaurant, grab a bite, and head home." Unfortunately, Alan's shift started within the hour, so my plan wouldn't work.

I did, however, have to return Annetta to civilization. We decided to take the car and drive to Pat's house. Annetta and I will both have to work tomorrow. Something I never did before, I dropped Annetta at Pat's place without going in with her. I did have an excuse, though, as if an excuse was needed between friends. I had to drive home for at least an hour and get up early for work in the morning. I called Annetta when I reached home. No anger or contention between us, just the sorrow we felt from parting. We arranged to meet next Friday again; she would take the train and please meet her with the bike if possible.

During the working week, I gave much thought to another foray behind the fence. I decided to tell Annetta and possibly Alan and Mary. Indeed, my intent was to ride the bike into my great backyard unknown, with or without Annetta's approval. As it happened, my expedition did begin with her authorization, almost. I met her at the station Friday evening and brought the bike to acknowledge her request. Cold though it was, Annetta was not troubled by the conditions. No Steakhouse this evening; Denny's fast food welcomed us happily.

As we ate, we talked briefly about my plan to take the bike through the gate and explore. Annetta listened, shaking her head but saying little. "So, do you have an opinion?" She smiled and nodded.

"Darling Em-Jay, you not wanting an opinion of me because you are already determined to do this foolish thing. So, I will give you an onion instead. My onion is you are opening a door with no idea what may be there behind you, watching you.

I have some knowledge of that place, of those mountains you see, but I would not attempt what you will try to doing. I love you, but that is a selfish emotion, eh? If you ask me to come with you, I say no. No, because I am afraid.

You are testing the work of God with no idea of the danger there. You are not ready to understand yourself, so how you know anything greater?" She interrupted me with an impatient wave of her hand as I made to respond.

"You are darling, a mouse, a mouse sitting in contemplation before a grand piano. As a mousy, you have no possible understanding of the machine before you and no hope of operating it, eh?" She made perfect sense as she always did.

"Thank you for the onion, my darling."

CHAPTER TWENTY-NINE

Saturday, about eleven in the morning, after a big Annetta breakfast at the house, I bought the bike through the back gate and motored slowly across the grass, stopping in front of the little magic fence gate. I planned to ride a few yards to test the surface for traction, then assuming all was well, ride at a moderate speed before turning in a large loop and heading back. During this time, a watchful eye on the fuel and oil levels. I pushed the bike through the gate as Alan walked to join us.

He and Annetta stood behind the gate as I made ready for launch. He had no inkling of what was happening, just a spectator watching with an attractive girl as her demented boyfriend rode a motorcycle in his desert backyard. I smiled, thinking of Annetta trying to answer Alan's inevitable questioning.

He pushed the gate open as I started the engine. I turned and then a big wave to Annetta and Alan as I rolled away. Beginning of December, but the weather was humid and unpleasantly warm, about the same as the last time I was here.

Rolling past the shed, I noted that the surface beneath me was firm. There was no deep sand here. With a touch on the brakes, quick-change second to third, and roll on the throttle, everything was normal except the engine exhaust note was quite different. A dull, muffled sound, unlike any big Harley I had ever heard before.

No matter what, despite all misgivings, I was riding a motorbike into the great magic backyard desert. The distant mountain range before me was my marker before me, flat carpets of sparkling sand. To my left or my right, the view never changed. To gauge motion or speed was difficult because the landscape never changed to provide any reference points. Looking at the speedometer, I was traveling at sixty miles per hour; this agreed with the engine tachometer. I felt as if I could step off the bike and run alongside.

I said nothing had changed as far as I could see. Something had or was changing, though. From the base of the mountain range, a bright, sparkling light caught my attention. A diamond far away in this desert land perhaps, but how far away then? A mile, one hundred miles? There was no way for me to judge.

The light appeared about as big as an egg from where I was. I shut the throttle, letting the bike coast for some time before shutting the engine down. I stopped, dismounted, and stood staring into the distance for a while, trying to focus on the mysterious light source—three things I noticed quickly. I was so dizzy and uncertain on my feet; It was necessary for me to hold onto the bike to prevent myself from falling. The other was that the light seemed to be approaching rapidly. Also, there was nothing with an odor. No hot oily gasoline smell from the engine or hot rubber from the tires. The usual smells that come to a rider after a run on a motorcycle. This strange place was sterile, a sterile titanium plateau without wind or sun: no rain or fog.

What now, then? I sat beside the bike for a while, which helped with my dizziness. A few minutes of sitting before I got to my feet again. Now, much better.

I gazed out across the flat desert plain. There was no light anymore; there was, however, a truck, an old faded red Ford pickup truck, about nineteen forty-eight or so. Staring at this astonishing sight, I felt no fear, only a sense of wonder. Here In this infinite deserted flatness, a sudden jolt of familiarity.

The same truck, undoubtedly driven by the same strange fellow who gave me a ride after my accident. But out here? Had he come from the other side of the mountains? Was there an old road out there still in use? He opened the driver's door and stepped onto the sandy ground gazing around him as if searching for something. It was the same skinny old bone bag I had met previously. Nothing had improved his appearance during that time, yet he was so familiar. And then I knew his face was that of Bob Dylan, a ravaged Dylan, but undoubtedly the iconic Bob Dylan himself, except this version was much taller.

He wore old faded blue bib overalls and a stained brown fedora hat. What the hell could he possibly be doing out here? He raised his hand in greeting, nodding at me.

"You have strayed far from your home; there is no reason for you to be here, no reason at all. See, you and I are talking now because I come to help you as I did before."

I stared at him, amazed and confused. Amazed because he spoke with the slow drawl of an old Southern farmer. Unlike our last meeting when he spoke with a thick Scottish accent. I was confused because there was a shabby tottering old ratbag cautioning me and suggesting I should not be here in my own backyard. Would he then presume to correct my choice of clothes?

"*Oh no, no, no, you can't wear that shirt with those pants; you better change the shoes as well; Brown is the wrong color to wear; it should be black. Your hair is rather long, haircut and shave will do you a world of good.*

There are bound to be questions and possible changes to my nasty lifestyle: *too much booze, those awful drugs, and the motorcycle. Everyone knows what bikers are like.*

"There is every reason for me to be here, Bob Dylan or not. This is where I choose to be. Not only that, you are trespassing on my land. So, that being the case, I would say *you* have no reason to be here at all."

"Well now, sonny, let me quickly put you straight about that. I am here on business, and you are that business; but no matter, only the

Chumash Indians have a legitimate reason to be here. They are the caretakers of this land, as they have been for ages. If you had asked most humbly, it might have been possible to stay with them and learn about this place. That choice is no longer available to you.

In many ways, you are privileged to be here at all. Houses and stores, factories, and hospitals were built everywhere. With the population growth came disruption and significant danger to newcomers here. It was and is necessary to make changes. Such changes require an enormous level of activity, attracting unreasonable and most unwanted attention. Now, do you understand me, boy? You do realize what I'm saying to you, don't you?"

I shook my head, trying to decipher his babbling and braying, rendering it into recognizable language. Possibly To glean From his nonsense information that I could process into a reasonable understanding of anything at all. I wondered why the dislike and hatred I felt for him. A deep-seated skin-crawling dislike for someone I didn't even know. Here was a harmless old man, probably a moonshiner, who had helped me previously, now trying to help me again.

"No, I don't understand what the hell you are bleating about. You don't appear to be drunk or fucked up, so; I suppose you must have a mental health condition. As for Indians? When did you last see a living Indian in this desert? "Suddenly, I knew why I hated him so much. It was not hatred at all but fear. I was terrified of him, and all my responses to his questions were bluster.

There was an unnerving resonance, a terrible hidden strength radiating from him. It was the embodiment of the horror I felt on my first visit as I ran for the gate. Perhaps he was the awful vicious spirit from the corner of my little London bedroom. The imagined crouching goblin that terrified me so many years ago. He shook his head slowly before continuing.

" You understand nothing, my boy. They are everywhere. You will see them in the quiet times; they are with us now, the intelligent shadows of things once living in your space. There are other intelligent things here that were never human."

Suddenly changing his demeanor, the antique vinegar-faced coot, that reeking old scroat, smiled thinly.

"And, mind your mouth, lad; I will not tolerate insolence or an irreverent attitude here in my classroom. Is that clear?"

I nodded. "Yes sir, sorry."

And once again, it *was* very clear, and I was as sorry as I had been so many years ago. A sudden wave of cold fear washed over me again, for the old overalls were gone, replaced by a long black gown and mortarboard, unmistakable curly brown Dylan hair mop visible beneath the cap. In his hand, the feared and well-remembered thin bamboo cane. No Southern drawl, that was replaced by a clear clipped—English accent.

"Good, listen carefully then. Your friend Annetta, the lady who showed you her little trick with the white stone? I nodded, waiting apprehensibly for him to continue.

"What she did was to show you possibilities; then, you began to realize those possibilities within yourself. You are beginning to develop perception and abilities that exist within you and most other people, dormant and unused."

And how, in God's name, *do I separate truth from imagination now?* Was I dreaming now? Did I shoot smack or smoke dope? No, these experiences had rolled past me with such clarity; they could not possibly exist in dreams. This was not opium; my memory was clear from the time I left the fence until I first saw the brilliant light. The awful black robe and stick so abhorred and feared during my school years were no longer visible. How could I be sure of anything now? I saw his gown slowly replaced again by the blue bibs and hat. The English accent remained as he continued.

"This space exists on another level of reality from yours. It is dangerous and unforgiving. Not for tourists or inquisitive bicycle riders. There is nothing to be gained by you being here, everything to lose. Enough random energy fields surround us that any one of them would melt the flesh from your bones if you inadvertently tried to cross one. You have staggered around here recently without any good reason, with no idea where to go or what to do. As always, you came close to hurting yourself in your ignorance and arrogance." He smiled gently, the antique leprous old sod, waiting, like unshaven reanimated roadkill, for my response.

"Look, sir, I'm a simple person, okay? I came through my garden gate just now as I'm entitled to do. There are no posted signs or warning notices. Perhaps you are the problem with all this secrecy and Indian land stuff." I shook my head but understood little as I continued.

"So this means then; I can never go out in my backyard again?"

"No, it does not, but you must learn to close your perception when you pass through the gate. Annetta will help you with that, a simple practice. Lovely girl and I knew her mother well. When you came through the gate on your bicycle, you were popping away nicely, carried along, riding on a ribbon of energy with no problems. Of course, you would not have been able to sustain that progress. Had you not stopped when you saw me, you could have easily traveled in a full circle, forever meeting yourself in passing. Have you any idea how far you have come?"

"Not exactly, less than sixty miles according to the clock."

My eighty-inch Harley Davison was now a bicycle. The sound of the exhaust was described *as popping away*. Okay, Farmer John, the only *popping* here is between the cheeks of your withered arse. I said nothing, of course; my bravado has its limits.

"A little more than that, boy."He replied.

"If we were to drop down directly into your old plane of reality, you would be in Calcutta, India. Time and distance, direction, and spatial positioning, all these qualities you hold so dear, all these ways you try to regulate your life in the other place are meaningless here."

I closed my eyes for a few seconds as a glimmer of understanding took hold.

"Is this like being dead, then?"

"No, dear boy, there are similarities, but not the same as here. Dead is another reality and a brief cessation of life's mysteries and confusion. One passes through a different gate, and then one is no longer dead. You must have passed through a gate to come here. Why? You talk about realities, but you have never explored your personal levels or your own reality.

Understanding will not be found in heroin or cocaine. That is only distortion." Another long pause in the conversation. I was fighting against the temptation to ask him when he last got laid. My guess would be about eighteen forty, perhaps a little earlier. But instead, not wishing to be rude and afraid of the repercussions.

"Do you live here?" I asked, trying to deflect a probable lecture on the evils of narcotic ingestion.

He stared at me for an uncomfortably long time before he replied.

"No, I came here for you to help you again. Self-centered wretch though you are, even you fulfill a higher purpose of which you are unaware. That purpose will be revealed to you very soon. You smacked your foolish head hard in the accident and rattled your little brains. Perhaps you should consider wearing a protective helmet, the type your mother wanted you to wear. Or learn proper control of your bicycle. Had the blow been harder than it was, all those dreams and fanciful visions would have spilled out in the dirt, leaving you like a broken vegetable. I came to help you before when you were wandering around with no direction on the road. I think you remember that time, eh?"

He smiled a sudden horrible grin; his teeth were white, gleaming in contrast to his face's dark, windswept features. I saw the teeth, even and pointed, sharp animal predator teeth. The eyes were black, dead, and endless, dull black glass, reflecting no indication of humanity. This was no Farmer John. I was listening to the voice of evil, a harmful demonic creature, probably waiting for the services of a deranged celestial dentist.

"Yes, of course, sir; I recognized you at once when I saw you again today."

"There is no today, lad, but time will always move as it should and as it always has in its mysterious fashion. It is always with us, deeper than any ocean. It has a beginning, but the beginning is also the end. Time for others is not the same as time for you. For you, it is nearly time to go back."

Out here in this wasted atomic desert ocean, this sub-particle refracted illusion there must be intelligence, which brought before me a destitute old philosopher telling, rather than hinting at the nature of life and living, a creature, a predator capable of changing its form and voice. Out here, I was alone, without courage or hope, without any memory to guide me. Out here, was this tottering old scroat who spoke to me much more than he appeared to be? Almost certainly, he was. Then perhaps I *was* talking with God?

No, surely not, and definitely not with those teeth, for God, he was never described as a shambling flatulent rack of bones covered with blue bib overalls. And that truck? Where was a golden chariot or great firey vessel attended by shining white angels? Any reference to the Almighty, in any religious writing, ancient or modern, always referred to our Holy Father as a being so brilliant and powerful that no mortal could look upon him or pronounce his name, let alone comprehend his purpose. If this were God and the old Ford truck his chariot, he would be unlikely to impress a group of sweaty Wall-Mart shoppers.

Okay, but when I first saw the truck, it appeared to me like a brilliant white light in the distance, so perhaps I was wrong about this. Maybe I did, in fact, gaze upon an angel's chariot.

So, if this tatty dung pile of a thing masquerading as Bob Dylan was a God, or *the* God, did I have the balls to tell him to piss off? But why would I do that? And if I did, would I be instantly vaporized or find myself wandering with my head between my legs and my reproductive system sprouting from my neck?

Was I dead? Was I dreaming? My waking state was nothing but a continuous dream of late. I was scared. For the first time, I was scared of my habit, scared that I thought of my using as a habit. Perhaps this is where I die; Perhaps I am already dead. Could this be the place where dead things come to die? An overdose? The cumulative effects of opiates and hallucinogenics have led me to this desert place, this worthless dreamland some would call heaven.

And suddenly I was very afraid again. Perhaps now, my life up to this time would be dust and ashes scattered in the breeze, nothing remaining to remind anyone I had ever lived in the world. My story of visiting this place would stay untold, perhaps a good thing. Who would believe my description anyway? A junkie's testimony, hardly a credible report, even I was unsure of the experience.

"There is no one to listen, no one to sing. And never again will be winter or spring."

This must be a dream. Everything around me is illusory, so I live and think. Time now to talk to the old farmer John fellow again. I promised myself to reign in my smartass mouth and speak with some degree of humility and respect. Just in case this was not a dream.

"If I have to leave, and I suppose I do as I have no choice in the matter, but I have so many questions for you. Could you please tell me about my Father, at least?"

"Your father was an honorable man, simple and hard-working. He never knew you, never knew you were born. Left your Mother to volunteer in the desert campaigns during the war. He died recently. Had you known him, you would have had great respect for him."

"And Aunt Jen? Why did she leave without saying goodbye?"

"Oh, the games we play. There never was any Aunt Jeanine. You were projecting a need for love and companionship. Had that woman existed as you wanted, it would have been a disaster. I think you know that."

"But I knew her; I loved her."

He was right, of course. I stood silent, overwhelmed by so many emotions as I thought about my Father. I thought about my life growing up with Aunt Jen; I knew her so well, the smell of sweat on her body and the scent of her hair. I needed time to digest this latest information and reassemble my life again. I tried to stall, for I had so many more questions.

"By the way, sir, how is your cat? Last time we met, you had a cat with you."

"Yes, the cat is with me now, waiting in the truck."

He beckoned to me as he walked the few yards to the truck. Opening the passenger's door, I saw the same small black and white cat sitting on the seat and reached to stroke it. "Hello, cattie, remember me?" The cat looked into my eyes, bright yellow lights, hypnotic and intelligent. I felt a sudden shock of recognition. Whatever lived behind those eyes was not a cat.

"Hello, Em-Jay; good to see you again, man. My name is Nikita now, just for a little while. I hear you had a few problems after your accident."

So much had happened to me recently that I felt only mild astonishment when the creature spoke. Memories of my cat God experience returned clearly. I think I was half expecting it when the animal spoke, in English, with a heavy East Coast accent. I understood every word and knew this was my cat, god.

"Hello, again, Nikita. I remember the last time we met.

"Oh yeah, the time in the truck. Before that, I remember the time of the party at Rubens House. I had an accident recently, not like yours, though. After my accident, I traveled and visited a few friends I used to know. Nothing much changes, eh?

I Went on to Pat's; then, after that, I came by your place a while ago; some broad answered the door, then let me out in the garden again. Sorry I missed yuh eh. Time is odd, and I hadn't even had my accident then. Nothing is in a straight line here; none of that weird shit matters, though. Saw the old 142nd for the last time. New York is my real home; I know that now. Whatup Em-Jay? What the hell you doin' here anyhow, man? Obviously, your accident didn't slow you down much?"

"Just exploring, came through here on the bike. Matter o fact, I was wondering if I was dead."

Nikita laughed, then shook its head.

"Hell no, you're a long way from that, brother. The dead men you're thinking about don't ride Harleys or do much of anything."

"Well, I hate to admit this, but when we spoke before when you were a cat, a God on my front screen, we had a long conversation. I can't for the life of me remember what we talked about."

"A cat, God? It never happened, Em-Jay. I did see you briefly after you shot smack one time, but a God...Nah. As for our talk, you were babbling about the navy. Nothing important, brother.

I was about to ask him if there was anything I could help him with at home, but the old bone bag called.

"Em-Jay, come now; we must go."

I apologized to Nikita for the interruption. The cat stood,

"Okay then, Em-Jay, no problem; take care, pal."

I walked back to the bike, looking at the bib overalls, then turning quickly to look at the truck again. I felt my short conversation with Nikita had changed me at a deep fundamental level. More so, the revelations about my Father and Aunt Jen. There were reasons and purpose now for all the journeys that I never saw or understood before. Perhaps my destiny was to speak with and be guided by a small cat. An understanding was almost within reach, Just a little time to think about my upended life. Perhaps I would find there was meaning to my cat-God heroin experience after all.

"I honestly don't want to go, at least not yet. How about I stay for a couple of hours? Perhaps you could tell me more about this place? Maybe, I could speak with Nikita some more? Then I really will turn around and go, promise."

He shook his head and laughed gently. Not possible at this time, son. And, where is around then? Is it up above you? Beneath you? In front of or behind you? All these things and all at the same time, perhaps, eh? Much better for you if I bring you back."

I nodded to him, walked slowly, checked the bike, and sat, ready to move on word of his instruction.

"Okay, well, thanks, mister. Your cat's name is Nikita, or my friend's name is now Nikita... what's your name; I thought you were Bob Dylan; you do look like him?"

And at that moment, I felt sick, with a great need to vomit, although there was nothing in my stomach. All the kaleidoscopic pieces of my unhappy fragmented existence shifted position, and I was falling into blackness, twisting like a dry leaf. But, as I fell, I saw the old creature standing behind me and spoke before I could turn again or stop my endless plunge. His voice rose and fell, echoing all around me, and I was very much afraid.

"I am known in the high company of angels as Uriel. You can read about me in books."

"As I came out of the wilderness, I heard Annetta's voice quite clear. She said, "Hurry back, my darling; salvation's waiting for you here.."

CHAPTER THIRTY

"We do have a few books in the waiting room, Mr. Oconnell, Anyone in particular? Would you like me to get one for you?" The light was too bright here, hurting my eyes. Something was very wrong. A woman's voice, echoing in my ears and bleeding all around, frightened me. I could see a clear plastic tube that ran from a fixture in my arm disappearing somewhere behind me. There was a device clipped to my finger, from which ran a small cable. I stared at a nice plump nurse, clean, white, shiny, and smiling, speaking with a pleasant chubby southern accent.

Long, plump blond hair was tied in a ponytail. On her breast pocket, a name tag was "Elaine." She was the sort of nurse who would never pass gas loudly in a crowded room, unlike other poorly educated girls, farting violently without restraint, turning, feigning innocents, and glaring at others. A medical maven such as Elaine would, whenever possible, avoid public restrooms with their poor maintenance and sour odors, never carry condoms in her handbag or scratch her bottom in a public place.

I knew beneath the crisp, healing angel uniform must exist another persona well concealed: tiny black frilly panties and matching brassiere, a device struggling ineffectually to restrain both wayward breasts. The lacy cups were overflowing delightfully with smooth, creamy flesh.

"Give some to me, my darling plum pudding, for you have much to spare. It would be a righteous and humanitarian gesture to share those things from your abundance."

Her ample Southern buttocks were gleaming whitely through black fishnet tights. Were these robust, blushing, beef-fed cheeks capable of seizing and cracking a walnut? I wondered. And look; her red high-heeled shoes waited brightly with a subtle purpose in the corner of the closet.

"Please, I need you to heal me, to love me, Elaine. Take off that uniform and heal me slowly but wear those red shoes when you do. Show me, please, beautiful inflated nurse, for I am just a lost city boy waiting for your sweet Southern salvation."

A near-death encounter? A unique fundamental and religious experience, perhaps an interview with one of God's chosen angels. And then, having returned from the brink of extinction, the first thoughts filling my mind were of women's breasts and buttocks.

"Are you a friend of Uriel, then?" I asked.

"What is this place? Uriel said I had to go and told me he would take me back. Who is Oconnell?"

I heard her reply echoing from a great distance, it seemed, sounding clear at first and then fading.

"Well, my dear, this is wonderful to talk to you. I don't know about a urinal, but It sounds like *you* are back; do not overdo it. Your recovery has only just begun. Please let me know if you need to use the bathroom."

I must have fallen asleep for a while. When I woke, it was to the sound of a distant radio playing an early Dylan song. The area around my bed was populated by medical stuff, instruments, and monitoring equipment. I was attached to some device that emitted regular and most annoying *ping* noises. There were two small plastic tubes feeding air into my nose.

Was this the half-expected biblical retribution? Perhaps a hospital, an asylum, or possibly, was I the victim of an alien abduction? The appearance of the same nurse brought some relief. She explained about concussions, maybe delayed effects, and symptoms. "You are resting and recovering properly now, something you should have done immediately after your accident."

I thought I did. Although I do have to work, there is always the paying the ole mortgage thing."

"May I have some water, please?" She filled a glass from a pitcher on a nightstand next to the bed. Looking around, I saw for the first time I was in a room alone.

"I am the only one here, then?"

"In this room, yes, most patients here are in separate rooms," I was happy she used the word patients, not inmates. "Now, a little blood draw and some medication, Would you like to sit up and read? Are you hungry? When you are comfortable, we need to talk about your drug use. Some friends talked to me, wanting to help. If you were using a needle, there are no marks on your arms. Nothing on your feet or legs, so perhaps they were wrong, eh?"

Before I could respond to her questions, I was asleep again. The nurse told me I slept through the night. A different nurse, young, dot, not feather Indian as far as I could tell, and a most attractive girl. She introduced herself. "Hello, my name is Sheena. Have you read your register book yet, sir?"

"I have no idea what that would-be, sweetheart. I have read nothing."

"Yes, no problem, sir, I can help you with that. You had several visitors while you were asleep. Every visitor signs your little book, a keepsake for when you leave." She reached into the bedside stand drawer.

"Here, you see." Then handing a small blue book to me. If I had been sick, I had made a sudden recovery, for when she leaned across the bed with the book, I was overcome by a powerful urge to fondle her breasts, perhaps pull her into the bed with me.

Instead thanking her and dismissing the wishful thinking, I took the register. On the first page, Annetta is missing me, and please get well soon. Beneath in brackets, *Get out the bed, asshole. Pat.*

And then something else," Sheena," I yelled, thrusting the book at her with shaking hands. "What's this, here? Look," She read the words I was pointing to. She stared at me with wide, anxious puppy eyes and then read slowly in a small frightened voice. "Bobbie darling, get well again. See you soon, Aunt Jeanine." And next to the extravagant flowing script, a small heart. Ruben, Dot, and Alice had signed, as had Philipe. Co-workers, then Alan and Mary. All in all, a nice souvenir.

Two or three hours before I was awake again.

Sheena perched on the side of the bed, smiling nervously.

"Do you have the little book, sweetheart?"

She retrieved the book from the first nightstand draw, passing it to me hesitantly.

"Will you sign as well, Sheena?"

"I would love to; probably the doctor and other nurses will too."

Nothing I could do to change the book. Aunt Jen's extravagant signature remained as I had first seen it. I remember running my finger over the small heart, then staring for a long time, unseeing, into some distant place. Aunt Jen had returned, from where, though? If she had, as Uriel said: "never existed at all."

The first thing I noticed after nurse Elaine and dot Sheena was the food. It was excellent, bland, but excellent. Same for the coffee. I was fed three times a day and given a restricted choice. Apparently, I had been here in bed for five days. Before that, in the garden by the gate for a day at least.

Annetta came early that afternoon. She told me about the start of my journey. She and Alan were watching as I rode into the wasteland. About the time I reached the shed, I vanished. At least vanished from their sight, she said. She told me Alan said I became transparent and faded away, said he could hear the engine for some time before it stopped suddenly.

"Poor Alan was very frightened and wanted to go after you in his SUV. I tell him please, no, because I need him to be with me. We both walk to the shed but no looking or hear from you, of course. I am two days then with him and Mary. I have to tell them about this place, which took many hours to explain. We look over the gate many times, and they see the white rock when they go by the gate as you can. I sleep at your house for the end of the week. I go back to Pat house, and Tuesday, Mary, see you on the grass, sleeping or dead. Your bike was standing a few meters away. We must speak with each other about this thing soon when you feel good again, yes? So, my darling fool Em-Jay, No more of this adventure madness, please."

The nurse Sheena told me it would be at least another four days before they released me. "Here for you," reaching with a plastic bag to give to me. "Three pairs of socks for you to keep. A company makes them to distribute to hospitals." Within the bag three pairs of thick, neatly folded socks. Bright yellow, purple, and dark brown, all with white rubberized inserts in the sole: the perfect underwear for my feet—socks without holes and three pairs of them. So, my wretched old sock drawer would now be elevated to a repository for gentleman's fine foot underwear.

Another week at the house, and then life would resume as usual. Usual, to include work and commute. So be it, then; I will enjoy the rest. Annetta and I chatted for another hour before she had to leave. Philipe had bought a car, an old Datsun pickup.

"It ugly but run well," Annetta told me. "He comes to me, my darling, soon; I meet him at the little burger on the corner. I am hungry." I nodded, knowing I would miss her when she left. We kissed for the last time that day, promising to stay in touch by phone. "Also, dearest Em-Jay, beautiful Mary will drive for you to your house. She will arrange with the hospital to say when you are good. Alan will call later.

My poor Mary, Em-Jay, she is so sad."

"Sad, why sad?"

"Of course, you know she has a cat, yes?"

"Yeah, only had it for a few weeks; I think Alan found it in the front garden. Pretty little thing she said, although I never saw it.."

"Something got it, darling. A dog, they think. She said it die in her arms. Die when she picks it up—covered in blood, a big hole in its back: poor little thing and poor Mary. You know how she love animals. Alan think it was a dog."

We chatted for a few more minutes sharing the sadness before she left to meet Philipe.

As Annetta pulled open the door, she turned with a smile, then a quick wave, and she was gone. As the door closed behind her, a black feather floated from her open shoulder bag. A large feather, too big for a blackbird, Probably from a raven or crow. It was pulled by the draught from the closing door, floating until caught and lifted by a slight current from the air conditioner. It twisted and turned before eventually settling at the foot of my bed—a dramatic contrast between the beige covers and white sheets.

I remembered Uriel clearly, but the sound of his voice eluded me; which voice should I remember, though? I had three from which to choose. So, was everything that happened to me recently an insubstantial dream? Were my newfound friends simply imaginary creatures conjured by the echo of a memory from a motorcycle accident and possibly too much smoke? What, if anything, around me was real? What was ever real? Perhaps with rest would come clarity. Had I learned anything from these recent experiences, or had I just gotten older?

I wanted to see Uriel again, sit down with him, and ask questions, but he had vanished, returned to the waste places from whence he came. Perhaps he would come to visit me again; I didn't believe that either.

My present reality now was the small blue register book Sheena had shown me. There were names and dates in there that should mean something; that signature, that note from Aunt Jeanine, did mean something. It meant everything. Propping myself upright against the pillow, I started to read, but the writing blurred before my eyes, and I suddenly felt drained. It was two days before the rosy Southern Elaine nursie came to talk about the evils of drug use and the attendant health risks. She sat on the side of my bed, notebook in hand, poised to dig and pry, even to understand me if I let her.

Oh, she was charming and sincere, a big-breasted loving mother type, lactating gallons of sympathy, and an earnest desire to improve my sorry lifestyle. And while she talked about alternatives, methadone, and family interdiction, I thought only of my face between her breasts or buttocks: a substantially rounded beauty, all jiggly and bouncy. I needed to pull at her nipples and bite them gently, as she apparently needed to steer me away from drugs.

Suddenly I was clean; an orgasmic epiphany visited on me lying in a hospital bed while supporting a growing erection. A realization that nearly two weeks had elapsed without dope or even the desire to use. Perhaps Uriel had returned me, laundered and clean. How could I explain that to Elaine? I thought about the juicy peach on the side of my bed, then to the smoke and needle. There is nothing, no desire, except the urge to perform extravagant sexual acts with my darling nursie.

The combination of bed, with me in it, and the proximity of an attractive woman was again proving very hard to bear.

"I have injected morphine and heroin and smoked opium and snorted cocaine. The last time I injected anything was a month or so ago. After listening to your advice, I realized I'm no longer interested in any drugs. I was never a heavy user, anyhow.

Look, I know you can't just stop using heroin; the stuff lives inside you, waiting. I was sick for about a month with withdrawal symptoms. That is, for sure, the sign of full-blown addiction; no one is immune; they all tell me that. Although I never told anyone, I'm sure people noticed. I wish I had never started to use the stuff, but I did. I can't change that. Do *you* think I'm healed, honey? Perhaps you have healed me, dear Elaine.

I feel healed; I feel good, better than I have for some time." It was a strange sensation; I spoke without meaning to, and the words tumbled from my mouth into the room. Almost as if There were two people, me looking down at another Em-Jay who was talking to the nurse, perhaps because I had new underwear, I was wearing the yellow socks of invincibility.

"Anything is possible, sweetie, but in my experience, you can't quit these things without help. Now I'm not the expert, but opiates cause an imbalance in the brain and affect the central nervous system. That is a proven fact and much more than wanting to return to pleasurable sensations. These are physical changes in the body you see. If you are interested, this hospital is affiliated with one of the best detox and rehab centers in the country. Would you like me to arrange for an expert counselor to speak with you?"

She smiled at me, parting her plump red southern lips, displaying shiny, chubby white teeth.

"I understand and hear what you're telling me, but what can I do? For the first time in about three years, I have no desire for dope. Although I do have a strong desire to kiss you slowly, dearest Elaine. Perhaps I have replaced one desire for another; now there's a thought, eh."

She stood abruptly, staring at me angrily, not amused.

"Please don't belittle this conversation; I do try to help. Anything we have discussed is for your own good, not my benefit; I hope you understand. Please think about what I have said."

"Will you at least hold my hand then?"

"Goodnight, Mister Oconnell."

And with that curt professional dismissal, she was gone, leaving me feeling like a jerk and wishing I had shut my loud mouth. Elaine had gone, but I was not alone in the room. Something familiar and most unpleasant moved in my peripheral vision; I saw it clearly for a moment before it slid away from the corner of my eye. A gray slinking animal thing, about the size of a large cat: with a cold shock, I remembered the creature from the desert. Was this the same horrible hairless beast that followed me here, then? Had it now attached itself to me? A visitor from a bad dream.

"Not possible, Em-Jay; no matter how real they seem, you can't bring flowers from a dream."

I wanted to scream and call for help, but before I could do anything, Elaine poked her head around the door again, grinning.

"You are quite cute though Darlin."

She waved as she disappeared again, too quickly before I could tell her of the thing I saw. The room was no longer a bright, friendly refuge. It had become a frightening box of shadows, the same dark, threatening place that was once my bedroom when I was a child. I wanted to go away, hide from the world, pull the blankets over my head, and be free of dreams, drugs, demons, and bad memories. I tried for a few minutes, but too many uninvited thoughts were pressing and clamoring for attention. Too much outside hospital noise is intruding. Perhaps I should have prayed to Jesus or some other distant Gods. Maybe I will when my head stops aching and it's daylight again.

I remembered the big black feather that floated, settling on my bed a few days ago.

I thought about my Aunt Jeanine signing the book. Had this room become another place where dead things came to die? Was I one of them? Perhaps I had been tricked and lied to; this was no hospital; it was an asylum. A mental institution, I had no way to be sure; no, the nurses were not to be trusted. I thought about that again for a long time and wondered if I would ever be free from my Past. These thoughts pressed all around me, keeping me from sleeping. And yet there was hope. Someway, out in the distance, a radio was playing softly. One of my all-time acoustic guitar heroes, Bert Jansch, was playing and singing *Black Waterside*.

At that moment, I knew my story would continue or be made to continue. If nothing else, Mary promised to document the past few months of my life for me. Perhaps our short time together will help, and I will tell her the whole story when the time is right and I am alive again. According to Annetta, She and Alan had witnessed the beginning of my journey, so perhaps my experiences were not dreams. Annetta would describe with some honesty the awful place beyond my fence and gate, although honestly, from Annetta was of late an elusive quality, seeming to shift with her prevailing mood. Or, perhaps that opinion was just part of my confusion and growing distrust.

Surely I was entitled to a bit of distrust; there was a powerful manipulative intelligence presently at work in my life, a mystery for sure in the manifestation of my Aunt Jeanine's book page signature. Was I presented with tangible evidence of a purpose beyond my understanding?

I wanted to locate the source of the music I was hearing and increase the volume, but I dare not. I was safe here beneath the blankets for the moment. Come daylight, what is real now or what was real will not matter; the heroin will not matter, and fear will be washed away. A while later, I thought the door opened slowly, but I really couldn't be sure.

And with the daylight coming, I stood by the bed alone, without fear. My life would continue as I wished and as I wished to live it. This was my road, not a road of grave misfortune, and every stopping place would be a new adventure and a new song. There was something else, though—a distant voice calling me, pulling like an old lover for me to return to that place. The road was straight without end, and the song had changed; now, it told of hope and promise for the future. I had yellow socks, socks of invincibility, and a drawer with many panties for my feet. Nothing could stop me when I wore them. There were always the purple socks of power should the yellow ones fail me. Uriel told me I had a purpose that would soon be revealed. I believed him then and believe him now.

Although I had not slept well, I was refreshed and happy. One of the nurses will come with coffee soon, and Mary will come for me in a few days.

www.ingramcontent.com/pod-product-compliance
Lightning Source LLC
LaVergne TN
LVHW041920070526
838199LV00051BA/2684